RACHEL'S DREAM

Books by Lisa Jones Baker

The Hope Chest of Dreams Series

Rebecca's Bouquet

Annie's Recipe

Rachel's Dream

Anthologies

The Amish Christmas Kitchen
(with Kelly Long and Jennifer Beckstrand)

The Amish Christmas Candle
(with Kelly Long and Jennifer Beckstrand)

Published by Kensington Publishing Corporation

RACHEL'S DREAM

Lisa Jones Baker

ZEBRA BOOKS
KENSINGTON PUBLISHING CORP.
http://www.kensingtonbooks.com

ZEBRA BOOKS are published by

Kensington Publishing Corp.
119 West 40th Street
New York, NY 10018

All Kensington titles, imprints, and distributed lines are available at special quantity discounts for bulk purchases for sales promotion, premiums, fund-raising, educational, or institutional use.

Special book excerpts or customized printings can also be created to fit specific needs. For details, write or phone the office of the Kensington Sales Manager: Attn.: Sales Department. Kensington Publishing Corp., 119 West 40th Street, New York, NY 10018. Phone: 1-800-221-2647.

Zebra and the Z logo Reg. U.S. Pat. & TM Off.

First Printing: May 2017
ISBN-13: 978-1-4201-4156-6
ISBN-10: 1-4201-4156-2

eISBN-13: 978-1-4201-4157-3
eISBN-10: 1-4201-4157-0

10 9 8 7 6 5 4 3 2 1

Printed in the United States of America

To my favorite people,
John and Marcia Baker,
who raised me in a loving,
Christian home.

ACKNOWLEDGMENTS

First and foremost, I thank my Lord and Savior for blessing me with publication after twenty-four years of prayers to see my work in print. I'm tremendously grateful to my kind, loving reading specialist mother, Marcia, for taking me to the library every weekend during my youth and also for listening to me read my own stories out loud for over twenty-four years.

Huge appreciation to Dr. Jennifer Ostrom, DVM, for answering medical questions and sharing her valuable expertise. My gratitude to computer expert and sister extraordinaire, Beth Zehr, for taking on my challenges day and night, and to writer Lisa Norato, confidante, critique partner, and true friend for playing a significant part in my writing journey for over two decades. I can't forget Gary Kerr, Brittany, Brooke, and Doug for assisting with technical issues at a moment's notice. Huge appreciation to Geek Squad expert Elizabeth Ray in Bloomington, Illinois.

Over the past decade, numerous individuals in Arthur, Illinois, have contributed greatly to my quest for publication. These amazing folks have answered questions, related stories, and even had me into their homes for dinner, further inspiring me to write meaningful stories. I have been fortunate to have had hundreds of authors in the RWA diligently critique my work, encourage me, and help me to hone my writing, especially author Gina Welborn, who picked *Rebecca's Bouquet* from a contest and referred me to my fabulous agent, Tamela Hancock Murray. Thank you! My deepest appreciation to *New York Times* best-selling author Joan Wester Anderson for helping me to launch my debut story, *Rebecca's Bouquet,* and for rooting for me to succeed. Of course, I couldn't write these novels without the invaluable input from my Amish go-to girl, who prefers to remain anonymous while loyally reading my stories, cover to cover. You have my full respect, admiration, and fascination. Thanks to Amber Kauffman, former executive director, Illinois Amish Interpretive Center. Last, but not least, I'm extremely blessed to work with my wonderful editor, Selena James, publicist Jane Nutter, and everyone at Kensington who has played a part in the production of this book.

Chapter One

Her situation required immediate attention. In Old Sam's barn, Rachel wrung her hands together and poured out her great fear of losing Cinnamon. She sat back in the chair opposite Sam's workbench and let out a deep, impatient breath.

While she awaited a response, the late May breeze floated in through the large open doors. Every once in a while, they creaked when the wind moved them.

Rachel could hear Sam's horse, Ginger, clomp her hooves as she stepped from her stall to the pasture. The pleasant scent of wood filled Sam's work area. Birds chirped from the upper window by the hayloft.

Finally, Old Sam met her gaze before carving into wood that would become another hope chest. The widower was well-known for his hope chests. Of course, many could put boards together, but his special talent lay in creating personalized etchings on the oak lids.

His voice was thoughtful, serious. Rachel sat up straighter. "Young one, we never like to see our horses sick. I'm glad that Dr. Zimmerman's coming tomorrow. I've heard he has a special knack for healing."

Sam gave a slow shake of his head. "Now, I know he's fresh out of veterinary school. That would usually give me pause, but in my opinion, his youth works to his advantage. Not to mention that he was mentored by Doc Stevens. You know how word spreads quickly around here."

Rachel grinned, because what Sam mentioned was an understatement.

"According to the Wagler family, this Doc Zimmerman is marvelous. There wasn't much hope for Martha's cat until Zimmerman treated him. Now he's as good as new."

Rachel breathed in relief. She'd heard the young vet's name, and much more. That Zimmerman was a blessing to the sick. And that he was as good as or better than the well-respected Doc Stevens, who'd gone to the Lord not long ago.

"The good doctor has helped Rebecca's and Annie's horses."

Rachel knew that to be true. Rebecca Conrad and Annie Miller were friends. Rachel shared Old Sam with the two girls, who also took care of him. His wife, Esther, had been like a second mother to the trio. When she'd passed, Rebecca, Annie, and Rachel had returned that kindness to Old Sam Beachy.

Now Rachel wasn't sure what she would do without the widower. She went to him for his wise advice and to listen to his horse-and-buggy stories. Sam had made Rachel, Annie, and Rebecca very special hope chests to store their private thoughts in. And inside Rachel's was her dream.

* * *

Dr. Jarred Zimmerman took in the Standardbred. He squatted before the horse, and his heart nearly melted. With great tenderness and affection, he stroked the beautiful cinnamon-colored face.

As he did so, the scent of fresh straw filled his nostrils. He swatted away a fly while the early June breeze cooled the inside of the Kauffmans' barn in the country between Arthur and Arcola, Illinois. He glanced at the healthy filly that had been purchased to replace Cinnamon while he was down.

Jarred stood and turned to the girl who'd introduced herself as Rachel. He motioned to the healthy animal. "What's her name?"

"Paula."

He lifted an amused brow. "Paula?"

Rachel shrugged. "Yes, Doctor. Daddy bought her at the auction, and that was what they called her."

The horse whinnied and stomped her foot before proceeding outside to the pasture. Jarred laughed. "You're a beauty, that's for sure. But right now, your pal needs me. Sorry about that."

As Jarred stood, he could hear hammering in the neighboring building. He knew from his phone conversation with Rachel's dad that he was a woodworker who also farmed the land behind their home.

Jarred glanced at Rachel. It was impossible not to note the distressed expression on her face. Her eyes held a silent plea to get Cinnamon well. A tan halo around her pupils accented large blue-green irises.

Even with her beautiful heart-shaped face and

high cheekbones, the halo did a fearful dance. Jarred was committed to saving her horse, but because of her obvious love for the gelding, he also yearned to put her mind at ease.

A kapp covered light brown hair that was pulled back tightly off her face. Remembering his purpose, he turned his attention to the helpless creature in front of him. Jarred ran a compassionate hand over Cinnamon's mane and spoke with conviction.

"Don't you worry, boy. I'm here to help. Just bear with me, and before ya know it, you'll be pulling that buggy again for Rachel and her family."

He turned to Rachel and smiled a little. "I fell in love with this guy years ago. Do you know that I even helped Doc Stevens deliver him?"

"Oh!"

Jarred furrowed his brow and softened his voice. "First thing, we've gotta get some weight back on those bones."

His optimistic words were directed to the gelding, but also to Rachel. From experience, he'd learned that the human's mental suffering needed almost as much attention as the sick animal.

He knew all too well that watching their loved ones suffer made the owners extremely vulnerable. So in his opinion, there were two in need of healing: Cinnamon and Rachel.

Ensuring that Rachel maintained her optimism was part of his recovery plan. Horses were exceptionally sensitive, especially to mood.

Now was the time to voice that. After glancing back at her, he offered a soft pat of encouragement on Cinnamon's face. "Getting you well isn't gonna be easy. But be patient. Your recovery will take all three of us putting out one hundred and ten percent. So you've got to promise to do your part, okay, boy?"

Not expecting a response, he turned to Rachel. "How about you?"

A quick, eager nod followed.

Jarred smiled in satisfaction, but the corners of his lips made a sudden drop when he turned back to Cinnamon. "I don't know if you're aware of this, but Cinnamon survived a grave illness at birth."

He heard Rachel's surprised breath.

Jarred rose to his feet. "But he's a fighter! Time to get down to business." After checking the horse's eyes, ears, nose, and mouth, he reached for his bag while asking if the animal had been anywhere and Cinnamon's history of eating, drinking, and slowing down to develop a time line.

After Rachel's quick responses, Jarred offered a nod. "First thing we've gotta do is check his temp." He unzipped his medical pouch. "You mind giving me a hand?"

"Of course not."

"First, let's tie him."

When her eyes reflected confusion, he explained. "Not that he's feeling good enough to go anywhere, but just as a precautionary measure."

She completed the task.

"Now, stand here." He motioned. She moved next to Cinnamon and stroked his head tenderly.

Rachel continued whispering to Cinnamon as Jarred removed and checked the thermometer. He gave the stick a second glance, shook his head, and frowned.

Rachel waited for him to speak.

"Just as I suspected. He's running a fever."

The corners of Rachel's lips dropped. While he observed her reaction, his heart warmed. A combination of compassion and determination floated through him.

He supposed that his immediate bond with this young girl was because of her obvious adoration for this beautiful animal that had once stolen his own heart.

Not only was his heart at stake, but Rachel's was, too. As he watched the expression in her eyes that was a strong mix of fear and hope, he vowed to pay extra care and attention to this special opportunity. He couldn't let this unusually kindhearted girl down.

"Just so you know, a slight fever's okay. You're probably already aware that horses have trouble getting rid of body heat. A hundred is normal for them, but this guy's temp is over a hundred and three. We're looking at all the symptoms of the upper respiratory virus goin' around."

His cell beeped and he glanced at the message from his next appointment.

"Will he be okay?"

The soft, worried tone pulled his attention from his phone. He shoved it back into its holder on his belt. Jarred's pulse quickened as he considered how to respond.

What Cinnamon suffered from appeared to be the very same virus that had claimed the lives of numerous horses in the area, but her question was posed with such innocence.

Jarred stood, slapped the dust from his hands, and shoved them into his jeans pockets to hook his thumbs over the tops.

When their gazes met, he could see that she was waiting for him to say something. He cleared his throat and forced a confident smile. "Cinnamon's definitely struggling. Unfortunately, there's no good vaccine for the illness, but we can do some things to try to jump-start him."

He pressed his cheek against the gelding's long face and whispered, "I'll do everything I can for you, you know that. Do you remember when you were born?" Not expecting an answer, Jarred went on. "I doubt it. But I'll never forget. We beat the odds then, and we'll do it again."

He straightened his shoulders and lifted his chin confidently. "We're gonna fix this guy up."

Rachel's cheeks glowed with happiness. Again, his heart melted at the vulnerable expression that was so genuine and sincere. She stepped beside him. When she spoke, a combination of gratitude and shyness edged her voice. "You can't imagine how happy I am you're here. I've heard all about you and how you studied under Dr. Stevens."

She hesitated. "I'm sorry for your loss. He was a great man."

Jarred nodded in appreciation. "Yeah, he was. And a good friend. True animal lovers are few and far between, Rachel. He was the most unselfish individual I've ever met. We docs are constantly learning, but his knowledge was unmatched. Not to mention his open mind. I would be honored to be half as good as he was."

Rachel's eyes lightened. "He helped us a number of times. He was special."

The recollection of Doc Stevens prompted Jarred to chuckle. "The man had a house full of cats and dogs." Jarred grinned. "I can't tell you how many times he pulled over to the side of the road to rescue a stray. He always made it clear that he'd find them a good home."

The corners of his mouth pulled up even more. "He never did, 'cause he couldn't part with them once he took them in."

Rachel giggled in amusement. "God must have been anxious to get him to heaven."

The statement made Jarred's jaw drop in surprise. For several speechless moments, he considered another death, one even more personal than Tom Stevens's.

Ready to change the subject, he turned to Rachel and forced an optimistic tone. The girl who loved Cinnamon every bit as much as he did depended on him to make things right. And time was of the essence. He couldn't let her down.

Rachel shook her head. "He isn't drinking water. He just kind of plays with it. You know, holds his face in it. And he won't even eat sugar cubes." Her tone filled with deep concern. "Usually, whenever he sees me, he begs for them."

She added, "You know, by licking my hand. He has a sweet tooth." She lifted a brow apologetically. "Course, we can't blame him for that."

He considered her statements and slapped his right palm against his left. "You mind giving me a hand?"

"Of course not."

Within a short time, he had hosed Cinnamon down to lower his temp. Jarred followed with flunixin before giving fluids through a tube up Cinnamon's nose, which was certain to be much easier than going through the mouth. He did this just long enough to deliver five gallons with electrolytes.

When his tasks had been completed, Jarred zipped his bag shut and stepped closer to Rachel. He caught her staring at the scar on his neck.

He decided to indulge her curiosity. "When I was a teen, I was thrown from a horse."

She gasped.

He chuckled. "It's all right. In fact, as often as I rode, I'm lucky it didn't happen more than once." He went on. "I grew up on a ranch not far from here."

"What was it like?"

When he darted her a curious look, she jumped in. "Growing up on a ranch."

As they walked from the barn to his truck, he pushed out a sigh. *What was it like? Was I happy? Did I miss my parents?*

When he turned, he saw the eager expression in her eyes and softened his voice. "I loved being with animals. Horses, especially. And we had lots of them."

He drew in a deep, uncertain breath before continuing. "Rachel, this virus won't make things easy, but I know with all of my heart that God will help us."

"I know. Old Sam—he's my friend—he always tells me to look at the glass as half-full. And my parents have always stressed how important it is to have faith." She paused before lowering her voice to a tone that hinted at shyness and uncertainty. "How about your folks, Jarred? Obviously, you've been raised with love. Otherwise, how could you do so many wonderful things for animals?"

The unexpected words nearly stopped Jarred's heart. Breathless, he froze. His fingers turned cold on the bag as he fought hard to view his glass as half-full, like Rachel had recommended. He didn't make a verbal response to her question. Reality hit him hard as he acknowledged the strange thing that had happened while he'd talked with this lovely girl.

Without thinking, he'd been pulled into a world where everything was positive. Sunny. Cheerful. A place of hope and optimism. He didn't know Rachel well, but his impression was that she was protected from life's ugliness.

But unfortunately, he couldn't change what had happened to him. Rachel was right: He had been brought up in a loving home. But he wished that his own parents had cared about him enough to have raised him.

That evening, Rachel stood in front of her bedroom window, squeezed her eyes closed, and drifted happily to her all-too-familiar imaginary land. She straightened, pressing her palms against the soft blue cotton dress that covered her hips.

Now that she was eighteen, she truly believed her greatest wish would come true because she prayed for it every night and because God took good care of her and her family.

Her thoughts turned to Cinnamon and the wonderful doctor who'd offered hope for her horse's recovery. She considered the young vet. When he'd begun checking Cinnamon's vitals, Rachel had taken advantage of the opportunity to get a good look at him.

She recalled his blue-gray eyes that reminded her of the sky before a dangerous storm. His dark brown hair bordered on black. The doctor's face was kind looking, but his fierce depths made her wonder if something had happened to upset his life. She knew he was kind and thoughtful. She'd barely met him, yet her acute senses told her, without a doubt, that they would be great friends. His soothing voice put Rachel at ease.

She smiled a little as she glimpsed Old Sam's barn in the distance. Her very deepest secret was recorded in ink on the solid blue lines of her journal and stored in her hope chest.

Every night, while she wrote in her journal, she jotted it down in expectation that seeing the words would ensure they would come to life. She breathed in the pleasant, comforting scent of apple and cinnamon emanating from the small candle on her desk.

As always, glimpsing the hope chest that Old Sam had made especially for her prompted a happy sigh. With great emotion, she dropped her hands to the work of art and rested her fingers on top of it. His artistic capability was so superb, his carvings looked real.

Without thinking, she reached for her feather duster and ran it over the few pieces in her room while she considered her dear friend. To her, Old Sam was much more than a hope chest maker. She liked him best for his horse-and-buggy stories. No one told them like Sam. He enjoyed reciting the interesting truths that had transpired over his eightysomething years. And she loved hearing them. Listening to him even trumped the numerous horse stories she'd read in the public library.

Sam was her confidant, too. His wife of over sixty years, Esther, had been like a second mother to Rachel until she'd succumbed to pneumonia. Rachel had looked up to Esther. And Rachel was fully aware that mammas in the community, including hers, had often sought advice from the woman who had seemed to have a knack for everything, especially cooking.

Sam's kind wife had been especially fond of animals, and her great love for horses, in particular, had bonded her to Rachel in a special way. Not to mention her delicious sponge cakes.

After Esther's death, Rachel had returned that extreme kindness to Old Sam, feeling that in a small way, she was repaying Esther·for all of the attention she had offered Rachel over the years.

She cherished her friendship with Sam. It didn't bother her that she had to share him with Rebecca and Annie, two of her friends who loved spending time with him, too. Sam offered wiser advice than anyone in the world. And most importantly, he was the one person who fully respected Rachel's love of horses.

Rachel stepped on her tiptoes to run the duster over the top of the closet door. When her bare heels met the wood floor, she caught her breath before moving on to her headboard.

Sam knew that horses were much more than work animals. Why couldn't everyone understand that? Because of Old Sam's adoration for their means of transportation, Rachel hadn't been surprised when she'd first glimpsed the beautiful horse and buggy on the lid of the hope chest he'd designed for her seventeenth birthday. Using his great talent, Sam had artfully etched an image of her beloved Cinnamon and their family buggy into oak.

Finally satisfied that she'd rid her room of every visible speck of dust, she moved over to her desk. As she sat on the soft blue cushion Mamma had made on her old Singer sewing machine, Rachel rolled her shoulders to relax as she took in her bedroom's familiar comforts. She glanced to her oak-framed bed on the left. Old Sam's piece was at her right. The desk and bed had both been made by her father in his woodworking shop, as had the comfy rocking chair in the corner next to her large window that overlooked their backyard.

The four white walls were empty except for two dress hooks. As the mouthwatering aroma of baked chicken and dumplings floated up the stairs and into Rachel's room, she said a quick prayer of thanks for all she had.

Bending, she opened the hope chest and pulled her journal from inside. As she did so, the sound of chattering cicadas came in through the open window. The air was a comfortable temperature that held the smell of freshly cut grass.

Rachel closed the lid of her hope chest and once again looked at Old Sam's work. Right now, the horse-and-buggy scene brought her spirits down. Her sadness had nothing to do with the four-legged animal in wood; it had everything to do with the suffering of her living horse, Cinnamon. She caught an emotional breath at the thought of Sam's inspiration for the art. She quickly pressed her palms together.

"Lord, please get him well. Don't let him die.

Amen." For long, heartfelt moments, her gaze lingered on the etching until she blinked at the salty sting of tears.

Finally, with great care, she placed her private book on the desk and flipped to the first empty page. The moment she did so, she eyed a speck of dust on the corner.

She ran a finger over it and quickly returned her attention to the lines. Mamma always told Rachel that her "thing" for dust wasn't bad, but that it was a bit extreme.

As usual, her heart picked up to a happy speed while she considered where to start. She aimed to preserve her most special moments for when she got old. If she lost her memory, she'd have a backup.

Her bare feet caressed the smooth hardwood floor when she inched them closer to her body, wiggling her toes as she did so. Writing was her favorite part of the day. She breathed in contentment while she reflected on what had happened.

She recorded the date. As words came, she crossed her legs at the ankles and shifted her hips for a more comfortable position. Even simple things were important, and she never wanted to take them for granted. But that wasn't all she wrote about.

She tapped her pointer finger against the stained wood for a moment, then stretched her arms. As she did so, a yawn escaped her. She put her palm over her mouth and continued writing. There were so many blessings. *My parents, six married sisters and their families, Old Sam, and a supportive community.* She paused. *My beloved Cinnamon. And Dr. Zimmerman.*

She began recording her thoughts.

God has blessed me with love. Of course, life is never 100 percent perfect. I expect challenges. They test my faith. But that's not a bad thing, because throughout Cinnamon's illness, I'm becoming stronger. And I'll need that strength to protect my children when I'm a mamma.

I enjoy everything about the Amish lifestyle.

She stopped a moment as her imagination went to work and her special goal pulled the corners of her lips up until her smile stuck. She referred to it as "the dream." It was on her mind when she woke up, at night as she drifted off to sleep, and during the day.

Old Sam taught me to look at my glass as half-full. To concentrate on the positives. Because all good things come from God. Our lives can be happy or sad. Happiness is a choice.

Although I strive to be satisfied, something makes my heart heavy. Cinnamon is very sick. Sugar cubes don't even interest him. I've tried my best to cheer him up. Sam has always told me that attitude plays a large role in recovery.

I've even tried relating to Cinnamon Sam's horse-and-buggy stories.

Several heartbeats later, she went on, increasing the tempo of her writing so her words kept up with her thoughts.

I respect Old Sam's opinion more than anyone's. I'm aware that a number of horses in the area have already passed from the virus going around. Right now, Cinnamon needs me to not give up.

At the end of her entry, she added her dream. She flipped her journal closed and considered what she'd written as she returned her attention to the hope chest.

Her fingers lingered with affection on the lid because touching the beautiful piece sparked her imagination. Hope. It was like a security blanket that offered assurance that the world was at her doorstep.

As she contemplated something that seemed somewhat impossible, yet doable, she stepped back to the window and gently ran her hand over the light blue curtain that was pulled to the side. There was just enough light to glimpse the old barn.

Chickens made their way into their roosts for the night. She glimpsed the haymow, propane tanks, daddy's large pile of firewood. Mamma's clothesline was empty. The family buggy was parked next to their two-story house, which had been built by her great-grandfather.

She knew the inside of their means of transportation like the back of her hand. Blue velvety material on the front and back benches. Three windows. Two metal steps.

She pushed out a deep, anxious breath because she couldn't look at the buggy without thinking of Cinnamon. She loved him more than anyone could imagine.

The moment Dr. Zimmerman appeared in her mind, she pushed out a sigh of relief. *Look at the glass as half-full,* she'd told him. The compassion in his voice gave her hope. The determined expression in his eyes was the reassurance she needed at a time when she was afraid. He loved Cinnamon, too. Maybe that was why she had immediately felt at ease with him.

She found herself wondering about the young veterinarian. The more she considered him, the more interested she became in the man who would help Cinnamon recover.

Did he have lots of pets when he was young? What made him want to become a veterinarian? So many questions flitted through her mind, and her pulse picked up to a curious speed that increased the longer she thought about him.

She'd wanted to talk much more to her newfound friend, but she'd known not to ask too many questions. After all, he was a doctor, and he probably had many more appointments after Cinnamon's.

For some reason, her heart skipped a beat as she recalled his eyes. She'd noticed that their conversation had ceased the moment she'd mentioned his parents. She wasn't sure why he hadn't commented, but she'd caught how he'd stiffened. She put a hand on her hip and gazed out into the darkening sky.

She thought of Old Sam, Cinnamon, how long it would take for him to rebound from the virus. But the kind veterinarian drifted into her mind—and stayed there.

Chapter Two

A couple of days later, Rachel was making her way to Paula and the family buggy after doing errands in town when she glimpsed Dr. Zimmerman's truck in front of King's Bakery. Just then, he stepped out of the bakery and glanced in her direction. Rachel smiled and waved. He returned her friendly gesture as he moved toward the sidewalk seating area outside the bakery.

As Rachel approached his table, voices from the locals floated through the air, morphing into one sound. The bright sun warmed her face.

"How's everything with Cinnamon?"

Rachel lifted her shoulders in a shrug. "No better, no worse."

As they stepped closer to each other, he motioned to the paper bag between his fingers. "Care to join me?"

He eyed the small circular glass-top table on the sidewalk in front of him. "My next appointment's not for another hour, and I just happen to have an extra roll." He winked.

Rachel's smile turned into a full-blown grin. "I'd love to. There's no way I'd turn down a cinnamon roll from King's. They're the best around!" She nodded in the direction of the well-known pastry shop.

"They do the yearly cinnamon drive around Christmas, right?"

She offered a nod. With great care, he used a white napkin to pull a roll from the bag and handed it to her.

"Thank you."

As she took the seat opposite him, he quickly moved to help with her chair. His hand brushed her wrist. At his touch, she warmed inside.

The slight drop in temperature in the shade of the building was a welcome relief from the heat. She'd certainly never complained about long sleeves, but often wondered what it would feel like to wear a summer top like English girls did.

"Are you thirsty? I'll get you a beverage . . ."

She shook her head. "No, thanks." She could have used a drink of water but didn't want to inconvenience him.

"You seem happy today. You haven't stopped smiling."

She beamed. "Oh, Dr. Zimmerman, I just learned the best news!" She scooted forward in her seat and rested her elbows on the table. "My oldest sister's going to have a baby! That means I'll be an aunt again!"

She paused. "Of course, I already have nieces and nephews, seven to be exact, but this little one will be particularly special."

He waited for her to continue.

She cleared her throat. "You see, Hannah has tried to have children for several years. We've all been praying for her to get pregnant."

The expression on his face was a combination of surprise and joy. "That's wonderful news, Rachel!"

"Thank you, Doctor. I've never been this excited for a new baby! Hopefully, he or she will be healthy. And Hannah, too. This pregnancy is an answered prayer."

After a thoughtful pause, Rachel moved closer to the edge of her chair. The legs made a noise as they scraped the concrete. "I can't wait till the baby comes! But it's six months away!" She drew her arms over her chest. "It seems like such a long time."

He laughed, sat back in his chair, and crossed his legs. "All in God's time, Rachel. Your niece or nephew will be here, and that little person will have as much love as any kid could ever have, I'm sure of it."

"I know. I love my family. And the best times happen when we're all together. Thank goodness, my sisters don't live far away."

The conversation continued until a light squeal of brakes sounded when a car driving past stopped for a pedestrian. As a woman crossing the street waved to the driver, Doc Zimmerman glanced at his wrist-watch and crunched the empty paper bag in the palm of his hand. He tossed it into the nearby garbage can and stood. "Time to get back to work."

As she got up, he quickly made his way behind her to pull out her chair. Again, his fingers brushed her hand, and like before, the pulse above her wrist did an excited jump.

"Here, let me carry that for you." He took the bag of spices. "I'll walk you to your buggy."

As they stepped side by side, Rachel tried to savor the happy sensation that floated through her entire body. She knew her prayers for Cinnamon would be answered. God had blessed Hannah with a baby inside her, so Rachel was confident that Dr. Zimmerman would be able to nurse Cinnamon back to health.

She swallowed as she considered the kind, gentle man next to her. She'd never felt this sort of excitement with anyone else and found herself wondering what it would be like to date him.

She quickly chastised herself. He wasn't a part of the Amish church. But to her dismay, she couldn't stop wanting to spend time with him. The thought prompted a smile. Some day, she hoped to be a wife and a mother, just like Hannah would soon be. But something Jarred had said stuck with her, and she silently repeated the words. *All in God's time.*

A few days later, Rachel stood close to Cinnamon, repeating soothing things to her horse while Dr. Zimmerman went through his checks. She looked around the large barn that Daddy and some neighbors had built after a bad storm had destroyed the old one.

A feeling of comfort settled in her shoulders. She loved the beautiful oak rafters leading up to the pitch of the roof where skylights allowed the sun to penetrate the tall building.

On the other side of the structure were nesting boxes for the twenty or so chickens. Behind them, her gaze followed the tall ladder up to the loft, where Daddy kept bales of hay and straw.

Next to the large entrance were shelves upon shelves filled with work tools, chicken feed, pails, and other paraphernalia. Her father liked things clean and in order. In that respect, she was a lot like him.

A mixture of farm smells filled the air. She'd grown up in this environment. Her familiar surroundings comforted her.

When Dr. Zimmerman finally spoke, disappointment edged his voice. "No significant improvement yet, unfortunately, Rachel."

The veterinarian gave a slow shake of his head before meeting her gaze. "His temp is still high. His lymph nodes are swollen. I'm giving him another dose of anti-inflammatory and electrolytes. After that, let's rinse him down again."

"Okay."

They worked together. While they wiped cold water off Cinnamon, Rachel struggled to stay positive, but it wasn't easy because Cinnamon was ill. What bothered her most was his listless expression and lack of appetite. She wished she could take some of his pain.

"Hey, cheer up." The corners of his lips lifted into a wide, contagious smile. "Just think of that little niece or nephew you'll get to hold soon." He swatted away a fly that buzzed in front of him.

She grinned at the pleasant realization, and a giggle escaped her as she imagined holding another new baby. "Jarred, I'm thinking of names. Have you ever helped to name a little one?"

He laughed. "Can't say that I have. Unless you include horses and dogs."

Rachel giggled. A light breeze coming in through the doors blew some loose straw across the concrete floor. "If you could name your first child, girl or boy, what name would you pick?"

He stopped what he was doing and darted her an uncertain glance. Several heartbeats later, he spoke. "Let me think on it, Rachel."

"Okay. Hannah wants everyone's input before deciding."

"I'm sure she does. Deciding your firstborn's name . . ." He let out a low whistle. "That's a big thing."

As he finished and began zipping up his medical case, she recalled why he was here. Her joy over the baby news competed with the sadness about her suffering horse.

"I wish there was some improvement. Even a little." She pretended to measure with her thumb and pointer finger.

He patted the horse while holding Rachel's gaze. "Upper respiratory viruses are tough. Unfortunately, there's no magic bullet to cure them. But from my experience, improvement can strike all at once. And I'm praying hard for a recovery."

The statement prompted her to step closer to him. "You are a true friend, Doctor."

The expression in his eyes reflected surprise.

"Thank you for that, Rachel. It means a lot. This guy here . . ." He glanced at the gelding. "He's my favorite patient." A frustrated sigh escaped his throat. "I watched him barely survive, and it broke my heart. Now I ache for him again. It's just not fair."

The way he said the words prompted Rachel to look harder at the man who seemed incredibly dedicated to getting Cinnamon well.

She cleared her throat. When she continued, her voice cracked with emotion. "Thank you for all you're doing."

The expression in his eyes became more haunted than before. Their gazes locked while she tried to guess his thoughts. The turbulence in his eyes grew. At that moment, she was certain something haunted him. She couldn't help but wonder what it was.

When he didn't respond, she gave a helpless shrug of her shoulders. "I appreciate you."

"I'm glad to be of assistance." He paused. "And it's all my pleasure to help such a lovely lady."

Her heart fluttered. She'd never had anyone say that about her, let alone a man that she admired so much. Members of her church focused on a person's inside more than the outside. All the same, what he'd said made her pulse jump to a happier pace.

For an awkward moment, she continued to look at him. Finally, for something to do, she threw her hands in the air and smiled a little. "Thank you for the compliment, Doctor."

He paused and brushed some straw off the front of his jeans. "Rachel, I want to clarify that I was referring to your heart. I always learned in church that beauty comes from within, but with you, beauty is inside and out."

Warmth flooded her face and she looked down at the ground to hide the color she knew was in her cheeks.

To her relief, he changed the subject. "I'm praying for Cinnamon's recovery." He glanced at the horse. "For Cinnamon." Then he lowered his chin and pointed at her. "And for you."

Not only was he trying to get her horse well, but he cared so much.

"I can tell by Daddy's lack of interest that he's already written Cinnamon off. I love my father with all of my heart, but I have never been able to make him believe that Cinnamon is part of our family."

She raised her palms to the ceiling in a gesture of helplessness. "Daddy only considers horses a means of transportation. And that's frustrating."

Finally the doctor offered a nod of recognition. "It'll be okay, Rachel. Nothing's ever perfect. Not for you, and certainly not for me. We're only human."

She immediately wondered if his statement was in any way related to his lack of reaction to her compliment about his folks a few days ago.

He looked down and smiled sadly. When he glanced up at her, he said softly, "You caught me off guard the other day when you commented about being raised in a loving home." He shrugged. "I've given your comment a lot of thought. Fortunately, I was brought up with unconditional love, but I wish my parents had cared enough about me to raise me."

Her heart nearly stopped as she digested his statement and the sad tone of his voice as he'd said it. "I'm sorry."

He offered a slow shake of his head. "No apology necessary. My mom and dad sent me off to distant relatives here in the area when I was only four." He shrugged disappointedly. "And the truth is, Rachel, that I haven't seen or spoken to my mother and father since. They're in Ohio."

His shocking words took her breath away. She was sure her eyes were as wide with surprise as the state of Texas.

He continued to gather his things and carefully placed them into his brown medical pouch. She stepped closer to hear him.

Rachel ached for him. Obviously, the turmoil behind his dark depths wasn't her imagination. There was a deep reason for the haunted expression in his eyes. She had an inkling that there was a sad story around Cinnamon's kind doctor and his mother and father. What had happened?

It was already the second week in June. Rachel's pulse on her wrist pumped with renewed energy and hope as Jarred pulled away in his pickup. After waving good-bye, she stood for long, thoughtful moments, watching his silver Ford disappear around the corner. The dust at the end of the drive lingered like a foggy cloud before finally settling.

The bright noon sun caressed her face, and she closed her lids to enjoy the warm, feathery sensation. When she opened her eyes, she placed her hands on her hips and turned.

Between the barn and where she stood, the welcome breeze picked up enough speed to move the damp garments on the clothesline up and down. The green leaves on the cherry trees rustled, and vegetable plants in Daddy's garden did a slight dip to the west. On both sides, farmers worked the fields. Rachel breathed in the fragrant aroma of Mamma's homemade tomato soup that was carried on the breeze.

Mamma's voice startled her. Returning to reality, Rachel automatically held out her hand to accept the lined basket with a smile. With a wave, Mamma looked toward the healthy plants.

"Tomatoes are ready. You should get a basket full. The Early Girls are lookin' good. And while you're in there," she waved a hand at the garden, "you might come across some bell peppers, too. By the way, your daddy just picked up our voice messages, and Hannah's doing great!"

When Mamma stepped back toward the house, Rachel smiled at the good news while she proceeded to the large area of vegetables. Careful not to step on the vines, she slowly and cautiously edged her way between narrow rows and carefully pushed tall plants out of the way.

The velvety leaves came higher than Rachel's waist. The combination of moisture and warm weather had produced record crops in the fields. This fall's harvest should be something to celebrate.

As she set the basket on the ground, the pleasant, fresh scent from the nearby pumpkin blossoms filled her nostrils. She glanced at the half-closed yellow blooms that were ready for picking, too. But she'd wait till early morning, when they were full.

With practiced care, she used both hands to pull the deep red tomatoes, holding the fragile stems to prevent the vines from snapping. Unable to resist the sweet cherry tomatoes, she rubbed a couple over her apron, slipped them into her mouth, and sighed with delight. They were her favorites. And she loved the juice she and her sisters would help Mamma can later in the summer.

A buzzing noise interrupted her thoughts. She

slapped at a mosquito that landed on her sleeve. From experience, she knew that her long dress wouldn't prevent bites. Produce was wonderful, but fresh food didn't come without pests.

As she filled her basket, she considered Cinnamon's doctor and the conversation they'd shared only a short while ago. To her surprise, despite their hour-long visit in the barn, she still didn't know much about him, other than his special interest in healing. And that he'd named a lot of animals. Of course, the purpose of his visit hadn't been personal.

She bent to add two medium-sized Big Boys to her growing collection. *Does he have brothers? Sisters? Why did his folks desert him?*

Before she'd even met him, she'd heard about his gentle, kind touch with animals. Everything from dogs to horses had made miraculous recoveries under his tender care. A huge sense of relief swept over her, and the tenseness at the back of her neck went away.

She returned her basket to the dry earth at her feet and crossed her arms over her waist to briefly enjoy her surroundings. She was a self-proclaimed dreamer, and this beautiful ambience was conducive to thoughtfully drifting away.

In the distance, she glimpsed Old Sam's barn. As she took in the view, a story came to her about his horse, Ginger. Rachel tried to recall specifics. Ginger had once suffered a serious malady. In fact, the illness was so grave, Dr. Steven's prognosis had looked hopeless.

But despite the grim prediction, Sam had never given up. Neither had Esther. Every day, they both prayed for Ginger's recovery. In the meantime, they gave their best care. Eventually, God had rewarded their faith, and Ginger rebounded. Rachel recalled how their tense weeks of tremendous concern had quickly evaporated like steam from a teakettle.

Look at the glass as half-full. She had no doubt that Cinnamon would follow suit. Rachel's faith was strong. Her Lord and Savior wouldn't take her beloved friend from her, not yet, anyway.

In a silent prayer, she thanked God for Cinnamon and for the recovery she was certain would come. After a slight pause, she offered another prayer—for Dr. Zimmerman.

The more she considered him, the more she yearned to learn everything about him. The soft-spoken healer who'd responded to Daddy's call was obviously special, and his presence eased her worries about Cinnamon. But something from the doctor's past saddened him.

There was a reason behind his haunted expression. Still, whenever she was around him, she felt unusually happy. In fact, for some reason, just the mere thought of him prompted a wide smile. She barely knew him, yet she was sure she knew his heart. And that's what mattered.

She'd been taught to focus on the inside of a person, not the exterior. But his eyes intrigued her. The dark-blue gray reminded her of the deep lake where Daddy fished for bass. On the surface, the water looked calm and beautiful, but she'd always wondered what it looked like beneath it.

Certainly, she was no expert at reading minds. She didn't have a college degree. Not even a high school diploma like the English kids in town got. But she had Old Sam. She nodded in satisfaction.

What she'd learned from him was more valuable than anything a textbook could teach her—of that she was sure.

He had commented more than once that the eyes were the windows to a person's soul, and she believed him. He knew everything. Of course, he had experienced a lot in his eightysomething years.

A monarch butterfly landed on top of her pointer finger. As she watched the insect gracefully fly away, she recognized that she definitely considered Cinnamon's doctor a special friend. She was glad she'd told him. She wanted him to know. Because . . . She wasn't sure why.

Letting out a deep breath, she knelt to reach a tomato nestled near the ground, close to the stem. For some reason, Jarred stayed on her mind. As she shoved a couple of Early Girls aside in the basket to make room for more, his kind, compassionate demeanor floated through her thoughts.

She wondered why his parents had sent him away when he was young. Mamma had always said that children are a product of their mother and father. In the vet's case, it couldn't be true.

She didn't want to be nosy; at the same time, she yearned to help him because he was a godsend to Cinnamon. Several heartbeats later, she decided that there was more to it than that. Definitely, there was something very special about Dr. Jarred Zimmerman. But how could she help him if she didn't know what was wrong?

Jarred had seen four other patients before he got home. Entering his house, he picked up two small feed bowls on his patio. Inside, he quickly filled them with food and water and stepped back outside to place them underneath the iron table.

He wiped away a bead of sweat that had slipped down his forehead. Since the tomcat's mysterious appearance a week ago, Jarred had maintained him with food and water to help him stay alive. He'd placed the small round table next to his back door for shade.

Jarred frowned. Unfortunately, it was common for unwanted animals to be dumped in the country. His opposition to such cruel actions only made him more determined to rescue the abandoned.

He smiled with satisfaction when the furry creature came closer. In the softest voice he could muster, Jarred said, "We'll be friends, you and I. I know you have trust issues, and I understand why because I do, too. But in time, you'll realize I'm your buddy. In the meantime, I'll offer you nutrition and shade."

Jarred adjusted the heavy cloth he'd placed over the table. This year's early June temps were unusually hot, and for now, this simple covering he'd cut out of material was the best he could do to protect the stray from the sun.

Still keeping watch on the golden fur, Jarred went to his back door. Inside, he listened as he clicked the lock into place and proceeded to the window to the open blinds for a better view of the poor thing feasting on scraps.

While the four-legged being that was barely more than skin and bones indulged, Jarred's stomach growled. He washed his hands, pulled premade chicken Kiev from his fridge, placed the breasts onto a baking dish, and shoved it into the oven. He turned the timer to forty minutes. While his dinner baked, he sat at the small kitchen table and opened his mail.

When the timer buzzed, he startled. He proceeded to the electric oven, removed the food, and pulled the foil. Admiring his efforts, Jarred smiled at the dish he'd taught himself to make when he'd first moved into this place.

He scooped the golden-brown stuffed breasts onto a plate from his cupboard and sat down at the table. Before taking a bite, he folded his hands and bowed his head. "Dear Lord, thank you for this food." He paused. "And I'm grateful for the chance to help Cinnamon. Please gift me the right knowledge to save him. Amen."

While he cut his dinner into pieces, he glanced out of the window in time to glimpse the stray finish the last bite and drink from the water bowl before rushed, timid steps took him away from the house.

Jarred tested his dinner and gave a slight nod of approval. His thoughts were still on the feline. He spoke under his breath. "You and me, buddy, we've got a lot in common. Someday I'll tell you my story."

Jarred focused on his all-time favorite dinner. With the help of the cookbook on top of the fridge, he'd taught himself to make a superb meal.

As he savored the buttery taste, he drifted back to his childhood. Unfortunately, home-cooked meals had been few and far between. The Mennonite couple who'd raised him had frequented restaurants. Of course, he would have enjoyed homemade dinners, not only for the taste, but to enjoy the family-type atmosphere.

He wasn't complaining, that's for sure. They had

loved him like a son. They'd done their best to comfort him during the long adjustment that followed after his folks had sent him to them. Most importantly, they'd raised him in a Christian home. For that, he was most grateful.

They'd both been taken in a car crash before his graduation from Purdue University. Every time he thought of the accident, his chest ached. He missed them. Wanted with everything he had to hug them and thank them for being there for him.

He focused on a happier subject: Rachel. A smile tugged the corners of his mouth up. Her comment about being a true friend stuck in his mind. He pressed his lips together and cupped his chin with his hand. The unexpected statement prompted a strange combination of joy and dismay.

Obviously, the honest remark flattered him. He didn't know Rachel well, but his instincts were usually right on target. His keen sense of reading people had kicked in at an early age. So had his lack of trust. By contrast, the Kauffman girl was unusually open and honest. Without a doubt, Rachel represented everything he'd yearned for growing up. When he was with her, an unprecedented sense of comfort and security filled his heart and soul.

But he had reciprocated her sentiment. And to his surprise, he'd confessed to her that his parents hadn't raised him. It was the first time he'd ever told anyone, but she was a good listener, and the sad story of growing up without his own mom and dad was something he'd carried on his shoulders for a long time.

He stood and paced to the living room to glance at the picture of his brother. At that moment, he knew he had to stay realistic about this sudden adoration for the beautiful Amish girl. Although she was of the Christian faith, the Amish way of life differed greatly from his own, so any feelings he had could only lead to a dead-end street.

That evening, Rachel knew something was wrong. After dinner, she began helping two of her sisters, Mary and Doris, clear the table. Married, they lived nearby and often brought their families for dinner.

To her surprise, her father interrupted them and motioned to her. Her siblings looked at each other and curiously raised their eyebrows as Rachel obediently followed him into the living room and claimed a seat on the couch.

Her dad sat opposite her. The expression of uncertainty on his face prompted Rachel to stiffen. Her pulse picked up speed. She clutched her hands together on her lap. "Daddy, what's wrong?"

He leaned forward and lowered his voice to a more sensitive tone. "Honey, I know how much you love Cinnamon."

Her gaze didn't leave her father's face. It wasn't like him to talk to her as the table was being cleared. Her heart jumped with anxiety.

"Rachel, Cinnamon's very, very ill. And he's not going to recover."

She jumped to her feet and cried, "Yes, he is, Daddy! Dr. Zimmerman believes it, too."

When her father pointed to the chair, she sat back down. She never disobeyed or talked back, but she couldn't bear the thought of losing her horse.

"Your mother and I have been talking, honey. We agree that it's best to put Cinnamon down."

Only one person could help Rachel, and that was Dr. Zimmerman. The next morning, the soft purring of an engine made her stop what she was doing and bound outside to greet her new friend.

She offered a big, desperate wave as he parked in their drive. She ran toward his truck, hiking her dress as she did so to avoid tripping. She watched him remove his sunglasses and lay them between his cloth seats before slamming the door shut.

Rachel and Jarred stepped quickly to the barn.

"Is everything okay?"

At first, her response was silence. As soon as they were inside the barn, she teared up. "Doctor, something really bad's about to happen." She threw her hands in the air.

Her sentences ran together as she poured out the details of the conversation she'd had with her dad. Then she pushed out a sigh and locked gazes with the veterinarian. "Can you help me? Please?"

Chapter Three

Jarred listened to Rachel's devastating words that came out of her mouth so quickly, they ran together. He blinked at the sun coming in through the large barn windows. As hard as he tried, Jarred couldn't control the helpless frustration in his chest as the girl sobbed uncontrollably into her palms.

He knew better than anyone what it was like to lose a being dear to one's heart. He faced it each day. Of course, every patient didn't survive. Saving every animal and each human—that would be impossible.

But he took this crisis more personally because of his longtime bond with Cinnamon and because of the extreme, rare love between girl and horse. *You've got to help her.*

He yearned to console her. At the same time, he was fully aware that it was improper to touch an Amish girl. Despite his knowledge, he embraced her in a tight hug.

Her tears flowed while he gently patted her back.

"It'll be okay, Rachel. Please, don't cry. Instead, let's talk about what to do."

Too conscious of the softness in his heart, he released her and apologized if he had offended her.

She wiped at her eyes while composing herself. "No. I'm sorry. This is my fault. There's nothing to apologize for, Doctor. What you said . . . about talking about what to do . . ." She sniffed and lifted her chin with sudden hope. "But we can do something, *jah?*"

He offered a firm nod and a swift wave toward two bales. They sat down on the straw, and he turned toward her. In a serious voice, he started. "Rachel, I want Cinnamon to recover every bit as much as you do."

He paused to consider the right words. "At the same time, I understand where your dad's coming from."

Her eyes widened with shock.

He raised his hand. "Hear me out. If you're a math person who looks at things in black and white, you'd probably focus on all of the horses taken by the virus. And I'm sure your father wants to spare Cinnamon pain. But if you're optimistic, as you are, you would focus on the chance that your horse would survive."

"What do you think, Dr. Zimmerman?"

He frowned. The words seemed so formal. "Call me Jarred."

He noted the surprise that registered in her eyes while he considered her question. "I truly believe with all of my heart that Cinnamon will rebound.

I don't really have evidence to support that; it's a feeling inside me."

He shrugged. "Unfortunately, recovery isn't a short journey. And I've met plenty of others who just won't stick it out." He shook his head. "Life is a miracle, Rachel. I understand people who want to end misery. And I agree, in some cases. Pain is evil. But life is precious. And if Cinnamon rebounds, and there's a chance, he's got a lot of living ahead of him. Sugar cubes, for instance. Not to mention that right now, he's in his prime."

He winked.

She smiled. "I don't want Cinnamon to hurt, Jarred."

The sound of his name from her mouth stirred something warm and wonderful within him. He wasn't sure what it was.

She choked. "But I just know he'll recover. Can't we give him more time?"

"Tell you what, Rachel. I'll talk to your dad. And if he'll allow me, when he's ready to throw in the towel, I'll take our sick guy to my place and care for him."

The expression in her eyes, a combination of surprise and extreme gratefulness, prompted a grin. Her reaction sparked something else that he didn't recognize, but whatever it was it made him feel good inside.

He softened his voice to make sure she understood that it would be okay. "Cinnamon will have every opportunity to get well if your dad will agree."

* * *

A short time later, Rachel swept two horse stalls while Jarred made a trip to his truck for medicine. *Jarred asked me to call him by his first name.* She closed her eyes in happiness and savored his words. It felt so good to say his first name.

Her dad's voice made her look up. "Your horse ain't improving." Several feet away, he cleaned his farm tools. She could hear the light whistle of metal scraping metal.

"Daddy, he's not just mine. He belongs to all of us. He's part of our family." She heaved out a frustrated moan. "He's worked so hard for us over the years. Don't forget when he's taken us to church in the freezing cold and on the hottest days in the summer."

"Honey, other horses can do that work."

The statement prompted the corners of her lips to turn down into a sad frown. She wouldn't argue with Daddy. That would be disrespectful. But she wished he would appreciate what Cinnamon had done for them. Why did most people see animals just as a means to get things done? Their hearts needed nurturing, just like humans'.

She realized he was awaiting a reply. "I'm really worried about him."

As usual, Daddy's voice was unbending. "I've already replaced him with a healthy filly."

"I know, Daddy." Rachel's heart sank. *Have faith. Look at the glass as half-full.* "But no horse can or ever will replace Cinnamon."

"Honey, I know you love him, but that bad virus goin' round is fatal. It's not right to make him suffer."

She bit her tongue.

He continued cleaning his tools. She was very

much like her daddy and so much unlike him. They were both unusually tidy. She kept the house free of dust. And his farm equipment must have been cleaner than anyone's around.

At the same time, she searched for the positive, and her daddy leaned more toward the pessimistic side. She'd even talked to Old Sam about it, but Old Sam had merely grinned and said that her father was too old to change.

"It's takin' a lot of good animals from us." Her dad paused. When he resumed his talk, he squinted as if what he said was agonizing. "I just don't want you to get your hopes up, honey. If he rebounds, it'll be a miracle."

Rachel lifted her chin. "Then it'll be a miracle."

At that moment, Rachel sighed in relief when Jarred walked through the doors. She spoke with hopeful conviction. "Dr. Zimmerman's gonna get Cinnamon well, Daddy. I just know it! Remember how Old Sam's Ginger recovered?"

"I'm doing the best I can to help your horse." Before Rachel's dad could respond, the doctor went on. "I understand why you don't like the horse suffering. Neither do I. But I'm hoping that he'll recover. Please give us more time, Mr. Kauffman. And when that window of opportunity expires on your end, I'd like permission to take Cinnamon to my place."

The expression on Rachel's father's face was of the utmost shock. Of course, he didn't understand Jarred's love or hers for the struggling animal. But he didn't have to. As long as Cinnamon got well.

Finally, Daddy offered a slow, thoughtful nod. "Let me think on it."

"I appreciate that, Mr. Kauffman. In the meantime, I'll give him meds to ease the pain."

Rachel glanced at Jarred before focusing her attention on her dad. She thought Daddy would give Jarred's offer serious consideration. She hoped so, anyway. She would pray that God would speak to her father.

As Jarred watched Rachel in his rearview mirror, he took a swig of soda and placed the can in the cup holder between the cloth bucket seats. He'd made his case for more recovery time. He checked his watch and accelerated before flipping on the cruise control.

As usual, he was running behind. He drove with his right hand on the wheel and his left forearm propped comfortably on the open window. When the bright sun reappeared behind a large, fluffy cloud, he pulled down his visor and slipped on his sunglasses.

He enjoyed the open countryside, trying to relax while he passed corn and bean fields. The scene should have provided some sort of comfort. But inside, he shook with uncertainty. He couldn't take seeing Rachel so sad. And he'd asked her to call him by his first name. Why?

It just felt right.

Without taking his eyes from the road, he opened the compartment to the right of his seat, stuck his hand inside a plastic bag, and quickly retrieved a cinnamon candy. He removed the plastic wrapper, tossed it onto the floor of the passenger seat, and popped the red ball into his mouth.

For most of his life, he'd attended the Mennonite church with Carolyn and Henry Zimmerman, who'd officially changed Jarred's last name to match theirs. Yet his Methodist start had a permanent spot in his heart. Sometimes, he wasn't sure if he really felt part of either.

Even though he currently attended the Methodist church closest to home, he was most impressed by the Amish. Something about them and their modest lifestyle comforted his soul. A soothing sensation caressed his shoulders. He'd never felt like an outsider around the Plain Faith. Through his work, Jarred had come into contact with plenty of them, and he'd never met an unkind one. The Amish called on vets frequently, as their livelihood depended on animals.

He couldn't blame Mr. Kauffman for his thoughts about Cinnamon. While he drove, he relaxed and breathed in the fresh air. No chaos. No noise. And no stress.

He braked at a T-intersection and looked around the corn, moving closer to the side of the road when another pickup met his. Automatically, he waved. The driver returned the gesture. After they passed, Jarred reclaimed the middle of the blacktop, where the road was slightly higher. He gave careful thought to Rachel's plea and to his solution.

He understood so well why she didn't want to say good-bye to Cinnamon, especially if there was a chance for a rebound. But Jarred never made predictions. Only God knew who would and wouldn't make it. In his heart, Jarred sensed that her horse would survive because he'd asked God for that special favor. So had Rachel. There was strength in prayers.

He didn't want to watch Rachel say farewell to her horse. He'd never forget the day he'd waved good-bye to his parents and moved in with Carolyn and Henry. An ache pinched his chest, and he frowned. That night, when he'd prayed, he'd begged God to protect him.

Jarred had only been four. But even at such a young age, he'd understood with great clarity that he belonged to the Creator of the universe. Not to his parents. Not to Carolyn and Henry. What mattered was that he pleased God, and he did that by healing the most vulnerable of the Lord's creations.

Jarred drummed his fingers on the steering wheel while that ugly day floated back into his mind like an unexpected storm. Before that, he'd believed that his parents loved him. He couldn't bear to think that they didn't.

A bead of sweat slipped down his forehead. As he wiped it away, he repeated his order to himself, the commitment he'd made years ago: *Don't go there. You don't have to. It's over.*

He coughed at the tightness of emotion in his throat, and to his surprise, recalled Rachel's words of optimism. *Look at the glass as half-full.* The uncomfortable quickness of his pulse slowed as he forced himself to see only positive things.

Matt had loved him. Every time Jarred thought of his older brother, he became more determined to start a shelter in Matt's name. His beloved sibling had been the ultimate animal lover, and Jarred awakened each morning of his life with that purpose in mind.

Salty tears stung his eyes. He blinked. *My Savior*

loves me, but there's no way to ever bring my brother back. Or to make my parents love me.

Look at the glass as half-full. When Rachel's face popped into his mind, his heart lightened. The girl was unusually wise for her young age. He wasn't sure but guessed she must be in her late teens. She stirred an emotion inside him that he'd never experienced. How he felt when he was around her . . . It was new to him.

She looked at the positive in everything. Of course, her life obviously differed from his in a huge way. He was certain she didn't have the mental baggage that he carried inside. On the contrary, he supposed she had a protective, loving family. He imagined the biggest drama that ever happened in their household. *A pot roast overcooking?* The thought forced a laugh.

To his relief, the more he thought of her, the more the ache between his shoulders eased. There was something so comforting and familiar about her, he could be himself around her. When they talked, he felt a welcome sense of belonging.

As he made his final turn, he acknowledged the great benefit to spending time with Rachel. The peaceful countryside helped him, too. Perhaps he was at ease in this landscape because he'd been raised on a large ranch. Maybe his comfort zone was away from crowds because he didn't feel the need to please anyone other than those who needed him.

Whatever the case, he knew his calling. Regardless of his past, God had given him a mission. He'd known it since Matt's death, and this time, Jarred wouldn't let his Savior down.

He'd never wanted an animal to recover as much as he yearned for Rachel's horse to. Matt would want it, too. And a large part of Jarred's determination to heal the horse had to do with its beautiful, kind owner.

That realization made him breathe in. He flipped the radio to the country music channel and drummed his fingers against the wheel to the beat. While Wynonna's big voice boomed through his small cabin, he considered what had happened today in the Kauffman barn.

He'd comforted a lovely girl who was frightened to death of losing her gelding. But that wasn't what had impacted him the most. He understood his incredible longing to take away her pain. His strong need to rescue her from sadness was logical.

What he didn't comprehend was what had gone on inside him while he'd comforted her, when he'd wrapped his arms around her to make her feel better. What disturbed him most was that he wasn't sure what he'd felt.

He contemplated the way his heart had picked up speed. His strong mission to help her. When she smiled, something wonderful had happened to him. He loved her soft voice. Her energy. Her determination. He finally acknowledged to himself that he was romantically interested in Rachel.

That evening, Rachel wrote on the lined pages of her journal. She breathed in the pleasant apple scent from her candle and sighed with satisfaction.

I can't wait for Hannah's baby to come! I wonder if it will be a girl or a boy? I don't care, as long as it's healthy. I'm so glad I have that to look forward to.

Then her thoughts turned from Hannah's happy news to Cinnamon's poor health.

Today, I confided in Jarred. I wonder if I should have confessed my grave concern. Mamma always tells me to keep my private thoughts to myself. But I'm more worried about my horse's fate than ever.

I'm disappointed that my parents regard Cinnamon as merely a means to pull the buggy. That they don't try harder to believe in miracles. How can they not love and care about him like I do?

She stopped a moment to close her eyes. A wrenching pain pulled at her insides until she opened her eyes and decided to deal with the disappointing situation on paper. If she could visualize her penned thoughts, perhaps she could better accept her mom and dad's view on Cinnamon.

Nervous energy made her stand, grab the nearby feather duster, and run it over the headboard before continuing to the windowsill. When she reclaimed her seat, she laid the duster on the headboard. Taking a deep, satisfied breath, she reached for her pen and continued her thoughts.

To my surprise, I found it easier to relate my dilemma to Jarred than I ever dreamed. He makes me so at ease. And when I watched his eyes, I could tell he mirrored my own sentiments. I know he absorbed every single detail.

Rachel rolled her shoulders to rid the kinks. She crossed her legs at the knees and continued her train of thought.

There was a moment today. It was after I poured out my heart to Jarred. Our gazes locked. The expression in his eyes left me breathless. They're deep, mysterious, and something else. I don't have the word yet.

I've never encountered such a look. And it affected me in ways I'm not sure are proper. My feelings . . . it was as if Cinnamon connected us in a way that will bond us forever. I've no doubt that Jarred loves my horse as much as I do.

But it's not simply because he's an animal lover. He was even there for Cinnamon's birth. Jarred helped to deliver my horse and prayed for his recovery when it was predicted he wouldn't live. Cinnamon's a survivor. He overcame obstacles once. He'll do it again. But he needs time. That I'm sure of.

What I'm not certain of is my reaction to Jarred in the barn this afternoon.

She paused to recall every detail of his expression. His voice. His physical reaction to what she'd told him.

Even now, alone in her room, thinking about him caused her heart to beat at an unusually fast pace. But she wasn't sure why it was uncomfortable, too.

My heart sprinted. My cheeks flushed. My lungs had to pump harder than usual, and I felt out of

*breath. I wasn't in control of my own emotions. Am
I falling in love with Jarred Zimmerman?*

The following morning, Jarred glimpsed Rachel
as he stepped out of King's Bakery. As she came his
way, he offered a big wave. "Hello!"

While the sun slipped under a large, fluffy cloud,
they locked gazes from a distance. She returned
the greeting and quickened her pace. When they
were face-to-face, he motioned to the paper bag he
held in his other hand.

"Care to join me?" He glanced at his watch. "I've
got ten minutes before I have to leave for my next
appointment."

"I'd love to."

As she started to pull the patio chair away from
the small table, he took over, and pushed it closer to
the table once she was seated. His fingers touched
her hand, the light caress sending a warm tingle up
her arm.

Across from her, he removed a cinnamon roll
with a white napkin and handed it to her.

"Thank you."

At the same time, they ate. She swallowed and
smiled. "How's your day so far?"

"Better now that you're here."

He noted how she lowered her gaze to the table
and blushed. When she lifted her chin, her eyes
hinted at shyness. He barely tasted his pastry as he
took in the rosy color of her cheeks, the softness of
her voice.

"Mamma's talking with a couple of friends from church. She'll be coming this way."

"So what plans do you have for the rest of the day?"

Her eyes brightened. "It will take a while to finish my chores. After that, I get to help Daddy weed the garden. Daddy's kind of a jack-of-all-trades. But in his heart, I know he most enjoys growing vegetables and making sure there's plenty of food on our table."

"What's your favorite chore, Rachel?"

She finished her roll, swallowed, and ran her napkin over her mouth. "This probably won't surprise you."

"No?"

"Helping Daddy in the barn."

He nodded. "Of course."

She sighed. "I like to be with the animals." She looked away, and when she glanced back at him, her eyes glowed with satisfaction. "They count on me to take care of them. And I know this might sound odd, but, Jarred, they're family to me." She paused and added in a gentle, compassionate tone, "I know you understand."

He gave a slow nod. And as he did so, he understood more than her love for animals. He knew that Rachel Kauffman had more in common with him than anyone he'd ever met. And he wished he could spend the rest of the afternoon being with her.

Chapter Four

In Old Sam's barn, Rachel swept loose straw into a pile in front of Ginger, who whinnied for attention. Rachel grinned and stopped to stroke the horse's muzzle.

Rachel looked behind her and raised her voice to get Old Sam's attention. "Sam, can she have an apple?"

He looked up from his work. "I just bought some Red Delicious. Her favorite. Just one, though."

While Rachel fed Ginger the apple, his beloved Irish setter tugged at the bottom of Rachel's navy dress. Rachel looked down and laughed. "I love you, too, Buddy."

Then she joined Old Sam on the chair opposite his workbench. "Your family's spoiled."

The corners of his lips lifted, showing deep creases around his mouth. "I didn't want to disappoint. Esther cared for them like children. I'm not sure I could ever make them as happy as she did, even if I tried. She knit clothes for Buddy to keep him warm in the winter."

Old Sam nodded at Rachel. "I hear you're going to be an aunt again."

"*Jah!*"

"Congratulations!"

"Oh, Sam. It's a blessing. And I don't know if I can make it through the next several months!" Her gaze landed on the hope chest lid Sam was working on. When she took in the detail, her jaw dropped in awe. "A fisherman?"

Sam nodded and continued carving what appeared to be a pond. "This one's for a Florida woman. Her young grandson loves to fish. Some day, he wants to be captain of his own ship and take people on excursions in the Atlantic."

Rachel smiled. "How old is the boy?"

"Only five."

Rachel giggled.

"But he's no stranger to water. He goes out on a boat every weekend with his dad. His mother's going to keep his favorite toys in this hope chest."

Rachel's jaw dropped. "Oh, no, Old Sam. It's too beautiful for that. It'll get scratched."

He smiled in amusement. "The chests are sturdy. I add a thick finish to protect them."

He pulled his work close to brush away the chippings. "I haven't seen you for over a week. How's Cinnamon? Better, I hope?"

How Rachel wished she could boast of improvement in her four-legged friend. But she couldn't. Finally, she offered a helpless shrug.

"Still running a high fever. He's so lethargic, Sam. And thin. Doc Zimmerman's helping to get it down."

Sam nodded in recognition. "He must be good at

what he does. He and Doc Stevens helped the Mast family get their horse well a couple of years ago."

"Jarred was able to get Cinnamon's temperature down a bit, but there's still a long way to go. I'll sleep better when he's healthy enough to enjoy sugar cubes again."

"Jarred?"

"Dr. Zimmerman, I mean." She lifted her hands. "He told me to call him Jarred."

Old Sam offered a slow, accepting nod.

Rachel went on to explain her conversation with her father and Jarred's resolution.

Sam raised a thoughtful brow. "You know the best weapon, don't you?"

"Prayer."

Old Sam nodded. "Our Savior is in charge of progress, young one, so your Cinnamon is in good hands. God knows how much you love him. He has our lives all planned out, even your beloved Cinnamon's."

"He's a part of our family, Sam."

"Of course he is. There's nothing like the bond between you and your horse."

The image of the helpless expression in Cinnamon's eyes pulled at her heartstrings. She wished God would heal Cinnamon faster. The more she saw him suffer, the more difficult it became to watch him in pain.

"Cheer up, Rachel. Remember the advice I always give you?"

Rachel stared at him a moment before speaking in a soft voice. "Look at the glass as half-full."

"That's right. And when you consider all of the positives, I'm sure you'll feel better. I've known you your whole life. And you've got a fighting spirit. You'll get through this. Sometimes, the things we pray for don't happen overnight. So in the meantime, you've got to stay upbeat. Besides, you've got a new baby coming soon. Your sister will need your help."

He paused to work. Rachel turned her attention to the hope chest and could see the art start to take shape. She was sure the incredible detail would make this chest one of Sam's best pieces.

"Rachel, I know getting through the sickness of a loved one is difficult. But when my dear Esther was ill, I never allowed myself to imagine that she wouldn't make it."

Rachel crossed her legs at the ankles. "You looked at the glass as half-full."

"That's right. And because of my strong determination to provide her my absolute best, I have no regrets. I can honestly tell you that I gave her everything I had." He wiped a teary eye. "A positive attitude plays a huge part in the healing process, no matter who or what you are."

Rachel pressed her lips together in deep concentration while she digested his words.

He glanced up a moment. "Rachel, I know a story that will give you strong hope for Cinnamon. Did I ever tell you about Strawberry?"

The name prompted her to smile. Rachel imagined a reddish-colored animal. As she considered the question, she arched an eyebrow.

"Did Esther name her?"

A low chuckle escaped Sam's throat. "You know us too well. She did, just like she named every other pet we've adopted. This little filly was unique in every way, Rachel. When we first took her, never in my imagination did I dream how much we would fall in love with her.

"But life is full of surprises. And the struggles test us and make us who we are as people. Let me tell you about when Strawberry became ill with a bad strain of flu that was claiming horses 'round here."

He pulled the hope chest lid to his face and blew the small chips. Rachel watched them float in the air before landing on the barn floor. Her first instinct was to sweep them into the duster, but that would have to wait, because Sam was telling a story. One she'd never heard.

A long silence ensued as Sam gathered his thoughts, and Rachel studied the kind face detailed with lines and creases. He'd explained more than once that each crease represented something wonderful in his life. That if God blessed you with old age, your face would reflect significant events that had happened. He claimed that the sad lines on his forehead represented the deaths of his sons and Esther.

"Esther and I took in the little filly that had been given to us by a family that moved from the area."

Rachel scooted closer and leaned forward to not miss a word because nobody related horse-and-buggy stories like Old Sam.

After studying the piece he worked on, he continued talking while he etched the beautiful wood. "With Strawberry and Esther, it was love at first sight. And you remember how animals stole Esther's heart."

Rachel gave a strong nod. "I'll never forget when

Annie and Levi found that poor little kitten at the creek. Esther let them keep it here in this very barn."

"That's right." His eyes glistened. When he spoke, his voice vibrated with emotion. "She was an angel to the helpless."

Rachel swallowed a painful knot. She knew of another angel to the helpless. Jarred. She wished Esther were still here to keep Old Sam company. And her.

"Anyway, Strawberry loved Esther's sponge cakes."

Rachel giggled. "Really?"

"Uh-huh. In fact, she made extras for Strawberry. I must say that as far as I know," he laughed, "this is the only horse 'round here who was privy to such treats."

While Sam talked in slow, thoughtful sentences, Rachel created an image of Sam's wife conversing with Strawberry while the horse delighted in Esther's cooking. Already, she wondered what happened. She hoped there was a happy ending.

"Anyway, one day Esther brought a cake out to the barn for our dear Strawberry and found her lying down. This was unusual during the day."

"Just like Cinnamon."

Sam nodded and continued. "Anyway, we got a hold of Doc Stevens." He cleared his throat. "He did everything he could for poor, sick Strawberry."

Rachel's heart skipped a troubled beat.

"Doc Stevens never gave us hope." Sam pushed out a sigh. "The prognosis looked grim. The poor thing practically withered away to nothing."

Rachel gave a sad shake of her head.

Sam's voice shifted to a more urgent tone. "This

went on for weeks. Esther and I prayed and prayed for a miracle, because God is good."

Rachel nodded in agreement.

"And He answers prayers. We know that. And in this case, God made a miraculous recovery for our Strawberry."

Rachel pushed out a happy breath. "Oh!"

"One day, Esther came out here early in the morning, as she always did to talk to her horse, and do you know that our Strawberry perked up?"

"Really?"

Sam nodded.

Rachel's jaw dropped in a reaction that was a combination of shock and happiness. If Strawberry could get well, so could Cinnamon!

"The doctor couldn't explain her recovery except that it was a miracle from above." Sam motioned up with his large, withered hand. "And that was our Good Lord at work."

As Rachel digested the happy ending, she said a silent prayer for God to reward Cinnamon for all he'd been through.

When Sam finished talking, she eyed the pile of sawdust on the floor around his work area. As soon as he stepped away, Rachel took the broom to the area. A satisfied feeling went through her as she swept the woodsy-smelling chippings into the dustpan.

When Sam returned, he grinned. "That's my girl." A chuckle escaped his throat. "I've never known anyone as tidy as you."

"I'm not sure if it's good or bad. All I know is that cleaning is like brushing my teeth," she said. "I have to do it."

"I would say that's a plus. And I have no doubt that when you're a wife and mother, you'll keep the cleanest house around here."

She smiled a little and contemplated his statement. When she was a wife, there would be a spouse. She looked away to imagine who it would be.

While she allowed her mind to dream, there were two requirements that couldn't be negotiated in a husband. First, the man had to be Amish. And of equal importance, he had to love animals as much as she did.

A few days later, Rachel anxiously drummed her fingers against her thighs and listened for the quiet purring of Jarred's truck. Chickens clucked. A goat meandered past the horse stalls. The warm, damp morning breeze floated in through the open barn doors.

She leaned against Cinnamon and caressed him with the most soothing words she could think of. To her dismay, there was no reaction. Not even a whinny.

He's not improving. Closing her eyes, she breathed in and concentrated on Old Sam's constant advice. "Look at the glass as half-full. Remember Strawberry. And Ginger. God rewards the faithful."

Rachel opened her eyes and smiled a little. *On the upside, Cinnamon isn't worse.* She continued to caress her friend's ears. When he opened his large, sad eyes, Rachel sighed in relief and continued to encourage her horse to eat. It didn't work. However, she had stronger weapons. Prayers. Faith.

She looked up and offered a desperate plea.

"Please, God. Let him live. Show me a sign that he'll make it. I'm so worried. Amen."

Rachel scooped dirty straw with the large pitchfork and placed the manure in the nearby spreader. Most girls didn't like barn chores, but Rachel did. She loved being around animals.

And Hannah's new baby was around the corner! Rachel drew in an excited breath as she contemplated possible names. Mary . . . Jacob . . . William . . . Lydia . . .

The sound of tires meeting gravel made her jump to her feet. She offered Cinnamon an encouraging pat. "Our angel's here, boy. Have faith!"

A few moments later, Jarred entered the barn. Rachel gave a large wave of her hand as she stepped closer.

"Hey, there. How's our boy doing?"

Rachel's heart warmed at his words. Every moment he spent here, he seemed to grow closer to her and to her horse. At the same time, she became fonder of the young doctor.

"You've got to step it up, Cinnamon."

To Rachel's surprise, Cinnamon threw his head back.

She looked at Jarred, and they laughed at the same time. "The glass is half-full!"

"And prayers work!" Jarred unzipped his bag and spoke under his breath. "If we're gonna get you well, boy, we'd better get down to business!"

Excitement edged Rachel's voice. "What can I do?"

"Let me check him out. Then you can help."

"Got it."

After he completed the preliminaries, they worked together to connect the hose to cool him off and remove excess moisture from his back. To their astonishment, Cinnamon reacted by giving a strong shake.

Rachel laughed as cold drops hit her. Automatically, she ran her hands over her face to rid it of the moisture.

"Now we're talking!" Jarred continued treating the large body with water and talked as he did so. "I knew you needed this cold bath. It's making you feel a whole lot better."

He patted Cinnamon's neck. "Hey, how's your sister doing? The one who's expecting."

"Hannah?" Rachel caught Jarred's grin from the opposite side of the animal. "She's been really sick in the mornings, but I know from my other sisters that having a baby isn't easy." She laughed. "Easy for me to say, right?"

He grinned. "I suppose."

As they laughed, she recalled how he'd comforted her and lowered her voice. "Jarred, I'm sorry to have lost faith the other day. I don't know how it happened, really. You made me feel so much . . . better. Thank you."

"Rachel, I'm glad I helped." He shrugged before meeting her gaze. "Watching you sad . . . it hurt."

Color warmed her cheeks. "I'm grateful for the comfort. When I thought of losing Cinnamon, I panicked."

He smiled a little. "It's okay. Life happens. If we were all perfect, we wouldn't need God." He went to shut off the water. When he walked back toward her, the expression in his eyes switched. It amazed her how quickly amusement replaced mystery in his deep depths.

"Not only that, but . . ."

"What?"

He toweled Cinnamon. At the same time, Rachel pulled a cloth from the pile of old rags and wiped him down on the opposite side.

When he didn't respond, she pressed him. "You were saying . . ."

She stopped to look at him, and to her surprise, he blushed. He waved a dismissive hand and continued his work. The pinkish color in his face made his jet-black hair look even darker.

"What I was about to say is that you seem pretty perfect to me," he said in a tone that hinted at shyness.

Rachel's heart skipped a beat. Jarred had just paid her a compliment she was sure she didn't deserve, but the affectionate, shy way the words came out indicated he was fond of her.

She tried to look at his statement objectively and decided a correction was a must. "Jarred, we Amish view humility as a strong point. You must know I could never even begin to think of myself as perfect."

As he tossed the wet towel aside, he winked. "And that's another thing I like about you. You're modest."

Her cheeks grew so hot that they must be a boiling temperature. She wasn't sure that it was proper to have this conversation with a single man. At the same time, she certainly wouldn't hold his words against him. They came out with such sincerity and kindness, she could never question his intentions. She could barely move the towel across Cinnamon's body as she digested what he'd said.

His smile widened. "Rachel, I'm sorry if I offended

you. That's the last thing I wanted to do. I'm fully aware that the Amish practice humility. But for some reason, it's important to me that you know just how special you are."

I'm on fire. I know Jarred's sincere. But I really don't deserve these compliments. There's no way I can live up to them.

He added, "Of course, you're not absolutely perfect. No one is. But there's definitely something unique and special about you, Rachel. I'm not one to confide my feelings, yet when I'm around you, it's easy to be myself. I've never really experienced such a comfort zone, but . . ." He looked down at the floor as if deciding how to continue. He pressed another towel on Cinnamon's wet body and ran it upward.

When he'd finished, he pushed out a breath and straightened as if he'd just made an important decision. "Let's just say that I've found a confidant in you. And when this sick boy gets well," Jarred gave Cinnamon an affectionate pat on the head, "We'll celebrate."

The thought of Cinnamon's recovery prompted Rachel to draw in a deep, excited breath. She couldn't wait to know her horse was okay. She yearned for a sign.

In the meantime, she struggled with the strange but pleasant emotions she was experiencing with Jarred. She wasn't sure why her cheeks warmed when he said something nice about her. She reasoned that it was because compliments were new to her. But in the back of her mind, she knew it was more than that.

Of course, she was far from an expert in being in

love. As she ran a long brush over Cinnamon's
mane, she tried to think of another time someone
had paid her a compliment. To her surprise, one
came to mind. Mamma had told her she kept their
furniture dust-free. But that certainly hadn't caused
her to blush. Nor had it made the pace of her heart
quicken.

Of course, it had come from Mamma. Perhaps
that was the difference. But Jarred's compliment . . .
Well, it was from a young, single man. That realization hit her as Jarred replaced wet straw around
Cinnamon with fresh, dry bedding.

As she watched him, a new sensation of excitement mixed with fear made her pulse skyrocket. She
couldn't define the feeling. She'd never experienced
such an emotion, and she struggled to comprehend
what was happening. She only knew that it couldn't
be bad. She was all too aware that when she was
around Jarred, her heart did crazy things, so her
reaction had to be positive; it couldn't be otherwise.

"Jarred, you cheer me up."

A surprised expression crossed his face. After a
brief pause, he tilted his head slightly. "That's the
first time anyone's told me that."

"Really?"

He nodded. She noted that he'd stopped what he
was doing.

"That's hard to believe."

"It's true." His phone beeped, and he checked it.
While he pushed in some numbers, he talked under
his breath. "My life hasn't been like yours, Rachel."

He looked up at her. "I mean, what I'm assuming
your life has been. As I told you, I wasn't even raised
by my parents."

She sat very still on a nearby bale of straw and listened. After he zipped his medical bag, he sat down on the bale next to her and turned. "Rachel, because I consider you my friend, and because you're a good listener, would you mind if I run something by you?"

After a slight hesitation, he pushed out a breath and glanced down at his feet before looking up. "It's about why my parents gave me away. Since we touched on the subject, it's been on my mind."

She nodded. "I'd love to listen. Maybe I can help. What on earth happened?"

He studied his boots and fidgeted with his hands as if rethinking whether or not to go on. When he started, his voice was soft. "It all started on my fourth birthday party."

His gaze drifted off in the distance, and his voice lowered to barely more than a whisper. "My parents let me invite four friends. Including my brother, Matt, and me, that made six. He was seven years old."

She watched his eyes illuminate when the sun shone in through the open doors. Flecks danced in his eyes, which lightened a notch.

"My mother baked an angel food cake. With white icing. It was my favorite. Dad made homemade ice cream. While we ate, I opened presents. I got a mini race car and track. We saved Matt's gift for later. He loved to draw. He was an artist."

"At seven?"

"I'm not sure where he got his talent, but he was a natural. And because he loved animals, he constantly drew them. He dreamed of living on a farm with lots of pets. In fact . . ." Jarred chuckled. "His bedroom walls were covered with pictures of horses."

He swallowed. "It was a beautiful day, and we played in the tree house. We chased each other around the backyard." Jarred raised his hands to the ceiling in joy before dropping them to his lap. "And that's what I loved most about my birthday."

He followed with a sad shake of his head. "Matt was my best friend in the world, Rachel." He paused before locking gazes with her. "He's with the Lord."

Rachel drew her fingers over her chest. "I'm so very sorry. I . . . I . . . had no idea . . ."

Without warning, the glow on his face did an immediate change to devastation. She watched in surprise as he lowered his face into his palms. Rachel's heart picked up to a nervous, urgent pace as she tried for the right words. She wasn't sure what had happened on his fourth birthday, but whatever it was had been awful. She could tell by the way Jarred stiffened. By how he held his face in his palms and looked down. By the way his low voice cracked.

When he lifted his chin, his eyes sparkled with moisture. His eyes reminded Rachel of morning dew on pumpkin blossoms. A long silence ensued.

"Jarred, whatever happened, it's okay. Before you came, I was worried to death about Cinnamon. In fact, I went through some pretty bad moments," she added. "But the second you stepped into the barn, I knew he'd be okay."

She softened her voice. "Jarred, you're my angel."

Chapter Five

That evening, Rachel still tasted Mamma's delicious dumplings on her lips as she stepped into her room and closed the door. Her temples pounded with great intensity as she considered this afternoon with Jarred.

At her desk, she pressed her palms against them to ease the pain. *My headache will pass, but Jarred's agony haunts him day and night. What happened? And what on earth could a four-year-old do to warrant his parents giving him away?*

They hadn't finished the serious conversation because his pager had gone off. He'd had to rush to an emergency.

She picked up her hope chest for comfort. Sam's hope chests weren't large, like some she'd seen. They were small enough and light enough to be carried around. She opened the oak lid and glanced with great appreciation at the detailed horse and buggy.

The beautiful art prompted her to think of her dear friend, Old Sam. Of her beloved horse,

Cinnamon. And of Jarred. Because he would make sure Cinnamon lived.

She pulled out her journal and pen and claimed her normal writing spot. The fire downstairs popped, and she automatically lowered her chin as pen met paper.

> *Today, Cinnamon looked better! He threw his head back and shook his body to rid it of water. I've asked God to tell me that Cinnamon will make it. I believe those were signs.*
>
> *And Mamma talked to Hannah today. She went to the doctor for a checkup, and everything's fine. But there's other news, too, that isn't as positive. About Jarred. I have no idea why he wasn't raised by his own flesh and blood, but I think he's almost ready to talk about it with me.*
>
> *After today, I'm sure the sadness I sense in his demeanor isn't my imagination. The lines around his eyes deepened.*
>
> *I cannot imagine what he did that was so terrible, he can't recover from it. But until I know, I'm helpless. I so want to make him feel better.*
>
> *He told me that his world was surely different than mine. Obviously, that's true. I haven't known him long, but one thing's for certain. My parents would never have given me away, even if I'd done the most horrible thing imaginable.*

She paused a moment to consider what that could be. She stretched her legs and glanced toward the window. The star-dotted sky looked like a puzzle with unfitted pieces.

She breathed in the fresh smell of detergent from

her bedding and Murphy's wood soap she'd used on her headboard. Despite the pleasant fragrances, she frowned, trying to understand how a mamma and a daddy could desert their own child.

She continued penning her thoughts.

Unfortunately, the past can't be changed. But the future can, if God will let me help Jarred. I know that as strongly as I'm sure that I love to dust. Today, I feel like Jarred and I stepped up our friendship to a more serious level. For him to want to confide in me must have taken a lot of trust on his part.

I hope he'll finish his story. I'm his friend. And because of that, I have a responsibility to look out for him.

He's done so much for me. He's giving. Kind. Thoughtful. It pains me to know that his parents gave up such a wonderful son.

She stopped, looked around, and smiled a little. A sigh of relief escaped her as she took in her comforting, familiar surroundings. The shiny oak floor. The nightstand next to her that her father had made. The blue curtains that decorated the large window overlooking the pasture.

The large kerosene light for night-time reading sat in the corner. The delicious aroma of Mamma's chicken and dumplings floated from the kitchen, up the stairs, and into her bedroom. She sighed happily. God had given her the best parents in the world.

She rested the book on her thighs and drew her legs up to her body. *Mamma and Daddy have helped to make me everything I am today. My thoughts, actions, my beliefs . . . they all stem from how I was raised. I don't understand why God doesn't give everyone two wonderful parents like mine.*

I'm not sure what happened in Jarred's past. She considered her dream. She thought about it as she drifted off to sleep and when she woke up.

As the noise from the crickets and the cicadas floated in through her screen, she came to a decision. She began writing with a renewed determination. With purpose.

I want my dream to come true. But I have another goal, too: to help Jarred find peace and to reconnect him with his parents. It's up to me to ensure it happens.

That evening, Jarred smiled a little as the tomcat finished the chunks of chicken. Jarred had fed him for a little over a week now. With July fast approaching, the golden tom had stuck around longer than usual.

Jarred spoke in a low tone, careful not to scare him off. "You're starting to feel at home, yeah?"

Inside, he breathed the pleasant scent of pork roast as the meat and veggies cooked in the Crock-Pot. He turned on the living room television, flipped to the local news, and relaxed back onto his soft, brown sofa.

He closed his eyes and said a quick prayer of thanks for all he had. When he opened his eyes, his gaze locked with the five-by-seven photo in the silver frame on the end table. With great care, he reached for the picture and held it on his lap with affection.

As he stared into Matt's deep green eyes, vivid childhood memories flooded his heart. Matt's love of horses. Matt's smile. Matt's unconditional brotherly love.

Thank goodness Jarred's folks had sent a picture of his beloved sibling with him. As Jarred looked into the photo, the familiar face stared back at him with tenderness. As always, when Jarred studied the seven-year-old, things they'd done together haunted him until he drifted back in time with his best friend. The boy he had looked up to and trusted.

Images popped into Jarred's head. Matt teaching Jarred to tie his favorite black-laced tennis shoes. Matt at first base in Little League. Matt helping him up the ladder to his bunk bed. Matt teaching him to shoot the miniature basketball into the hoop on the front drive. Matt encouraging him to blow out the four candles on his birthday cake.

Jarred opened his eyes. He longed to be with his only sibling, if only for a moment. Salty tears stung Jarred's eyes, and he blinked. But the sting in his eyes couldn't compare to the piercing sting in his heart.

He sat very still, taking in Matt's endearing features, even though he knew them by heart. Jet black hair. Two small freckles on the bridge of his nose. A Cubs hat. An ear-to-ear grin that showed two crooked teeth.

Jarred's heart filled with a combination of excitement and devastation as he relived them chasing each other around their two-story house. As Jarred focused, the scene became clearer and more real. At his birthday party roughly two decades ago, he'd struggled to keep up with Matt. When Jarred had reached out to tag the tail of Matt's Cubs T-shirt, Matt had surged ahead.

Jarred's heart pounded as the pleasant aroma of grilled hamburgers and hot dogs floated through the air like a tasty cloud. At the same time, two other kids at the party jumped from the tree house in the nearby catalpa tree.

Jarred pushed out a wistful sigh, and his grip on the frame tightened until his knuckles turned white. When he laid the photo on his lap, his fingerprints imprinted the gold before slowly disappearing.

His gaze wouldn't leave Matt's face. For the first time since his death, Jarred had shared some of what had happened. He'd begun to confide the story that had destroyed his entire family. Telling it to Rachel had seemed like the right thing to do. She had listened. Without a doubt, he knew she had his best interests at heart.

He was fully aware that she admired him by the adoration in her voice. The sparkle in her eyes. In fact, her respect for him was a bit overwhelming. He relished her faith in him, and he wanted desperately to tell her the rest of what had happened. It was his hope that she would be able to help him accept the truth.

The last half of June started with the early morning breeze floating into the Kauffman barn. The air smelled of straw and manure. Jarred eyed the pool of flies buzzing around the dirty pile waiting to be boxed. He checked the thermometer a second time before meeting Rachel's hopeful gaze. "His temp's down."

Rachel jumped up and down. Her voice shook with excitement. "Cinnamon's going to be okay! Because our prayers are strong, and so is our faith."

He enjoyed her happiness; at the same time, he knew that the struggling horse was far from the recovery finish line. He tried for the right words. "Rachel, you've probably never seen a horse race."

She hesitated. "No. But I can picture it."

He nodded. "If you could view Cinnamon's recovery as just that, the gun has been fired, and Cinnamon has left the starting line, but he's far from the finish."

She lowered her chin a notch. "Would you say he's equal distance between the start and finish?"

Jarred tapped the toe of his boot while he carefully considered her question. "The last thing I want is to stymie your hopes, but I'd say he's closer to the starting line."

He forced an optimistic tone into his voice. "So keep the prayers going. That's our strongest weapon."

She pushed out a sigh and squared her shoulders. "I will, 'cause they're working."

Jarred talked to her while he continued his checkup. "His lymph nodes are still inflamed. But he drew up water."

"So the glass is half-full!"

They laughed.

Rachel went to the nearby cabinet and put a lone sugar cube onto the palm of her hand, smiling at Jarred. "This will be the true test of Cinnamon's recovery." She knelt in front of her horse with her open hand extended toward him.

Jarred looked on in dismay as Cinnamon expressed

little interest in the treat. "Rachel, let's be patient. As I told you, recovering from a virus isn't easy."

She offered a slow nod. "I know." Rachel went on to relate Old Sam's story about Strawberry. Then she threw her hands in the air in a satisfied gesture. "That just goes to show you that God *does* work miracles. I believe that sometimes, He tests our patience first."

Jarred responded with an understanding smile.

"Like Hannah's pregnancy," Rachel said. "We prayed for years and never gave up on a baby. God rewarded our faith."

She looked at him. Their gazes locked. "Jarred, I'm praying to help you deal with whatever is bothering you." She lifted a hand defensively so he couldn't interrupt. "I'm not begging you to tell me what it is, but I gave a lot of thought to what you said. Something must've happened on your birthday to change your life."

She harrumphed. "This, I know. You can't control your past, but with God's help, you can own your future."

After she finished, she lifted her fingers in the air and pressed her lips together, thinking about the advice she'd just offered. And she smiled a little because she'd told him exactly what she'd intended to.

A long silence passed while they locked gazes. Rachel hoped she hadn't intruded in his business. That wasn't her aim.

Finally, he offered a slight nod. "Rachel, you're very astute for your age." He paused. "How old are you, anyway?"

"Eighteen."

After he absorbed her young age, he straightened his shoulders. "Someday, I'll finish my story. Today, I'd rather not. Trust me, it's complicated."

She stood and lifted her chin. "Jarred Zimmerman, don't you dare give up! It says in the Bible that if you knock on God's door, He won't turn anyone away. Even though we make mistakes, God is about forgiveness, and we'll be in heaven for eternity if we believe. Nothing, bad or good, can even begin to compare with that."

Reality prompted her to close her eyes and tear up. "Don't you see, Jarred? There's nothing God can't fix."

An expression that was a combination of shock and uncertainty filled his eyes. The longer the silence ensued, the darker his depths became. Finally, they became so stormy, a chill crept up her spine. She shivered and pulled her arms close to her chest.

She was certain he wasn't going to share what disturbed him. So she laid her thoughts on the line. "Jarred, I can't change what happened. But I like you so much, and I want more than anything to help you with whatever bothers you. Just like you asked Cinnamon to do his share to get well, I'm requesting that you do your part in your own recovery. How can I help you if you won't let me?"

Chapter Six

The first weekend in July was almost here, and Rachel did a happy rock on her toes on the kitchen floor as she continued her chores.

Cinnamon's temperature was down. He had also drawn up water from his trough. Rachel smiled while she went through Mamma's list and checked off the chores she'd finished.

Mopping the kitchen floor was next. She much preferred dusting to the other things on the list but fully recognized that there was a lot to do in a four-bedroom house, so she couldn't pick and choose.

Rachel added hot water to the oversized cleaning bucket, and a renewed energy swept through her as she breathed in the fresh scent of Mr. Clean. White bubbles floated on top of the sudsy water. She flexed her fingers in front of her and considered Strawberry's miraculous recovery. Sam's story had boosted her hope that Cinnamon would recover. And when that day came, Rachel would give extra praise and thanks to God.

At the same time, her last words to Jarred continued

playing in her mind. She stopped to put her hand on her hip and tapped the front of her black shoe against the tiles.

Was I too tough on him? Or was what I told him right on? I didn't intend to be rude or intrusive.

How can I help you if you won't let me?

She wondered if she'd been too direct as she stepped onto her tiptoes and reached into the top cabinet for the feather duster. Rachel couldn't resist swishing it over the windowsill. Mamma often commented that her feather duster was like a weapon in her hand. That dust didn't have a chance when Rachel came in contact with it. The thought prompted a giggle.

"What's so funny?"

An inquisitive voice broke Rachel's thoughts. She turned as Mamma stepped inside.

"That you call my feather duster a weapon."

The door clicked into place, and Mamma sighed and ran her fingers over her forehead. "My, it's hot out there. I'm glad your father replaced the battery in the kitchen fan."

Rachel watched as her mom bent for the air to caress her face. A few moments later, she stepped to the bathroom sink. Rachel heard running water and knew her mom was washing her hands.

"Those tomatoes are growing like weeds. There must be at least thirty or forty ready for picking."

"I'll get to them after the chores," Rachel responded, loud enough for her mother to hear down the hall.

When her mom returned, Rachel caressed the banister with the duster. As she stepped up the stairs, she whistled.

Mamma looked up. "You're awfully happy today."

Rachel continued running her duster between the rails. "I have every reason to be. Cinnamon's getting better." But that wasn't the only reason for her bliss. Jarred was on her mind, and she couldn't stop thinking about him.

That evening, Jarred organized paperwork on his small kitchen table. He'd paid eleven visits during the day. He frowned as he regarded the stacks in front of him. Eventually, he would hire someone to do the desk stuff. But until he caught up on his school loan, that wasn't an option.

The microwave above the sink beeped, interrupting his thoughts. He laid down his pen, got up to remove the salmon he'd thawed, tossed the deep orange fish into cookware, added olive oil, and placed it inside the preheated oven.

He returned to his duties. But as he used his calculator to tally up expenses, he mentally drifted away. Unable to focus on his work, Jarred shoved his hands into his pockets and meandered toward the barn, stopping to admire what was in front of him. He relaxed and smiled a little, breathing in the familiar scent of hay.

He'd bought the house after his recent graduation from veterinary school. It needed work, and the barn could use new paint, too, but what mattered was the open land in front of him. Tom had once commented that you could always add to a house. But you could never move land.

Jarred's heart warmed while he remembered his mentor. Jarred wished the kind doctor could see this place. He drummed his fingers on the wooden post and glimpsed the large barn, imagining the day the stalls would be filled.

Jarred made his way around the wire fence that encompassed the alfalfa pasture. As he walked, he took in the country smells and closed his eyes in delight. He'd always dreamed of having a place like this. He opened his eyes, making mental plans. He'd eventually fill the barn with animals that needed homes. The house, too. Maybe the stray cat would eventually be tame enough to keep him company inside.

He laid his hand on a wooden post and looked out at the sunset. Rachel's last words before he'd left the Kauffmans' came to mind: "How can I help you if you won't let me?"

While he pondered the astute words, he regarded in awe the melting colors in the western sky and pushed out a sigh of astonishment. If God could create a sunset, surely He could resolve what disturbed Jarred more than anything in the world—his past.

Looking down, he stepped over a dip in the earth and caught his balance. The crickets and cicadas made a continuous humming sound.

Jarred acknowledged that what Rachel had said was true. She couldn't help him if she wasn't privy to what bothered him. No argument. Without thinking, he picked an alfalfa blade and chewed on it while he stepped around the property.

The beauty in front of him helped to ease his pain, but what he'd done was permanent. It couldn't be reversed. So in a sense, if he related the devastating truth to Rachel, his confession wouldn't benefit him in any way, because even the best advice in the world couldn't change the past. And there was no good way to deal with it.

A warm, gentle breeze caressed his face while he meandered back toward the house. As the sun dimmed, he slowed his pace. A mixture of gentle sounds hummed through the air. Mosquitoes. Two rabbits rustled in the butterprint. Lightning bugs disappeared as quickly as they appeared.

As he approached his patio, the tomcat drank from the water bowl. "Hey, pal. I'm glad to see you're finally putting on some weight."

With a slow, cautious motion, Jarred bent to pet the stray, but the moment his hand touched the animal, it darted away. Still, Jarred smiled in satisfaction because he had made progress with his new friend.

Another four-legged being entered his mind. Cinnamon. Jarred rested his hand on the door handle. The horse showed improvement. Jarred opened the back door.

Inside, the delicious aroma of baked salmon filled the room. When he opened the oven, his stomach growled. The wall clock revealed it had been eight hours since he'd eaten. He looked forward to tomorrow. He would see his favorite patient. He paused and smiled. And his favorite person.

The following morning, Rachel waved from the living room window as Jarred pulled into their drive. She made her way to the side door that they used to enter and exit the house.

"Hello!"

As he got out of his truck, she stepped quickly to greet him.

Jarred's voice was upbeat. "How is he?"

Rachel walked alongside him as they made their way to the barn. There was no question about who "he" was.

She gave a hesitant shrug. "The same. That's good, *jah*?"

He turned to offer her a smile. "Yup."

Rachel sighed in relief. "*Gut.* The meds you've been giving him are working, Jarred."

Jarred did his routine check while Rachel talked to Cinnamon. "When you're better, you can have as many sugar cubes as you want. Promise. How's that sound?"

As she looked into Cinnamon's large, hopeful eyes, she kissed him and turned to Jarred. "I can't tell you enough how grateful I am to you, Jarred."

He smiled. "I'm happy for the improvement." He lifted an eyebrow. "But remember the race scenario?"

She nodded.

"The finish line isn't close." Jarred eyed the stall and turned to Rachel. "Let's get some fresh straw in here." He looked up to the second floor where her father stored the bales.

"Daddy's in the field today."

"That's okay." He checked his watch and nodded. "I've only got three more appointments. So I've got time."

Holding the base to steady the tall ladder, she watched as he climbed up to the loft. As he made his way up, the steps creaked.

When he reached the top, she hollered, "Don't

carry them down. Daddy drops them over the side.
I'll take it from there."

When he pointed to an area close to her shoes,
she stepped out of the way and watched as he pushed
a bale from the loft. As soon as the bedding was near
Cinnamon's stall, he climbed down to join her.
Sweat gleamed on his face and neck.

She went toward the water bin. "It must be terribly hot up there." She handed him a bottle. "Here."

"Thanks." He took it, removed the lid, and took a
couple of swigs. "You mind if we step outside a
minute to catch the breeze?"

"Of course not." She sat down next to him on the
bench to the side of the barn. "The temp's supposed
to be in the nineties today."

He nodded.

"Daddy said it would be the hottest day of the
year. It must be hard." She crossed her legs. "I mean,
working in stuffy barns all day."

He smiled and downed more water, blowing out a
deep breath as the breeze lifted his hair. "It's all
right. I'm following my heart."

She sat up straighter. "To heal animals?"

He shrugged. "Sort of. It's actually more than
that." He lowered his voice to a serious tone. "Like
I told you, my ultimate goal is to start a shelter to
protect lost or rejected animals. For my brother."

"What a nice dream, Jarred."

"I want it named after him." Jarred hesitated. "He
died on my birthday."

Chapter Seven

The moment Jarred uttered the truth, he regretted it. He watched Rachel's eyes double in size. A long, tense silence ensued while Jarred absorbed the surprised expression on her face. He'd never shared his past with anyone, not even Tom, but for some reason, he couldn't drop the subject.

"I've been thinking about what you said, Rachel. That you can't help me if I don't tell you what bothers me."

He sighed and stretched his legs, fully aware that she was waiting for him to go on.

He respected Rachel as a friend. *It's more than that. I really like her.*

His pain was so deep, he couldn't contain it inside any longer. As he contemplated his agony, his appointments didn't matter. Jarred's palms started to sweat. He breathed in and closed his eyes, fighting the heart-wrenching truth that had changed his life at four years of age.

"Jarred?"

The soft voice pulled him back to reality. "Rachel,

I've never trusted anyone like I trust you. I've never shared my past, but I'm going to ask you to listen and hopefully, you can tell me something to help me deal with it." He paused. To his dismay, his knees shook.

"Jarred, what happened at your birthday party?"

Salty tears stung his eyes.

"It was the best day of my life. And the worst."

Trying to gather strength, he shared everything he could remember about the day. "We ate cake and ice cream. I opened gifts." He smiled sadly. "I used to collect little race cars. I got some of those, and my folks gave me a Hot Wheels track. After that, we played outside. It was a bright, sunny day. July fifteenth. We started kicking the ball around."

Jarred closed his eyes and paused. He wished he could stop the devastating pounding of his heart. "Our backyard was large. The front was small."

He stopped to consider his words. "As usual, my parents had warned us to stay in the back, and we did, but somehow, the ball ended up on the street in front of the house."

He pressed his lips in a tight line before continuing. "While the rest of us played around, Matt rushed to get the ball."

Jarred's heart nearly stopped as the nightmare unfolded in his mind. He lowered his chin and clenched his palms together in his lap. "Next thing I knew, my mom was sobbing uncontrollably as my dad went with Matt in an ambulance."

He locked gazes with Rachel, but he didn't see her. His head pounded with such fierce intensity, he pressed his palms against his temples and caught an emotional breath.

"Later, I found out that a driver had run the stop sign in front of our house at the moment Matt was in the road."

Rachel's expression reflected dismay. "Oh, no."

Jarred watched Rachel cover her eyes as if she were trying to block out the ugly scene. His arms tingled and began to go numb as he related the rest of the story.

"Later that night, Matt went to the Lord." When Jarred turned toward Rachel, tears slipped down her cheeks. The horrified expression on her face was something he'd never forget.

"My brother's gone, Rachel. Shortly thereafter, my parents sent me away. They must have blamed his death on me."

Rachel's jaw dropped in shock. At a loss for words, she digested Jarred's heartbreaking story. *Don't be down. Look at the glass as half-full.*

Now she fully understood the haunted expression in his eyes. She knew why he didn't feel deserving of love. A pain stabbed at Rachel's chest until she pulled her arms over her midsection to warm herself.

She had to respond. He'd trusted her enough to confide in her, and he expected a response. *I can't let him down. I have to talk. But what do I say?*

He threw his hands in the air. "I'm sorry to hit you with this. I should have kept it to myself. The last thing I want is to burden you."

She gave a sad shake of her head. "No, no. There's nothing to apologize for. And you're not burdening me. Not at all. It's just that . . . you took me by surprise."

Some moments later, she went on. "Jarred, I'm so deeply sorry. I had no idea you'd been through so much. I can't imagine. I'm not sure this will do any good, but first of all, you've got to recognize that this isn't your fault. Not at all. You do know that, right?"

His pupils widened in surprise. "But if it wasn't for my birthday party . . ."

"Oh, Jarred." She paused and struggled for the right words. "I'm short on experience with things like this, but something my mother used to say sticks in my mind. She used to tell us kids that a mamma's responsible for her children."

She took in the quick, thoughtful lift of his brow while she studied his face. "Mamma's always right about things like this. Jarred, you were only four. And if your house was that close to the road, there should have been a fence, right? So something like this wouldn't happen. Maybe there should have been more adults supervising the party?"

She shrugged. "I'm in no way placing blame on anyone because I wasn't there. Besides, things happen in life that aren't anticipated."

A long, thoughtful silence ensued before she continued. "I remember when I was young, Jarred. Of course, we lived in the country, so we didn't have to worry about wandering out onto a busy street. And it certainly wasn't your brother's fault for chasing the ball. After all, he was only seven."

She pressed her finger to her lips for a moment. Then she said, "I thought of something. Okay. Before Daddy built the new barn, I remember my mom telling me to close the henhouse door when I finished collecting eggs." Rachel shrugged. "I said

I would. But I forgot, and the chickens got out. Of course, kids sometimes forget what they're told. And you certainly can't be blamed for what happened because it was your birthday party."

"But that was a harmless mistake, Rachel, because no one got hurt. Yeah, mine was an innocent mistake, like what you did. It's just that, unfortunately, the circumstances were different, and because of me, something horrible happened."

"Jarred, four-year-olds can't be accountable for things. And neither can seven-year-olds! Parents are supposed to protect their kids. It's the child who asks the adult for permission. You never see a daddy asking his little one for something, right? There's no way that what happened to your brother was your fault. How could your parents blame you for that?"

"I get your point, but I don't think my mom and dad deserve the blame, either. It all happened so fast. It was just hard when I got sent away. I missed them so much."

I have to help him. What else can I say to convince him he's not at fault? What words will ease his guilt?

Focusing on answers, Rachel thought of Old Sam. He was the wisest person she knew. But she'd promised Jarred to keep his story confidential. And she intended to do that. They regarded each other in silence.

As she gazed into his tormented eyes, her heartstrings pulled at her with a strength that was difficult to fight. She ordered herself not to cry. "Jarred, I'll pray about your situation."

"Thank you, Rachel."

Jarred stood and smiled a little. As Rachel looked

at him, she wondered if Cinnamon had been God's
way of connecting her to Jarred to help him.

"Jarred, you've been Cinnamon's angel. What
you're doing for him, and for me . . . I can't thank
you enough." As she spoke the words, she realized
that when Cinnamon got well, there would no
longer be a reason for Jarred to come over.

That sudden acknowledgment hit her with such a
strong emotional ferocity, she wasn't sure what to
say. *I will miss him. I have grown accustomed to his soft,
kind voice. And I feel such a bond with Jarred, like I've
never had with anyone. What will I do without him?*

As if sensing her thoughts, Jarred stepped closer.
"Rachel, thanks for lending me your ear. There can
never be a happy ending for what happened to me.
But I want you to know something. Even when Cinnamon's well, I still want to keep in touch."

His statement prompted a sudden relief. "Of
course."

As Jarred stepped out of the barn, Rachel yearned
for him to stay. To tell him everything she was feeling. So many emotions flitted inside her heart—
frustration, compassion, gratefulness, sadness, and
others she didn't recognize—as he stepped into his
truck and started the engine. He wanted to keep in
touch. The words came as a relief because she never
wanted to be without him.

I have to do something to ease Jarred's anguish. That
evening, after Rachel washed and dried the dishes,
she went upstairs to her room and closed the door.

She stood over her beloved hope chest and eyed
the lid with special appreciation. While she did so,

the pleasant aroma of Mamma's peach cobbler filled the air. Rachel gave a happy lift of her brows.

She pressed her lips in a straight line while her thoughts migrated to Jarred's devastating confession this morning. Since he'd related what haunted him, she'd thought of nothing else all day. She lifted her head to look at the off-white ceiling as frustration stabbed at her from every direction. She planted her hands firmly on the wooden chest and shook her head.

"Old Sam," she muttered, "I can't wait to talk to you. I'm going through something I've never experienced in my life, and I don't know how to help Jarred."

With that, she reached into the chest and pulled out her journal and pen. As she stepped to her desk, she considered the day and all that had happened. She still couldn't understand Jarred's parents sending him away.

She gave a sad shake of her head. Finding a comfortable position in her chair, she flipped to the first open page of her journal and drummed the tip of her pen against the blank paper.

Disbelief swept through her as she struggled to accept the truth. Jarred's brother was dead. Jarred believed he'd been responsible in some way and that his mother and father had blamed him.

Rachel's heartstrings pulled at her until an ache pinched her chest. She considered Jarred and blew out a deep, thoughtful breath. Already, she counted him as a lifelong friend. She'd become close to him the day he'd comforted her. There was something so gentle and kind about him.

She considered their moments together and

treasured them. Even though she hadn't known him long, she didn't doubt that she could trust him. His love for her horse bonded the young vet to her in the strongest way imaginable. Automatically, she considered her great dream and imagined Jarred as part of it. Then she rolled her eyes.

She looked down at her journal, not sure where to start. She checked to ensure there were plenty of blank pages because she would need a lot of space to sort out her thoughts.

She closed her eyes to say a quick, soft prayer. "Dear God, Jarred needs help. So do I. What happened in his family can never be fixed. But, Lord, there must be a way to comfort him. Please help me to share Your abounding love with him. Amen."

After recording the date in the upper right-hand corner, the conversation she'd had with the veterinarian floated through her mind.

She put pen to paper.

Cinnamon's better. I hope Daddy shows more patience and gives him time to recover. The threat that he won't looms over me every day like a rain cloud. Thank goodness Jarred will keep my horse if that happens. But Daddy hasn't actually given permission for that to happen.

She breathed in a deep, happy sigh while she envisioned Jarred's dark eyes. But she no longer wondered what was behind the turbulence. She knew.

She pressed her lips together and continued.

I learned why Jarred didn't discuss his family at first. And the reason they gave him away. It's hard to believe any parent would desert their four-year-old. I'm only eighteen, but I know that's not what God would want.

Jarred blames himself for what happened. It's a torture I can't imagine carrying. He told me that Matt was an animal lover, too.

I believe in my heart that's why Jarred became a vet. It's also the root of his dream to someday start a shelter in his brother's name. Jarred puts all of his hurt and pain into healing. So in a way, what he's doing connects him to Matt.

There has to be a way for him to deal with his suffering. He's doing his best to help Cinnamon feel good again. I must owe him something in return.

But I'm really not out to make him feel better just because I want to repay him. It's because I like him.

She stood and stepped to the window, where she breathed in the smell of freshly mowed grass. And then she realized something as potent as Jarred's confession that caused her heart to skip a beat: *Is it more than that? Am I in love?*

The following evening, Rachel dried dishes after Mamma had placed them in the strainer.

"When's the vet coming again, honey?"

"Tomorrow." As Rachel ran a dry towel over the plates, she smiled at her mother. "Jarred's wonderful with Cinnamon. And with all of the prayers between us and Old Sam, there's no way God won't heal my horse."

Mamma stopped what she was doing and frowned. "You're calling the doctor by his first name now?"

Rachel shrugged before offering a nod. "*Jah.* He asked me to."

Rachel didn't miss the look of disapproval. "Mamma, you must know that any friend of Cinnamon's is a good friend of mine."

Mamma swished her hand around the bowl to make more suds. As she dunked a glass in clean rinse water, she sighed. "Honey, your daddy and I know how much you love that horse. But I wish you didn't become so attached to everything we bring to the barn."

Rachel tensed. The tone of Mamma's voice was far from optimistic. Perhaps her pessimistic signal was due to fatigue. Rachel hoped that was the case.

Rachel stuck up for her horse. "I love Cinnamon so much, Mamma. I can't wait till he's well and I can do buggy rides with him. And I want Hannah's baby to take rides with us. Cinnamon loves little ones. You know that every time my nieces and nephews come, he lets them pet him."

A long silence passed while her mom furrowed her eyebrows. "Rachel, your father and I are concerned that you're overlooking how sick he really is."

Rachel frowned.

"What I'm saying is . . . We're worried about Cinnamon, too. We don't like seeing animals in pain. You don't want that either, do you?"

Trying to hide her disappointment, Rachel kept her tone even. She didn't want to broach the subject of putting her horse down again. She couldn't bear the thought. And she was sure she would never convince her parents to view Cinnamon as part of the family. She'd tried.

"Mamma, I don't know how you could even go there. He's so much better." Rachel recalled Jarred's offer and changed her tone to a more enthusiastic one. "Daddy said he'd think about sending Cinnamon to Jarred's."

Mamma's eyes looked tired. "We need to be realistic, dear. Sometimes, we want our pets to live forever. Of course, that's impossible. Besides, this nasty virus goin' around . . . we were talking about it after church, and there's not one horse around here that's survived it. We've let this go on too long."

Rachel's heart ached. She longed for Mamma to have faith, like she did. And Jarred, too.

"Mamma, Old Sam's always tellin' me to look at my glass as half-full because God knows how strong our faith is when we ask him for something important."

She paused to consider her words carefully because she sensed that her parents were on the verge of giving up and she needed them to root for Cinnamon.

She made a sound of disapproval with her lips and shook her head. "Mamma, I hate to tell you this, but you're looking at this as a half-empty glass."

Mamma's lips curved into an amused smile. "I'm sorry, Rachel. You are the eternal optimist, aren't you?"

"That's what I get for hangin' out with Old Sam." Rachel followed with his miraculous story about Strawberry.

Afterward, Mamma offered a thoughtful nod.

"I remember that. Old Sam has such a kind heart. And Esther . . ." Mamma's eyes glistened with emotion at her name. "There wasn't an animal she'd turn away. Bless her."

The tone of Rachel's voice was a combination of desperation and disbelief. "Cinnamon needs time."

Mamma continued the task at hand. Rachel looked out the window in front of her, taking in the simple view of deep green pine trees that lined the lane leading to the blacktop country road. Chickens scouted the yard looking for food. The empty buggy sat next to the barn where Cinnamon used to look over the fence and eat sugar cubes from Rachel's hand.

Rachel's shoulders sank as she took in Paula. An uncomfortable sensation swept up her spine and to the back of her neck. At that moment, a negative thought hit her. She silently chastised herself for even thinking the glass was not half-full. Old Sam would be ashamed of her, and she was not proud of it.

"Rachel, I think it might help if you see this from a more logical perspective. We need a horse for transportation, and Paula's healthy. Horses . . . they don't live as long as we humans do. You've got to know in your heart that things aren't looking good for our Cinnamon."

Rachel tensed. Determined that Cinnamon not be in the "failed" club, she met her role model's gaze.

"Okay. So we need a working horse. We've got one. But I'm still counting on Cinnamon to survive. And when he does . . ." She flung her hands in the air. "We'll just have an extra horse. I'll make sure they're both well cared for."

Rachel slapped her palms on her thighs as though

an important decision had been made. "We can always use a backup for transportation!"

Her mother stayed quiet. Rachel wished she could erase the dismal expression on her mother's face. *Why is Mamma acting like this? I've got to convince her to be optimistic.*

"Mamma, we can't control what happens. But in the meantime, Jarred's healing Cinnamon. I know things don't look promising, but with God's help, anything's possible."

She paused and lowered her voice. "Now . . . Could I ask you a question?"

"Sure."

Rachel drew in a breath. "Have you been thinking of names for Hannah's baby?"

A long silence ensued while Mamma ran a wet rag over the countertop. She stopped and met Rachel's gaze. A smile lifted the corners of her lips.

"Your father and I have been talking about it. We're thinking Jacob, if it's a boy, and Martha, if it's a girl. Honey, we're so blessed. God surely is looking after us. And someday, Rachel . . ."

"Mamma?"

Her mother said affectionately, "Someday we'll be choosing names for your little ones. And I'm sure they'll love horses every bit as much as you do."

Chapter Eight

The following day, Jarred and Rachel followed their normal routine with Cinnamon. Rachel considered her parents' name choices and lifted an eyebrow skeptically. She had been thinking more along the lines of Eli or Mary. But in the end, her sister and brother-in-law would have the final say.

Rachel's thoughts were interrupted as their rooster chased a chicken into a stall. She could hear their milking cows moo in the pasture. A goat stopped in front of her and regarded her with curiosity. Rachel ran her hand over its head before it rushed outside.

She focused her attention on Jarred, who did a double-take at the thermometer. Rachel looked at him with hope.

"You won't believe this."

Rachel hugged her hands to her hips and rocked once on her tiptoes. "What?"

"His temp is down half a point!"

Rachel's heart pumped excitedly. She jumped up and clapped her hands. Relief swept down her arms, and she interlaced her fingers before stretching and straightening them. Happiness flooded her heart, and she wanted to shout with excitement. Her automatic reaction was to hug Jarred. Of course, that wasn't appropriate. Still, gratitude abounded for the quiet, kind man who cared about her horse's recovery as much as she did.

They hosed Cinnamon and toweled water from his body. Jarred finished up with Cinnamon while Rachel replaced dirty straw with fresh bedding.

She swept the old into a pile to the side. While she continued to stuff it into boxes, she eyed Jarred and contemplated what she'd written in her journal. That she liked him a lot and that she'd even wondered if she loved him. She immediately forced that thought from her mind. Still, the realization warmed her cheeks.

The sun coming in from the roof windows landed on his eyes, revealing those familiar tan rings around his pupils.

"You're a born healer, Jarred."

"Thanks for your vote of confidence."

"It's true. When I watch you with Cinnamon, I've no doubt why God planted you on this earth." Her voice expressed her gratefulness. "Thank you, Jarred."

For several moments, his gaze locked with hers. She took advantage of the opportunity to study his face. His expression was a combination of surprise and gratitude.

"A healer." He offered a quick nod. "Now, that's a compliment!" Surprise edged his voice.

Rachel lifted a brow in disbelief. He didn't know what a blessing he was!

"Jarred, I've never met anyone as modest as you.

I wish your parents knew what a wonderful person you've become."

The moment the words came out, she regretted them. The happiness on his face evaporated like steam from a teakettle. The look that replaced it was a combination of sadness and lack of confidence, like he'd done something wrong.

She lowered her voice to a whisper. "I'm so sorry."

He pushed out a deep breath and gave a conceding roll of his eyes. "I don't think it would matter if they knew, Rachel. What's done is done."

A sense of helplessness stabbed Rachel in the chest until it ached. She was responsible for Jarred's sudden change in demeanor. It was her responsibility to change it. She carefully considered her words.

"Jarred, no matter what you think, what happened to your brother was never your fault." She motioned to the empty bales. "Can we talk?"

He lowered his gaze and nodded. "Of course."

She claimed the spot next to him and hooked her hands together on her lap before running her fingers across her apron to brush off some straw. "I've been thinking a lot about your situation. And I'm sorry. But . . ."

He eyed her with a combination of curiosity and skepticism.

"For what it's worth, you've got Cinnamon and me. We'll always be here for you, Jarred."

He blinked at the light coming in from the windows. "Know what I think?" He raised his chin.

"What?"

"That people give me way too much credit. Of course I pray for God to make the right decisions

for my patients. So the healing I'm able to do . . ."
He shrugged and motioned to the sky. "It all comes
from above."

She tried to suppress her amusement.

"What?"

She laughed. "You're modest, too," she said, and
added, "To be honest, Jarred, I haven't dealt with
sickness very much. But I've known people in the
hospital. In church, we prayed for them. I've been
taught that God has His own plan for each of us,
but I'm saying strong prayers that He will have
my good friend here"—she paused to clear an
emotional knot from her throat and to wave a
hand at Cinnamon—"pulling our buggy and eating
sugar cubes."

She nodded. "Every night, when I write in my
journal, I end by writing a special blessing God has
given me. And I list good things in my life." She
paused to pluck a lone piece of straw off her navy
sleeve.

"And that picks your spirits up when you're down?"

"Uh-huh. And that way, when something bad
happens, I realize that my life still is amazing."

"Is that how you deal with Cinnamon's illness?"

The question made Rachel's jaw drop. She'd
never really thought of it like that, but finally she
nodded. "In a way, yes. But, Jarred . . ."

"What?"

"There's something that bothers me. It's worse
than Cinnamon being sick."

The halos around his eyes darkened. A sense of
temporary relief loosened her shoulders. Her tenseness went away. She had his ear.

She decided to approach him with her concerns. After taking a deep breath, she sat very still, crossing her legs at the ankles while she poured out her sadness at what had happened to his family. "It bothers me so much, Jarred, that you could even begin to believe you were at fault for what happened to your brother."

He looked down at the floor and tapped the toe of his boot against the cement, flexed his fingers and released them until finally resting his palms on the bale of straw.

As Rachel considered what she'd just confided, she wondered if she'd said too much. She leaned forward and rested her elbows on her thighs while she awaited a response.

Jarred's voice broke her reverie. She glanced up, and their eyes locked. At that moment, the beat of her heart quickened to an uncomfortable speed. To her dismay, her emotions whirled at the speed of the blades of their battery-powered kitchen fan.

But his eyes . . . she was absorbed in the deep, mysterious colors and the barely visible tan halo around them. She was fully aware that she was staring, and that what she felt at the moment was definitely inappropriate. But what was it? An attraction? Or was it true love?

As she contemplated her feelings, color warmed her cheeks again. She looked away, trying to compose herself, to not feel anything for Jarred that she wasn't supposed to. Because attraction was wrong, wasn't it? She'd ask Old Sam. She didn't dare approach Mamma with her question. It would raise great concern, and the last thing she wanted was to worry her parents about her and Jarred.

"Rachel?"

The low pitch of his voice made her turn so she gazed at him again. This time, she forced a smile.

"I'm thinking about what you've just told me."

Talking to him was so easy. And it had relieved her a bit to relate her huge sadness.

"And there's something I need to say."

She waited for him to continue. The expression on his face was so sincere. Serious. She turned closer to hear him.

"I've never talked about Matt's death to anyone but you. And I don't regret it. In fact, opening up about what happened has lightened the burden I've carried for years. There's something about you, Rachel."

He breathed in. "You're a unique individual. And I don't want to scare you, but you deserve my honesty."

Her heart did a somersault. What was he getting at? She straightened and pressed her palms harder against the straw.

"You're on my mind more than you should be."

That evening, Jarred crushed garlic and transferred the potent-smelling clove with veggies to his skillet. Giving the veggies a quick toss, he turned the burner on medium and made a quick call to leave a message for a colleague he'd come to know when Tom was alive. After Tom's death, Jarred had stayed in contact with Joseph Conner, who Jarred referred to as Dr. Joe.

Olive oil sizzled, and steam floated above the skillet. The delicious aroma of fried garlic filled the small kitchen. As he placed the lid on the pan, Rachel popped into his mind. He frowned. He'd embarrassed her when he'd confessed that he thought about her. Her cheeks had reddened. He'd noted her chest rising and falling more quickly. And she hadn't responded.

He pulled in an uncertain breath and glanced out the window to calm himself, but his property took second place to the beautiful Amish girl and her beloved horse. He silently scolded himself for his forwardness. Still, he'd meant every word. Even if he'd shared too much.

As he'd watched and listened to her, he'd taken note of everything. High cheekbones. Large, hopeful eyes. Her generous mouth and flawless skin. He wondered what she'd look like with her hair down.

The more he talked with her, the more he respected and admired her. She wanted to help him cope with Matt's death, and he yearned to open up to her. He really liked her.

At that thought, he silently chastised himself. *Don't go there. Rachel's world and yours are as different as night and day. She's open and loving. I could never allow my heart to love like she does. It broke when my parents gave me away, and it will never heal.*

Rachel is trusting. But I can't blame her for that. In fact, I wish I had that innocence about me. Rachel's from supportive parents who dote on her. Just the opposite of me.

Jarred bit his lower lip and squeezed his eyes closed. Over the years, he'd shed enough tears to fill an ocean, and he'd silently vowed to never mourn again.

I could never allow myself to love someone like she cares about her family and Old Sam. I couldn't bear for my heart to break again. The people I depended on most in the world didn't love me enough to raise me.

The biggest healer, he'd found, was time—and helping four-legged souls that knew only loyalty. *They're innocent. Their love lasts a lifetime. Their hearts never fault.*

People, on the other hand, were fickle. Unpredictable. They changed their minds with the quick snap of two fingers, and just because they said something certainly didn't mean they could be held to it.

He gave a strong shake of his head and straightened, wondering if Rachel's outlook would be like his if her parents had sent her away. For long moments, he pondered the question. A dull pain in his temples prompted him to press his palms against his forehead. He closed his eyes and massaged the sore area.

He tossed the veggies when they sizzled and turned off the burner. His stomach growled.

While he contemplated sharing his past with Rachel, his brother's face popped into his head. He said a silent, urgent prayer. "Dear God, please heal me. Please forgive me and bless me with Your love."

His thoughts migrated to Cinnamon. The horse had improved, but not much. There was still hope. He recalled Matt's love of horses. His dream to open a shelter for animals needing homes. Ironically, Jarrod would fit right in with the abandoned. Perhaps that's why he bonded with them. They were powerless over who did and didn't love them. Matt was the driving force that guided Jarred to protect everything needing love.

Right now, Cinnamon was alive. Obviously, Rachel

still didn't realize the severity of the horse's illness—
or she wouldn't admit it. That admission drew a
frown. Cinnamon depended on him. So did Rachel.

As he transferred the food to his plate, his
thoughts lingered on her. He hadn't been able to
define what the girl had for him, but now he recognized it as faith. He straightened his shoulders and
lifted his chin with a newfound confidence. No one
had ever had such belief in him. Nobody had
counted on him to such a high degree, and he cherished the feeling. He wouldn't let her down. He
couldn't.

At the table, he barely tasted the vegetables.
When he finished his meal, he laid his plate and
fork in the sink and stepped to the living room to
turn on the evening news. He clicked the remote,
but Rachel's face lingered in his mind. As he
glimpsed the picture of Matt on the end table, his
eyes watered. He didn't bother to wipe away the
moisture.

Matt wasn't here on earth. But Rachel was. She
was good for his soul. He knew it like he was sure
of his scar. Without thinking, he ran a hand over
the area on his neck. He would have to control his
emotions before they grew, because feeling such a
strong need for someone was risky. Especially for
someone who wasn't sure he deserved to be loved.

The following morning, Rachel swept Old Sam's
work area. A yawn escaped her, and she put a hand
over her mouth. She had been up since four thirty
to do chores. There were still more, but Mamma had
given Rachel special permission to visit Sam.

All the while, Buddy stayed at her heels and whimpered as Rachel tried out baby names. Finally, she glanced down at the attention-starved canine before turning her attention to Sam.

"Have you ever thought about getting another dog?"

Old Sam darted her a surprised expression.

Rachel giggled, bending to kiss Buddy's head. "Obviously, he doesn't get enough TLC. Maybe it would be nice for him to have a pal."

Keeping his attention on his task, the corners of Sam's lips lifted into a huge grin. "Unfortunately, that wouldn't help."

Rachel gave the broom one last stroke before squatting to brush the wood chippings into the silver dustpan. As she stood, she pushed out a breath while Buddy followed her to the trash can in the corner of the barn.

When they returned, she sat on the chair opposite Old Sam. She doubtfully lifted an eyebrow and rocked back and forth. "Why not?"

Sam gave a decisive shake of his head before returning his knife to its spot in the nearby toolbox and rubbed his palms together. "Because Buddy's a people dog."

Rachel considered the statement.

"He doesn't care for other canines." Sam rolled his eyes. "Won't give them the time of day."

Rachel laughed. "No?"

"When Esther was alive, we kept a cocker spaniel while friends went out of town. Esther thought the company would be good for Buddy. But we were surprised."

"He didn't like the spaniel?"

"On the contrary. Whenever we paid attention to our guest, Buddy would vie for our time. I'd never seen anything like it. Finally, by the third day or so, he retreated into the corner of our living room and wouldn't budge. We thought he was sick."

Rachel threw Buddy a pretend look of sympathy.

"Had Doc Stevens take a look at him. Stevens told us there was nothing wrong, 'cept Buddy was depressed. When the couple picked up the spaniel, Buddy immediately returned to his old self."

Rachel laughed as Buddy wagged his tail. He whined and lifted his nose. In reaction, she stroked him behind the ears. He closed his eyes.

"Animals are so smart, Old Sam. Sometimes it's frustrating when people don't see how loving and loyal they are. They don't sin. And I'm sure God sends them straight to heaven."

"I agree with you. Is Cinnamon better?"

The question prompted all sorts of things to float through Rachel's mind. She longed to tell Old Sam so much, mostly, about Cinnamon's doctor. She wanted Sam's opinion, but she was afraid to talk to him about Jarred since the doctor wasn't Amish. The last thing Rachel wanted was to worry Sam that she might not join their church.

At the same time, this was her opportunity to converse with Old Sam about Cinnamon and her dad's determination to put him down.

Curiosity edged his voice. "What's on your mind?"

The creases around Sam's eyes deepened with concern. He stopped working and locked gazes with Rachel. Rachel finally let out a deep sigh and rested her hands on her lap, clasping her fingers together so tightly, her knuckles turned white.

"Sam, something bothers me right now. I'm going to run it by you to hear what you would do."

"Let's have it."

Rachel related her fear that her father would give up on Cinnamon.

Sam spoke in a low tone while he worked. "Rachel, you have a heart for animals. That's one of the things that makes you special. But unfortunately, there are some 'round here see them as a means to get work done."

He gave a sad shake of his head. "I hate to be the bearer of bad news. And I don't know if there's a solution to that."

A pigeon flew in and perched on the upper windowsill.

"Fortunately, if Dad gives up, Jarred offered to take Cinnamon to his place to continue the recovery. But Dad didn't commit one way or another."

A long silence ensued while Rachel realized another issue. She ached to tell someone. She decided to tell Sam what was on her mind. She trusted him.

"Old Sam, I really like Jarred."

Sam frowned, and Rachel knew that it was too late to take back her words. It was no secret that Jarred wasn't Amish. Nor was he what was expected of Rachel as an Amish girl.

"You're a responsible young woman, Rachel. And I'm sure I don't need to remind you that your parents plan for you to join the church. And it's what you want, too, I'm sure."

She raised a hand defensively and sat up straighter, pulling her feet closer to the chair. "Of course, Sam. But he loves my horse, which makes him a life-long friend."

She paused. "But something bad happened to Jarred when he was young." She drew in a breath. "Old Sam, how can I help him?"

To her surprise, he chuckled and continued etching into the oak. "Young one, you're determined to save the world. Cinnamon, now your doctor friend."

He shifted in his seat before continuing his work. "Rachel, you want to fix everything so there's nothing but love and happiness."

After a lengthy pause, he lowered his voice. "But unfortunately, you can't make everyone be like you. It sounds like this doctor is a good person, but I don't know what has happened in his past."

She contemplated his response. Jarred had intended his past for her and her alone. But she was at a stop sign concerning helping him. She chose her words carefully.

"Sam, just imagine that your mother and father gave you away when you were only four years old. That you believe you let them down, yet you want them back in your life."

She watched the corners of his lips drop into a disapproving frown. A long silence ensued while she considered Jarred's devastating situation.

Finally, Sam cleared his throat. "That's a tough one, Rachel. Parents I know offer unconditional love to their children. So I would think that, if a person finds him or herself in this situation, the only thing that could bring him together with his folks is his own mother and father's desire to be with him. They're the ones to talk to."

* * *

That evening, Rachel pulled her journal from her hope chest. The July warmth floated into her bedroom through the window. For a moment, she breathed in the summer scents. She'd always been fond of the smell of freshly mowed grass.

She brushed a hand over the lid of her hope chest and took in with great appreciation the detail of the beautiful horse. She didn't know how Sam was able to create such detail in wood. No flaws. It was as if the design had been imprinted with a stamper, like they used at the local post office, not physically etched with a hand and knife.

While she stepped to her desk, she breathed in the light fragrance of her apple-scented candle. To her right, her kerosene flame illuminated the lined pages in front of her. The thought of holding a new baby prompted her to relax. But there were issues that needed her attention. After all, life was complex, unfortunately. She put black ink to paper.

Tonight, I have a lot on my mind.

She stopped and wondered what she was feeling for Jarred. The thought of him prompted a warm sensation in her chest. She'd decided it was best to not share more of it with Sam when she'd noticed the concern on his face and his reminder to join the church.

As she contemplated Jarred and how she reacted to him, mentally and physically, she grabbed her feather duster. While she considered her dilemmas, she nervously stood and proceeded to the window, where she ran the duster over the sill. Quick steps took her back to her desk, where she laid down the duster and focused on her written thoughts.

> *I broached Old Sam with the situation Jarred faces with his parents. Old Sam was right. He told me that Jarred's parents must want a relationship in order for them to be close. Now I'm really at a standstill. Should I contact his mother and father?*
>
> *It's certainly doable. All we would need is their phone number and address. But I fear their reaction. I don't want Jarred to feel worse than he already does. Their response might be hurtful. After all, they've never tried to see or talk to him. On the other hand, he'll never see them if he doesn't make an effort.*

She let out a sigh that was a potent combination of frustration and determination.

> *So there's only one option to connect Jarred with his parents. And that's to reach out to them.*

The following morning, Rachel stroked Cinnamon's long nose. As she took in the horse's lack of reaction, she pleaded, "Please, boy, feel good. I can't stand to see you so sick. You were better. What happened? I want you to stick around to meet Hannah's baby that's coming soon. We're gonna have a new niece or nephew. You'll pull us in the buggy, and she'll love you like I do."

A firm voice made her turn. Her father stepped into the barn and joined her. "Honey, it's time to talk."

Rachel tensed. As she studied her dad's face, she

could tell that he came with bad news. His eyes hinted at seriousness; his jaw was set and the tone of his voice was unbending. "Allowing an animal to suffer like this just ain't right."

Her heart jumped with a combination of anxiety and denial. She cleared the stubborn knot from her throat and attempted to remain calm. "But, Dad, he was doing better."

He gave a firm shake of his head. "That's how viruses are. Sometimes, they fool you. But your horse is going south. It's time to put him down. That is, unless the doctor still wants to accept responsibility for him."

Rachel was fully aware that it was July 15, Jarred's birthday—and the anniversary of his brother's death. A lone tear slid down her cheek as she waved good-bye to Jarred and Cinnamon. She ached for Jarred, and she hurt for herself that she was losing Cinnamon. At least with Jarred, her horse had a chance.

She stood very still as the truck turned onto the blacktop and eventually disappeared. She dropped her arms to her sides, drew in a determined breath, and tried to accept the situation. As she struggled with this, the bright sun slipped behind a large cloud that reminded her of a helping of Mamma's mashed potatoes. The breeze dropped the air a couple of notches to a cooler temperature. A shiver darted up her spine and she threw her shoulders back to dispel the sensation as she glanced at the garden.

As the breeze picked up speed, the plants did a dip to the east. The wind let out a light whistle as it met the barn's roof. The pans connected to the posts in the garden clicked against the metal. Rachel looked on as chickens, goats, cows, and Paula stepped from all directions into the barn. When a raindrop touched the back of her hand, she glanced up at the sky to see that it had suddenly filled with dark gray clouds.

She wondered about Cinnamon. *I hope Jarred gets him to his barn before the rain hits them.* The thought of Jarred prompted a sigh of relief.

Cinnamon's with Jarred. And there's no one I would trust him with more.

Half an hour later, Jarred readied Cinnamon's new stall and smiled a little. "You'll be comfortable here, boy. Only thing is, you'll have to look at me every day instead of Rachel. Sorry about that."

As he smiled at Cinnamon, Rachel filled his thoughts. Night and day, she was on his mind. And to his surprise, he was giving consideration to joining the Amish church to be with her.

He focused on what was in front of him and frowned. Transporting the sick horse hadn't been easy. Jarred vividly recalled Rachel's expression, a urgent combination of sadness and relief. Now that Cinnamon was here, Jarred could give him his full attention. But was it too late?

Jarred eyed Doc Joe while he checked Cinnamon's vitals. He knew second opinions could be game changers. His acquaintance checked Cinnamon's vitals.

"The bad news is, the horse has a hard fight ahead.

The good news?" He shrugged. "I wouldn't do a thing differently."

Jarred gave him a friendly pat on the shoulder. "Thanks for checking him out. I wouldn't have bothered you, but this is my most important patient." He winked. "I want to do my best by him."

"How long has this been going on?"

Jarred was thoughtful a moment. "About a month." He went on to share the miraculous story of the horse's recovery at birth.

Doc Joe hesitated a moment. "You're a Good Samaritan, kid. Doc Stevens would be proud of you. I respected him, and I've no doubt that he'd want me to help you save this beauty. But unfortunately, there's not a whole lot more we can do."

Jarred nodded his agreement. "I appreciate the professional opinion."

Joe cleared his throat. "Uh, I know your good intentions, Jarred, but you've gotta realize that the odds are stacked high against him."

Jarred lowered his gaze to the ground and shook his head in dismay. "It's a bad virus, and watching an animal suffer isn't easy. But the Lord seems to bless you with special healing powers."

Joe chuckled. "This guy has his best shot if he's under your care."

Jarred patted him on the back and thanked him. After they waved good-bye, Jarred made himself comfortable next to Cinnamon, stroking him and tempting him with sugar cubes. Of course, Jarred didn't expect him to eat. Cinnamon's chance of recovery was fast disappearing.

The ride in the trailer had been hard on him since the horse had been so weak to begin with.

And now as he met Cinnamon's large, sick-looking eyes, he spoke with as much conviction as he could. "Cinnamon, you'll rebound. I know it."

Slow steps took Jarred to the door of the barn. He stopped and returned to the stall, where he knelt and pressed his palms together.

"Dear Lord, only You have the power to heal this special horse. It's too late to fix the situation with my parents, but please create a blessing on this sad day. Please work a miracle on Cinnamon."

In her bedroom late that afternoon, Cinnamon was on Rachel's mind. As he'd left in Jarred's trailer that morning, she'd said an extra-strong prayer for her horse's recovery. Cinnamon's empty stall left her with an odd combination of relief and sadness.

Relief because Cinnamon was with Jarred. Sadness because she missed Cinnamon. She breathed in the comforting aroma of her apple-scented candle as she mentally recapped the day's events. She still believed with all of her heart that her horse would rebound. In fact, in a way, it eased her mind that he was with Jarred. She didn't carry the stress on her shoulders of her father putting Cinnamon down.

Emotionally drained, she closed her eyes for a moment. When she opened them, she blinked at the bright light floating in through the window as the sun left the sky.

The air smelled of rain. The unexpected downpour had forced her parents inside for a while. Now they were outside putting things away.

With great optimism, Rachel focused on her hope chest and opened the lid, automatically reaching for her journal and pen. Before stepping to her desk, she paused, as usual, to admire the horse and buggy. As she took in the beautiful artwork, a tear slipped down her cheek.

Leaving the lid open, she took another look at the sky before getting comfortable in her chair. The kaleidoscope of colors mimicked many different paints dumped into the same can.

If God can create such beautiful colors in the sky . . . If God will give Hannah a tiny baby, then surely He will heal my beloved Cinnamon. If not for Jarred, I would have already lost him. I don't blame Daddy. He truly believes that putting Cinnamon out of pain is the best thing. How can I hold that against him? But I know better. Life is precious. And I also believe with all of my heart that Cinnamon will recover.

Old Sam always taught me to look at my glass as half-full. To respect a beating heart and to preserve it, because life is a miracle. Although I understand how Daddy feels, I am praying to understand why my parents don't have stronger faith in God's healing powers.

Rachel gave a frustrated roll of her eyes and silently ordered herself to heed Sam's advice. *Being upset will get me nowhere. How can I see what happened today from a positive view?*

Deep in thought, she tapped the end of her pen against the blank journal page. As she did so, the earthy scent of manure floated in through her window. Rachel supposed most would find the smell offensive, but she looked at it as God's natural fertilizer to help the produce grow.

She pressed her palms together and squeezed her eyes closed to whisper the Lord's Prayer. Then she continued with her own personal words to her Savior. "Dear Lord, thank You for sparing Cinnamon's life."

She caught a powerful breath. "Please work a miracle on the horse I love with all of my heart. And please comfort Jarred on the anniversary of losing his brother. Amen."

As she opened her eyes, a new sense of peace welled up inside her chest. She smiled and wrote.

While praying, I just realized what I haven't recognized all day. The glass is half-full. I was focusing on losing Cinnamon. Now I should be thankful that God spared his life. God planted Jarred here to save my horse, and I have faith that He will help me to reconnect Jarred with his parents. I am as sure of this as I am of the tiny freckle on the top of my hand.

She pulled her knees closer to her chair for a better view of her words.

God has my life planned out. Because of that, I realize that setbacks are necessary in order for me to have the ending He has planned. Sam told me once that good comes from bad.

Today was the turning point for Cinnamon's recovery. I am blessed that Jarrod took responsibility and that my father allowed him to. I respect my dad. I love him and look up to him.

God is blessing me because of my prayers and my faith. And He sent an angel to rescue Cinnamon. The angel's name is Jarred, and I don't know what I'd do without him. Oh, why can't I feel this way about someone who's within my own faith?

* * *

Two days later, Jarred followed his daily routine with Cinnamon. Since the ride in the trailer, Rachel's horse had lost ground. Jarred had done everything he could to save the gelding, to get him better.

Jarred stood with his hands on his hips. "Dear Lord, I know it's wrong to let this horse go through more pain if he won't make it. Please work a miracle on Cinnamon. And please help me to do what's right. Amen."

Jarred's chest pumped with a combination of frustration and uncertainty as he pushed out a sigh and stroked Cinnamon's mane. "I know you've tried your hardest to get well." He planted a firm kiss on Cinnamon's wet nose.

He thought of how devastated Rachel would be if she had to say good-bye to her horse. As usual, his pulse picked up when he thought of her beautiful face, her soft, compassionate voice. He'd tried to suppress his romantic feelings for her, but now, he was in over his head.

He let out a deep sigh. While he took in the struggling horse, he frowned and squeezed his eyes closed as the realization hit him. When he opened them, he gave a slight nod of acceptance. It was time to put Cinnamon down. For the first time since Cinnamon's illness, he knew what needed to be done. *I've got to talk to Rachel first.*

Before leaving the stall, he did what he could to aid Cinnamon's chance of survival. To ease the pain. Telling Rachel what he was about to do would be difficult, but a voice inside of him told him that he'd done all he could.

After washing up, he got in his truck. During the drive to the Kauffman farm, his chest ached. "Please, Lord. Have her understand."

When he pulled into Rachel's drive, he decided to speak to Mr. Kauffman first. He pulled the key from the ignition, stepped from his pickup, and gave the door a shove. Slow steps took him to the wood-working shed behind the barn.

Rachel's father came out to greet Jarred with a firm handshake. "Doc Zimmerman, I didn't expect to see you today."

Seriousness edged Jarred's voice. "Mr. Kauffman, I'd like to talk to you about Cinnamon before I tell Rachel."

Before Mr. Kauffman could reply, a soft, familiar voice made him turn. "Tell me what?"

Chapter Nine

Rachel struggled to accept that putting Cinnamon down was best. Sitting in the passenger seat of Jarred's truck, she attempted rational thought. As she contemplated the agonizing truth, she sat up straight and interlaced her fingers into one fist on her lap.

Thank goodness she was with Jarred. Being with him filled her with a most-needed sense of peace. After talking with Jarred, her father had given permission for her to ride with Jarred to his barn to say good-bye to her beloved horse.

Jarred's concerned tone interrupted her thoughts. "I'm sorry, Rachel."

"I trust your decision." She lowered her voice to barely more than a whisper. "You've done everything humanly possible. I've prayed for a miracle." She paused to close her eyes. When she opened them, she turned to him. "I still am."

"Me, too."

A lone tear slipped down her cheek, and she caught it. "I have to let him go. But it's hard."

"I wanted for him to rebound. I've seen miracles happen. I mean, viruses are unpredictable."

He lifted his shoulders and glanced at her before returning his attention to the road. "Maybe I've been too optimistic. By the time I got him to my place, he had already failed a lot. That ride was tough on him. But it's certainly not to blame."

She nodded agreement.

"But, Rachel, let's look at the glass as half-full."

His statement made her smile. A laugh escaped her. "You're starting to sound like Old Sam and me."

Jarred's lips curved in amusement. "That's a good thing, right? Your positive attitude is rubbing off on me. I know God will take Cinnamon into heaven."

She turned a bit. The seat belt over her chest prevented her from directly facing Jarred. "I'm praying that God will bless Cinnamon with eternal life." A combination of uncertainty and hopefulness edged her voice. "Jarred, do you really believe that will happen, or do you say that to make me feel good?"

She watched the corners of Jarred's lips turn up.

"I'm far from a Bible expert, but I seem to recall that the Book of Revelation talks about horses in heaven."

Rachel sighed with relief. She relaxed her hands across her lap. "How could I forget? *Jah.*" That realization filled her with new hope.

Jarred's voice was soft, but reassuring. "Our days on earth aren't many, when you think about it, Rachel. But eternity is a long time. When we're in heaven with Cinnamon, we'll probably wonder why we were so upset about putting him down."

She considered his calming words and pressed

her lips together thoughtfully, taking note that he'd acknowledged himself as responsible for Cinnamon and his fate.

"Jarred, I don't know how I would get through this without you. You're my rock."

What seemed an eternity later, he pointed. "This is it."

As they pulled into the long drive leading to a small one-story house and an old barn, Rachel's chest ached because of what was about to happen. The back of her neck tensed and she stiffened. A pain filled her chest until she felt light-headed.

Jarred parked in front of the barn and turned off his truck. He proceeded to open Rachel's door. She breathed in and tried for composure as they walked side by side to the barn.

Jarred stopped a moment and faced her. "Are you sure you want to be with me when I do this?"

Salty tears stung her eyes, and she blinked. She squared her shoulders. "*Jah.* I want to pray one last time for a miracle. With you."

He helped her to kneel, then joined her on the damp clover. His side touched the fabric of her dress. She didn't care that this contact was inappropriate; on the contrary, she relished its comfort.

"Dear Lord, I pray one last time for a miracle. If You take him, please bless him with eternity in heaven. Amen."

They stood and regarded each other in a mutual understanding. As they stood at the large barn doors, a sound stopped them.

* * *

Cinnamon threw his head back and whinnied. Jarred and Rachel looked at each other in astonishment as the horse snorted and clomped its hooves impatiently.

Jarred's jaw dropped in a combination of shock and surprise while Rachel threw her arms around the long, cinnamon-colored nose.

"Cinnamon! I love you, love you, love you!" Rachel closed her eyes as if taking in what had happened. When she opened her lids, she flung her hands in the air. "God answered our prayers! It's a miracle!"

Still trying to comprehend what appeared to be a healthy Standardbred, Jarred stepped over to Rachel.

They looked at each other in joyous disbelief before bursting into laughter.

A chuckle of relief and disbelief escaped Jarred's throat as they both planted affectionate kisses on both sides of Cinnamon's long nose. Rachel cried tears of happiness while she nuzzled her face to the horse's.

As Jarred watched the two, he mentally confirmed what he'd already admitted. Rachel was special. Unique. He knew a lot of good people, but God had made this girl with an especially kind heart. Because of her strong faith, and his, God had blessed them with a miracle. Reality nearly pulled all of the breath from his lungs.

Excitement filled Rachel's voice while her gaze stayed on Cinnamon. "Jarred, is this for real?"

"I hope so." He looked at her as she caught an emotional breath.

"You're truly my angel."

Color warmed Jarred's cheeks as he took in the compliment, as always, uncomfortable with the credit she gave him. In response, he offered a slight nod of appreciation. "I just happened to be here at the right time."

Rachel shook her head. "No, Jarred. This wasn't circumstantial." She paused.

Before he could say a word, she jumped in. "Without you, Cinnamon wouldn't be here."

"With strong prayers from both of us, God wouldn't let us down." Automatically, he checked Cinnamon out. He glanced up as Rachel dusted straw from her dark blue dress with her fingers.

The thought of joining the Amish church entered his thoughts again. The more he thought about Rachel, the more time he spent wondering if he could live like the Amish.

"Jarred, you're a wonderful doctor. I remember when you first came to Cinnamon. You told me that time plays a vital role in recovering from a virus. And you stressed prayer."

He offered a slow nod. "Time and prayer."

Cinnamon put out a loud whinny.

Jarred threw his hands in the air. "And some people don't believe in miracles." He pushed out a deep breath. "Now . . . the true test."

He went to a box on the nearby shelf and took out some sugar cubes. He returned to Rachel and held them in front of her, dipping his head.

"I'll give you the honor."

She took the treat between her fingers, pulled in a deep, hopeful breath, and grinned. "Here it goes."

Jarred watched in utter amazement as Cinnamon licked the sugar cube from her hand.

Rachel's eyes glistened with moisture as she said two words to Jarred: "Thank you."

Jarred swallowed an emotional knot. There it was again. Her faith in him. The strong admiration Rachel offered him was something he'd never experienced. "I don't deserve such praise. You know . . ."

She lifted her chin. "*Jah.* You've told me about Matt. I also know his accident wasn't your fault. You've helped me. Now it's my turn to come to your rescue."

He smiled. "First of all, I'd like to talk about us." He paused before looking into her eyes. "Rachel, I like you."

On opposite sides of Cinnamon, they looked around the horse's nose and conversed. She laughed with excitement. "I like you, too, Jarred."

"Rachel, would you consider dating me?"

He noted the slight hesitation. Several heartbeats later, she lowered her voice to an uncertain tone. "But . . . you're not Amish."

He motioned to the bales against the wall, and they sat down next to each other.

"Rachel, this is a day to celebrate. I know that we've never had a serious talk about us, and I don't know if there's a proper time to discuss it. How about now?"

She drew her hand over her heart and breathed in. "I would love nothing more than to date you, but, Jarred, my parents expect me to marry within the church."

He smiled a little. "Joining the Amish church has been on my mind, and I've decided it's what I want. For me. For us."

"Jarred!"

"I plan to ask your father's permission to court you. Today." Several heartbeats later, he added in a soft voice, "I love you."

Jarred loved her. Later that day, he filled Rachel's thoughts as she collected eggs. But did she love him?

The afternoon sun coming in from the roof windows prompted a happy smile. Her heart did a joyous beat as she recalled how God had taken sadness and turned it into a huge blessing for her, Jarred, and Cinnamon. She reached into the chicken roosts and carefully placed brown eggs into her cloth-lined basket.

Cinnamon's miraculous recovery wasn't her only blessing. The other miracle was the strong feelings she and Jarred shared for each other. His desire to join the church that she loved with all of her heart. Today, he would ask her father's permission to date her.

Suddenly, she tensed while she considered the big step they were taking. The sound of men's voices floated into the barn. They morphed into one continuous sound, so she couldn't understand the words.

Her pulse jumped to a speed that was a combination of excitement and nervousness. From the small window, she glimpsed the two walking into the woodworking shop.

Surely Daddy will let me date Jarred. There's no one else I'd rather be with than Cinnamon's doctor.

* * *

Jarred tried to stay calm as he walked the fence around the Kauffmans' pasture with Rachel's father. Jarred respected the man. At the same time, his hands shook.

He yearned more than anything to spend time with Mr. Kauffman's daughter, and convincing Mr. Kauffman to allow him to date Rachel might not be easy.

After chitchatting about Cinnamon's miraculous recovery, Jarred stopped and faced Rachel's dad. He cleared the stubborn knot from his throat and squared his shoulders with forced confidence.

"Mr. Kauffman, I'd like permission to court your daughter."

Later that afternoon, Rachel worked in the kitchen. Daddy's stipulation to Jarred wasn't unexpected. He wouldn't give his blessing for Jarred to date her until he'd joined the church. Rachel rolled her eyes. *Look at the glass as half-full. That day will come, just like my new little niece or nephew and Cinnamon's miraculous recovery.*

The corners of Rachel's lips stuck in an upward position as she considered her future. God guided her life, and she was grateful. She wiped the metal lids and carefully placed them on glass jars of tomatoes and juice. The large fan couldn't put out enough air to compete with the boiling mixture that made the air hot and damp. Fortunately, her dad had replaced the fan battery again, so she didn't have to worry about it going dead.

As she glanced out the window, her gaze traveled to the barn. Cinnamon's stall was still empty, but not for long. A grateful sigh escaped her when she imagined her beloved horse eating sugar cubes from her hand. Her thoughts of Cinnamon included Jarred. The doctor and the horse were now an unbreakable pair, no question.

The popping sound of a jar sealing stopped her thoughts a moment, and she moved that quart to the box of sealed jars.

"Mamma, it's a good year for produce."

"*Jah.* There'll be plenty of veggies to sell on the roadside."

The comment drew a frown. "Let's keep plenty for ourselves."

Mamma laughed and blew a loose hair that landed in the middle of her nose. "You sure do love tomatoes. Don't worry, we'll can extra so we won't run out."

"Last year, we ran short, and there's nothing like chili and vegetable soup in the winter."

Mamma softened the pitch of her voice. "That's a nice young man, Rachel."

"Jarred?"

She nodded. "I'm sure you understand why your father and I want him to join our church before you date."

"Of course." Rachel closed her eyes and drew in a happy sigh. "I care about him so much, Mamma. I just love talking to him."

"Cinnamon's story is nothing less than a miracle. I suppose Jarred will bring him back now that he's well."

Rachel paused to consider the statement. "Mamma, you once told me that if you truly love someone, you'd be willing to give up what you love most to make them happy."

Mamma eyed her with an odd combination of dismay and curiosity.

Rachel carefully wiped excess juice off the clear canning jar and gave a small lift of her shoulders. "I have the utmost respect for Jarred. And he loves Cinnamon. In fact, he helped bring him into the world."

Rachel paused. "I watch the two of them together, and I can't imagine separating them."

"But you and Cinnamon are so close."

Rachel nodded. "*Jah*. But he's alive because of Jarred."

In the garden the following morning, Rachel considered her dream and smiled. Her heart fluttered with happiness. She still wasn't sure if what she felt for Jarred was true love. When would she know?

As she glanced at the tomatoes to be picked, she blew out a deep, happy breath. "Thank you Lord, for everything."

She blinked at the bright sun and hoped for a breeze. In the distance, she glimpsed Daddy in the field on a seat while Paula pulled the tiller. Cinnamon was doing well. Jarred wanted to date her, and he would even join the church.

What more could I ask for? She parted her lips as she recognized the answer. During their waiting time to date, there was work to be done. In fact, Rachel's goal was clear.

It was to reunite Jarred with his parents. This wasn't an option or something to be considered and thought about, and it was definitely not to be put off. It was a must. She wanted it for Jarred and for their relationship, because she yearned for that emptiness inside of him to be filled.

She would do whatever was necessary to ensure that the reunion happened. But how?

She squatted and shoved a loose hair back under her covering. With one hand, she pulled a bright red tomato off the vine and added it to the growing collection inside her lined wicker basket. She paused a moment to enjoy the welcome breeze that caressed her forehead and rustled the deep green plants surrounding her.

Nature's fan didn't last long. Rachel pulled her apron out of the way to reach some vegetables at the bottom of the vine. Her thoughts remained stuck on Jarred. She knew now that she had to repair his relationship with his parents. Who could help?

She pressed her lips together thoughtfully. She'd already gotten advice from Old Sam. But how should she heed it?

The next day, Buddy wagged his reddish-brown tail as Rachel rushed into Old Sam's barn. "Sam!" she hollered. While she awaited a response, she glimpsed the hope chest maker on his bench. His expression reflected deep concentration as he carved into a board that was held down by two metal planks.

The enticing aroma of freshly baked dessert filled the small area. Rachel stepped closer and licked her lips. She lifted an eyebrow in amusement, now fully understanding why the canine had appeared more hopeful than usual. She glimpsed half of a sponge cake on a napkin next to Sam and caressed Buddy's head.

"Sorry, Bud." Rachel held up a set of empty palms. "I'm not Annie." As the dog whimpered his disappointment, Rachel giggled. The widower stopped to look up, and Rachel smiled. "I see Annie's been here."

He chuckled. "Oh, yes. She makes sure I don't go hungry."

They referred to Annie Miller. Rachel had recently attended the large tent wedding of the young Amish girl who had married her best childhood friend, Levi. Levi had been English for over a decade before joining the church with Annie and marrying her. Despite what the couple had gone through, God had blessed them with a happily-ever-after ending.

The newlyweds were building a new home on the vacant lot next to her family. Despite her new "Mrs." status, Annie kept her commitment to feed Sam her home-made sponge cakes.

Catching her breath, Rachel plopped down on the chair opposite Sam's bench. As she eyed his project in progress, her jaw dropped. "It's a hand holding another hand."

For a moment, Rachel considered the simplicity of the art and thought it odd. Sam's pieces were usually filled with great detail. "It's touching. Who's it for?"

"A woman from Texas. And this special request is quite interesting."

Rachel eagerly leaned forward to rest her elbows on her thighs. Sam was about to tell her about the Texan.

As he realigned the board in front of him with great care, he shifted, offering a gentle lift to his wooden seat to move closer to his work.

Rachel tapped the toe of her hard shoe against the concrete floor, dying to hear what was behind this unique hope chest lid.

Sam proceeded to carve into the oak, lowering his voice to a more thoughtful pitch. The wrinkles in the corners of his eyes deepened as he spoke. "Her name is Audrey."

Rachel waited for him to continue.

"The story's intriguing, to say the least. She and her younger sister, Jordan, were separated when they were toddlers. Nearly forty years later, they found each other."

"Oh!"

"She wants to fill the chest with memorabilia from her childhood, picture albums and such, to give her sibling for Christmas."

"Why were they separated, Sam? How did it happen?"

Sam glanced up and gave a sad shake of his head. "It's devastating, but unfortunately, true, young one. They were in a park, five and six years old."

Rachel leaned forward and met his gaze with intense curiosity. "I can't wait to hear the rest."

Sam went back to work. Rachel took a deep breath. *Be patient.* Everything Sam told her was well thought out. He never spoke precipitously; that was one of the things Rachel loved about him.

He cleared his throat. "It started when they were playing at a family reunion."

Rachel pressed her lips together. She sat very still,

not wanting to miss one word of how the girls were torn apart.

While Sam blew sawdust off his tool, she took in his artistic-looking hands with admiration. *I wonder what it would be like to make such beautiful designs. To personalize each hope chest for the person who buys it. Sam is a true artist.*

"It was on a Sunday afternoon. Apparently, the park was quite large, and there were numerous gatherings that day." He squinted when a bright beam of light flooded in through the open doors.

"If you use your imagination, you can see kids playing and running around, people eating grilled steaks and hamburgers—you get the picture. It was most likely a happy day, like family things are."

Rachel didn't have trouble envisioning the scene. At the same time, she didn't even try to guess what was coming. She sighed in contentment and mentally placed herself at the park with her family, cousins, aunts, and uncles.

Sam stopped to hone his work. He used numerous tools to give detail to his work to make it look real.

Finally, he continued his story. "The two were swinging. Jordan stopped and rushed toward the merry-go-round. Audrey, the older, waited for her swing to slow before following suit. But when Audrey reached the merry-go-round, her sister wasn't there. The merry-go-round was packed with cousins. At the time, Audrey wasn't too concerned. After all, she was only six, too young to know about foul play. Besides, the kids were surrounded with relatives, young and old. I remember what it was like to play when I was little."

He looked away a moment as his voice drifted. "Not a care in the world."

Rachel couldn't imagine Old Sam running around with other kids, but it must have happened, because he only told the truth.

"Audrey asked around if they'd seen her sister. No one had. Then she ran to her mom and dad at a nearby picnic table." He stopped. "Well, you guessed it. Jordan had gone missing."

Rachel couldn't control the long *ahhh* of disbelief that escaped her throat.

"Now, nearly forty years later, with help from a private investigator, Audrey found her. What evidence they have indicates that Jordan was abducted and sold to a couple without children. Jordan doesn't recall anything about the day at the park, and the people who raised her are dead."

Rachel let out a sigh of amazement. "I can't believe her sister found her again, Sam."

Sam nodded. "It's a miracle, just like Cinnamon. And when we think about it, what went on could happen to anyone. That's why it's so important that kids have vigilant supervision."

The statement made Rachel stop and move her hands to her lap, where she pressed them firmly against her thighs. After a lengthy pause, Rachel made a decision. "Sam, I really need your advice. But in order to tell you why, I would betray someone's confidence. What should I do?"

A long silence ensued. "Life isn't perfect, young one. Sometimes you can't have what you need without compromising something else. The question is, which is more important? Not revealing what you're not supposed to, or getting help?"

Rachel considered the question. Finally, she threw her hands in the air. "Getting help." She added seriously, "Sam, I'm telling you this because the situation is dire."

He laughed. "I don't have answers to everything, you know. But I'll listen and try to steer you in the right direction."

Rachel hesitated. "Okay." She briefed Sam on Jarred's situation with his parents, then fell silent.

The late July sun floated in through the upper window of the barn. Rachel blinked and turned her chair so the brightness didn't hit her in the face, then watched as a brown squirrel rushed in through the open door, sat on his hind legs, and looked around the four corners of the large structure before rushing back outside.

Rachel breathed in the familiar aroma that was a combination of straw and fresh oak chippings. She smiled a little and looked down at the oversized workbench that separated her and Old Sam.

I'm glad I confided in Old Sam. Soon, he'll tell me what to do. I have to be patient. A warm breeze floated in through the large open doors and nudged a hair from Rachel's kapp. The loose tendril fell down her cheek. Without thinking, she tucked it back beneath her covering.

Rachel took in Sam's serious expression. He had once told her he didn't draw designs on paper, that when he envisioned the idea to put into the wood, he was able to take a mental picture that would be the end result. Rachel was sure that Sam was a genius. While she considered the brilliant artist, she thought of the devastating story she'd just shared.

Her pulse picked up speed. She rested her palms under her hips and leaned forward, searching her heart for a way to help Jarred. Rachel wasn't very old or experienced in worldly matters, but she was certain that when a mommy and a daddy gave their four-year-old son away, the story was sure to have an unhappy ending.

She knew there had to be a way for her to help Jarred not feel guilty about what happened. Sam would tell her what it was. She eyed the widower with optimism and hopefulness.

Small wood particles dropped around his feet. While she waited for a response, she turned her feet for Buddy to make himself comfortable. The canine moved around until he was finally satisfied, then he closed his eyes and let out a satisfied breath.

Sam cleared his throat. "I can't imagine my mother and father ever deserting me. But I was fortunate. So are you, Rachel. Never take your family's support for granted. There are people in this world who would give anything to have such unconditional love. In Arthur, we don't often see folks with what I call deep situations. But in today's world, there are problems I was spared."

Without looking up from his work, he continued. "We live in a rural area. In the good ol' Midwest. Our lives are simple, Rachel. The way God intended us to live, I believe. Of course, everything isn't perfect, but in many ways, you might say we're protected. For instance, we don't have illegal drugs that cities deal with on a daily basis."

He waved a hand. "Oh, I know. We get sick. People around us break rules sometimes. In certain cases, we have to shun those we've grown up with. Members of our church die. But in the English world, there seem to be much more complicated matters." He paused. "At least, that's the way I see it."

Sam pressed his lips together in a straight line. "I can tell you this. Parents are responsible for their offspring. Their beliefs. Most of all, you must raise your kids to believe in God and to follow His commandments, because time on this earth is short. Eternity is forever."

He took in a breath and tapped the board in front of him. He appeared to focus on the oak, but Rachel knew that he was contemplating with great care what to say. Sam didn't offer information without giving his advice great thought.

"Whatever the circumstances, I would feel compelled to see my parents."

"Okay. But how would you contact them?"

At Rachel's side, Buddy pushed his face into her chest and whined. Automatically, she stroked the soft reddish-brown fur just above his nose. The dog closed his eyes and let out a contented whimper.

Rachel's shoulders relaxed. When Sam finally stopped what he was doing, she was sure she would have her answer.

Buddy inched closer.

"Like I said, if I hadn't heard from my parents for over two decades, I would definitely want to see them. At the same time, I'd be afraid they wouldn't reciprocate. So . . . to do this . . ."

Rachel lifted a curious brow.

"I would sit down and write out my thoughts. Express my love and tell them of my strong belief in God. Tell them how important it was for me to see them."

"You would call them?"

Sam shook his head. "I would organize my thoughts into a heartfelt letter. And mail it."

Chapter Ten

Jarred had told Rachel he loved her. She hadn't responded. Did she love him, too?

He smiled as Cinnamon licked sugar cubes from his palm and his long tongue tickled Jarred between his fingers. He chuckled. "That's my boy. My fighter. I knew you'd come around. I'm sorry you went through so much."

The docile animal's health was a good cause to be happy. *Thank you, Lord.* Today, Jarred's energy level was unusually high. He was more optimistic about the future than ever. But Cinnamon wasn't the only reason he whistled while he filled the metal trough with water. Although the horse's vast improvement was grounds to smile, there was another one, too.

Rachel. He had talked to her bishop about joining their church. And the process wouldn't be fast. It would take a while to go through the classes, and before they started, he would be required to drive a horse and buggy.

To his surprise, he didn't see the change in lifestyle as an inconvenience. He viewed it as a great opportunity. At the same time, he was sure he spent too much time thinking about the Amish girl and how she made the impossible seem possible.

In fact, he enjoyed everything about her. What he loved most, though, was her optimism. Since he'd known Rachel, her attitude had rubbed off on him, and that was something to be thankful for because he was happier than ever. He had decided to risk his heart to be with her. To his surprise, Rachel's confidence in him had bolstered his regard for himself. He liked the way she always insisted on looking at her glass, and his, half-full.

Cinnamon drew up water, sloppily splashing drops onto Jarred's arm. With a swift motion, he wiped them with his free hand and chuckled.

"I need to teach you some manners."

He looked at the wooden stairs that led to the loft and glimpsed his last bale of straw. He'd get more. When his thoughts quickly returned to Rachel, he whistled. Since they'd become friends, he woke up thinking about what to do to better the lives of others. More than ever, his brother's dream of starting a shelter was so vivid in his mind, he almost considered it a reality.

Matt's death still weighed heavily on his mind. The difference was that now, he balanced negative with positive. Rachel had convinced him of his self-worth. Of what he could contribute to four-legged creatures.

He wanted to do something special to thank her for upping his confidence. But what could he give her? Since they'd met, he'd noted her compassion for animals and was keenly aware of her strong

faith and of her love for her family and her friend
"Old Sam."

But what did he know about her interests, really?
What did she think about when she went to bed? His
dream was to start a shelter and provide veterinary
care for God's vulnerable. Surely Rachel had goals
of her own. He was sure she must want a family of
her own. But what else? There were surely ideas she
toyed with. Thought about.

What was Rachel's dream?

Inside their barn, Rachel scooped dirty straw into
a pile. As she worked, her pulse beat at a steady,
happy pace because Cinnamon was healthy and
because in the near future, she and Jarred would
date.

She smiled at Paula and paused to swat a fly that
buzzed in her face. "You're gonna have to share the
attention, girl. Thought I'd prepare you. Cinnamon's coming home."

While Paula drew up water, Rachel talked to herself. "But when you think of it, that's not all bad,
really." With the pitchfork, she pushed the pile
closer to the wall to make it easier to load the
cardboard box that she used as a waste container.

"On the upside, girl, it means you'll have someone to split your workload with."

The soft purring of an engine caught her attention. Excited energy swept through her because the
familiar sound meant Jarred was here. She rested
the wooden handle against the wall, rubbed her
palms roughly over the front of her stable apron to

remove the straw, and walked quickly out of the barn to offer a huge wave as Jarred came toward her.

Rachel stepped to the side to avoid a chicken. As she took in Jarred, her lips lifted into a big smile. She liked being in control of her feelings, and this inexperienced sensation made her vulnerable. She didn't know what it was because she'd never felt it before.

She shrugged it off and greeted him with a big smile. "How's Cinnamon?"

He offered an encouraging nod. "Asking to come home."

Rachel laughed. "I'm cleaning a spot for him in the barn. And warning Paula that she'll have to share the attention."

"I suppose I need to talk to your dad about bringing him back home."

"*Gut.*"

"How's the filly?"

Rachel motioned toward the barn. "Come and see for yourself."

He followed her into the barn and greeted Paula with a pat on the head. "Hey, there."

"I'm getting Cinnamon's stall ready so he'll feel right at home."

Jarred chuckled. "This *is* his home."

"I know, but you've been spoiling him. To be honest, I'm not sure he'll want to come back." She teased, but at the same time, her voice hinted of seriousness. She made a faux pout with her lips.

"Thank you, Rachel."

"For what?"

"For making me feel good." He paused. "I really like that about you."

She looked at him to go on.

"Your confidence in me. Since we've become friends, I'm a better person."

She lowered her eyelids to hide some shyness. "You didn't need improvement."

Contentment edged his voice. "I appreciate that, too. But I'm making a concerted effort to heed your advice." He added, "About seeing my glass as half-full."

She looked up and smiled. "I'll tell Old Sam. That originated from him, you know."

Jarred rested his hands on his hips. "Then you can thank him for me."

She raised her chin a notch and grinned. "I will." She tried to restrain the emotion that edged her voice. "And as far as you, Jarred Zimmerman, I don't want you to ever doubt your worth as a human being. Just look at what you've done for me. For others. Horses have passed from this awful virus, and Cinnamon survived."

Several heartbeats later, she regained full composure and squared her shoulders with confidence. "You're a born healer, Jarred. God gave you a special gift, and there's no doubt in my mind that you were put here to take your mentor's place. I hate to tell you this," she swished her pointer finger back and forth in front of her, "but you'll always be a busy man."

To her surprise, her heart nearly stopped as they locked gazes. She found herself unable to divert her eyes from the blue-gray depths that once again reminded her of the calm before a dangerous storm.

Jarred broke the silence. When he turned to

proceed to the door, she struggled to figure out why her mind had suddenly gone numb.

No one had ever affected her this way, and she must figure out why this had claimed her emotions. Of course, she liked him. She also admired him for what he did. But her heart fluttered every time he looked at her. At that moment, she knew she was in love.

The next day, Rachel blinked in excitement. She pressed her palms together and gave a prayer of thanks. Cinnamon was coming home. Jarred helped Rachel to step up into the passenger side of his truck. His fingers tenderly caught her wrist before she landed in the soft gray bucket seat and crossed her legs. Again, she reacted to his touch, fully aware that this wasn't the first time.

He paused, closed her door, got in, and turned the key. He glanced at her and lifted an eyebrow in amusement. As if reading her mind, he said, "I'm fully aware of the rules, Rachel. But there's one problem."

"What do you mean?"

He chuckled, and she smiled at the baritone sound.

"In this particular case, the Amish rules conflict with my personal set of standards as a gentleman." He looked into the rearview mirror before returning his attention to her.

She waited for him to continue.

"It's not my nature to allow a woman to step up into my truck without giving her a hand." He darted her an expression of sympathy. "I wouldn't want you to fall."

She softened her voice. "I appreciate your efforts, Jarred. Of course. It's common courtesy." She lifted her palms and dropped them onto her thighs. "I've heard more than once that we Amish are a bit stricter than other churches."

"I won't hold it against you." He winked at her. "But there's something you need to do before we get Cinnamon."

She looked around.

His voice was edged with gentleness. "Your seat belt?"

"Oh!" She quickly fastened the buckle. The click confirmed the job was complete. "Thanks. I don't do a lot of truck rides. I should've remembered from last time."

She watched in the side mirror as he backed out of the drive. She smelled something sweet. When she looked at the floor, she glimpsed red candy wrappers and grinned. So Jarred had a sweet tooth, just like Cinnamon.

As he put the truck in DRIVE, he said, "Rachel, I respect that the Amish hold themselves to high standards. That's something to be proud of."

"*Jah?*"

He nodded. "In fact, one of the reasons I like you so much is because of your values." He changed his voice to a shy tone. "I hope you don't mind me saying this, but you're truly special."

She laughed. She wasn't sure why; she finally concluded that her reaction was a combination of embarrassment and uncertainty of what to say.

Jarred was the only man she'd ever ridden alone

with. For some reason, it seemed different than being alone with him around the horses. She always enjoyed her personal conversations with him, but she wasn't exactly sure how to act at times. However, there was one thing she was sure of: Her heart fluttered with joy at his approval of her.

Satisfied she'd decided that, she looked at the rows upon rows of corn on both sides. The crop was over knee-high. She relaxed and enjoyed the engine's soft purr as they cruised along the blacktop.

Rachel was certain that this drive wasn't something to be taken lightly. She was sure that Daddy had allowed it because of Rachel's strong bond with her horse. Her father had been frank. He really didn't want Cinnamon back because of cost and work, but he allowed it especially for Rachel, and also because he believed God was responsible for the horse's miraculous recovery.

Rachel had never given her parents any reason to not trust her. On the contrary, she'd always done what they asked. It was important to her to please the people she respected most in the world, and they had enough faith in her to allow her to make this trip alone with Jarred, fully aware of their plan to date.

She was at ease with the kind man next to her. Since she'd heard Jarred's devastating story, she'd become more curious about him. But she didn't pry. Mamma had taught her not to ask too much. It was rude.

Twenty minutes later, when Jarred slowed, Rachel took in his house and barn. Last time, she'd neglected noticing details. Today, she looked more closely at the modest dwelling. It needed work, but at the same time, there was something homey and comfortable about its appearance. Maybe it was the soft blue shutters in front. Perhaps it was the large, partially fenced outdoor patio.

When he stopped his truck, she unfastened her seat belt. By that time, Jarred had opened her door. His wide smile curved his lips up in amusement.

In silence, she followed him inside of the barn and rushed to the cinnamon-colored horse. She regarded the gelding with intent interest before glancing at Jarred.

"I still can't believe his miraculous recovery."

"The day I came to your house and glimpsed this fella, I knew his chance of recovery was small. But in my heart, I believed he would make it. And he did. I confess . . ." He swallowed. "I'm really gonna miss this guy."

She was quick to note the moisture glistening in his eyes. Her heart warmed and ached at the same time.

He motioned to the nearby shelf while raising an amused brow. "Be my guest."

His soft encouragement pulled her from her reverie. When Jarred glanced at the box next to the stall, Rachel immediately understood. She retrieved some sugar cubes, held them out for Cinnamon, and smiled while her horse's tongue tickled her hand.

As he licked the sugar from her fingers, she laughed, but the moment she glimpsed the regretful expression in Jarred's eyes, a dull ache replaced her happiness.

She lowered her voice to reflect a special understanding. "You love him, too."

After offering a nod, he smiled a little. "Always have."

He smacked his lips together. "From the moment I first laid eyes on him. It was love at first sight."

"I'm sure Cinnamon would thank you, if he could." She grinned.

He chuckled before seriousness edged his voice. "In all honesty, Rachel, I'm grateful he's got you."

He cleared his throat and pulled in an emotional breath. "You offer him as much, or more, than I ever could. And I don't suppose anyone would argue that too much love is not better than not enough."

Rachel offered a nod of agreement. "Jarred, any animal would be fortunate to get your care."

"Letting him go won't be easy." Several heartbeats later, he gave a helpless lift of his shoulders. When his mysterious dark eyes penetrated hers, she couldn't look away.

When he finally looked down at the ground, he shook his head before leveling his gaze with hers again. "Having Cinnamon here has opened my eyes to something very important."

She looked at him.

He shrugged. "I'm reminded what it's like to experience a strong bond with another being."

The unexpected confession took her by surprise. She stood very still, watching the honest expression on his face while she digested his comment and its significance.

While Jarred paced to the other side of the barn and back, she couldn't imagine so few bonds because she had so many: her mother, father, Old Sam, her sisters, cousins, aunts, uncles. And countless others.

At that moment, Rachel recognized how very different she and Jarred were. She considered her good fortune. Having love and relying on others for emotional support was something she'd often taken for granted.

She'd never realized that there were those who didn't have what she'd always thought normal. After all, love didn't cost anything. Rachel had more support than any girl could dream of. Her mom and dad guided her, protected her. The man opposite her didn't even have parents. At least, they hadn't raised him. He was all alone in the world, except for helpless animals who counted on him.

She was sure his patients adored him, but it wasn't the kind of nurturing a person needed to survive. As this deep recognition hit her, she struggled for the right words. But as hard as she tried, none came.

When she looked at him, his profound depths pulled her into a place she'd never been. She wasn't sure, really, how to describe it, but to her pleasant surprise, it was a haven of unusual comfort.

Finally, her last conversation with Old Sam came to her. So did his advice. She forced herself to look away for fear of drowning in the mysterious pools of bluish gray.

She lowered the pitch of her voice for emphasis. "Jarred, have you thought about reconnecting with your parents?"

The moment she posed the question, Jarred turned his back to her. Rachel fully recognized how inexperienced she was with such situations. She just had an eighth-grade education. Yet she'd offered the only question she could think of.

She had to make things right. But how? While she contemplated what to say, slow steps took him out of the large barn doors where he faced west with his hands in his jeans pockets.

Rachel returned her attention to Cinnamon, saying a silent prayer for God to ease Jarred's pain.

An uncomfortable lump stuck in her throat, and she tried to swallow it, but it lingered, just like the ache Jarred must feel every single day of his life. Eventually, the obstruction in her throat would go away. She wasn't sure Jarred's pain would.

While she contemplated the uneasy tingle that swept down her arms, she whispered to her horse for something to do. "You see how special you are, boy? Everyone who meets you falls in love with you. Aren't you lucky?" She sighed. "You're a heart-breaker."

While Cinnamon nuzzled his nose deeper into Rachel's neck, she glanced back at Jarred. He hadn't budged. When she returned her attention to her four-legged friend, she laughed at the tickly sensation of the hair brushing her nose. She stepped back to rub her face.

When the tickle stopped, she embraced Cinnamon as tightly as she could, planting affectionate kisses on both sides of him, acknowledging the miracle of his recovery and how close she'd come to losing him.

So many emotions fought within her, the chaos made her tense. Eyes closed, she thought of Cinnamon and how happy she was to get him back. She considered Jarred and how her beloved gelding had brought love to the doctor's lonely heart. At the same time, she admitted that her gain was Jarred's great loss. She lowered her gaze and pondered the sad reality.

She wanted to repay him for Cinnamon's life. "Dear Lord, please tell me what to do. Amen."

The sound of boots meeting cement made her turn.

Slow steps brought Jarred to Cinnamon, where he stood on the opposite side. "Rachel, reconnecting with them, as you put it, might seem easy, but it's not."

She didn't argue. Instead, she pressed her lips together for fear of uttering the wrong words.

Jarred looked straight ahead and continued stroking Cinnamon. "My parents want nothing to do with me. That won't change."

Don't open your mouth.

"When I was little, they loved me."

She stood a little straighter. Her heart pumped harder.

"But the day of my party, everything changed."

A long silence ensued. Finally, he began to prepare the horse for another trailer ride.

"Like I said, it was the best day of my life. And the worst."

The unusual softness of Rachel's voice stunned her when she finally spoke. "I wish I could change the ending."

He patted Cinnamon with affection, stepped past Rachel, and took a seat on a bale of straw. She looked on with curiosity while he rested his palms on his thighs.

After giving an uncertain shake of his head, he met Rachel's gaze. The light coming in through the open doors and the window above illuminated Jarred's face. She took in the tan halo that danced mysteriously around his pupils.

"Why not write them a letter?" Before he could

respond, she cut in. "You wouldn't have to see them face-to-face. And you could take your time and put your thoughts on paper. Then?"

She shrugged. "They might very well respond. And if they don't, then you know there's nothing you can do. But isn't it worth a try? If you don't, you'll never see them again."

"I don't know."

She stepped closer and waited for him to continue.

He paused before pressing his palms over his face. When he removed his hands, his eyes glistened with moisture. "Rachel, how can I look at the glass as half-full?"

Before she could respond, he snapped his fingers. "I can answer that."

She curved her lips inquisitively.

"I met you, Rachel. I don't have family, but I have you." He glanced with fondness at the stall. "And Cinnamon."

He looked down at his boots before lifting his chin. "Even though he won't be with me, I'll have him right here." He motioned to his heart. "But enough about me."

She parted her lips in surprise.

He paused. "I'm looking forward to dating you."

She blushed. "Me, too, Jarred."

"You know my deepest thoughts. But I want to learn more about you. And since it might be a while before we see each other again, tell me one thing. What do you really want out of life? What's your dream?"

* * *

The loud crackle of thunder made them startle. As they sat on the straw, an unexpected downpour of rain began to pound against the roof. Cinnamon let out a loud whinny.

Rachel rushed to him and stroked his neck. "It's okay, boy." She glanced at Jarred. "He never has liked thunder."

When the wind started up, quick steps took Jarred to the large barn doors. With one swift motion, he pulled them closed and locked them with the large metal latch to stop the rain from blowing in.

He reclaimed his seat and rubbed his hands together to dry them. "Looks like we're stuck here till it lets up."

"I'm glad we didn't load Cinnamon. It would have been a mighty wet ride back to my place."

Jarred took in the happy, satisfied glow in Rachel's cheeks. Suddenly, for some strange reason, as the lightning crackled and the rain beat against his old barn, he yearned for closure with his family. He wanted it more than anything. But was it possible?

She faced him. "Write a letter, Jarred. To your parents. If you want, I'll help."

"I'll pray about it."

"Me, too."

"It's getting late. We might have to postpone taking Cinnamon home." He went on, "But I'm serious about knowing your dream. I want to make you happy, Rachel."

He watched as she fidgeted with her hands. Finally, she breathed in, straightened her shoulders, and faced him. Her eyes brightened.

"I've never told anyone my dream," she started. "This will be the first time."

He waited for her to continue.

Her face glowed. "My dream is made up of three parts."

He lifted a curious brow.

"The first is to marry a good, honest Amish man."

He grinned. "Okay. Simple enough. What's the second?"

She gave a shy roll of her eyes. Her cheeks took on a rosy shade of pink as she looked down at her hands. "To have tons of children."

"Oh!" He chuckled.

"I really want a large family, Jarred. A continuation of what my grandparents started. How about you? Do you want kids?"

He considered the unexpected question. "I've never really considered it. But," he gestured with a lift of his chin, "it's certainly something to think on."

Rachel stood and looked down at him. "Right now, Dr. Zimmerman, I hate to change the subject, but I've made a very important decision."

He eyed her.

"Mamma told me that if you truly love someone, you can give them what's most important to you."

He waited.

"Jarred, I'm giving you what's dearest to me. Cinnamon." After a brief pause, she continued in an emotional, serious tone. "Because I love you."

Chapter Eleven

It was hard to believe it was already the first of August when Jarred stared at the blank sheet in front of him. He was checking out buggies since he was expected to be driving one before beginning classes to join the church. And Rachel loved him.

A warm sensation filled him until a wide smile pulled the corners of his lips up. He planned to marry her—after he joined the church, of course.

Paperwork cluttered his kitchen table except for the area he'd cleared to write his folks. With a slow, undecided movement, he reached for his black pen. Before ink touched paper, he thought of Matt. Of Jarred's shock when the car had hit his brother. He tapped the tip of his pen against the glass top for a few seconds, then laid it down again.

Rachel would write a heartfelt letter. But I'm not Rachel. Maybe I'm not as strong as her. If my folks don't reply, I'll feel worse than I do now.

His fingers shook. *They'll never forgive me.* He closed his eyes and sighed in frustration while contemplating whether or not to contact them. Rachel's kind, concerned face popped into his thoughts. The tighter he closed his eyes, the more he could hear the convincing timbre of her soft, urgent voice: "Write a letter, Jarred. To your parents."

When he opened his eyes, the sun's rays shone through the open window and onto his face. He blinked and turned to avoid the brightness. But his mind lingered on Rachel's advice. Should he take it?

Decide this like you determine everything else, based on pros and cons. He leaned forward to prop his right cheek on his hand and stared straight ahead at the off-white wall.

I could finally apologize for what's been a heavy burden on my shoulders for most of my life. At the same time, it would be an opportunity for me to tell my parents how much I love and miss them. Cons?

Resting a firm hand on his hip, he stood, shoved back his chair, and hooked his thumbs over the tops of the pockets of his blue jeans. With great focus, he contemplated the blank page and what to do about it.

What's the worst that can happen? Pondering the loaded question, he tapped his socked toe against the tile. *They might tell me they never want to hear from me again. Or maybe they won't even respond. Are these two scenarios worse than my current situation?*

He shrugged and watched as the rays dimmed to a softer shade. *Write a letter, Jarred.* Rachel's soft, but convincing voice haunted him. He remained standing, silently ordering the beat of his heart to slow. At that moment, reality hit him; he squared his shoulders and crossed his arms over his chest.

A combination of shame and embarrassment fought inside him until he bowed his head and prayed.

"Dear Lord and Savior, please give me faith to cope with what happened. Help me not to fear because You are by my side. And please forgive me for not having the strength You expect from me. Amen."

As he lifted his head, he pivoted and returned to the table. Taking a deep breath, he scooted the chair closer to the glass top and took the pen between his fingers.

> *Dear Mom and Dad,*
>   *I hope this finds you well. I've been searching my heart and feel compelled to write to you. I wish I could relive my fourth birthday party. I never would have taken the ball outside. I miss my brother terribly. And I miss you. I wish the driver had hit me instead of Matt.*

For a moment, Jarred went on to tell them about his mentorship under the late Dr. Stevens, his recent graduation from Purdue University's College of Veterinary Medicine, and his plan to join the Amish church with Rachel.

He blinked at the sting of salty moisture.

> *I am truly sorry for what happened. I love you.*
> *Jarred*

With slow, deliberate movements, he creased the paper into thirds. A nervous bead of sweat dripped down his neck. Before he could second-guess his actions, he shoved the letter into the envelope and sealed it. Stretching his legs, he relaxed in the chair, pulled in a deep breath, and dropped the letter onto the table.

Mail it.

After taking a swig of water, he dutifully stood and proceeded outside to the mailbox. The warm breeze caressed his forehead. It was like a good-luck kiss. He placed the envelope in the mailbox, flipped up the red flag, and nodded in satisfaction.

He wasn't sure what would come of his correspondence, but he was fully aware that nothing in life was guaranteed. Now communication between him and his parents was in the Lord's hands. Jarred reasoned that was a good place for it to be. Offering a nod, he whispered a quick thank-you prayer.

Quick steps took him toward the white fence surrounding the barn. Leaning against it, he focused on Rachel. He yearned to talk to the girl who'd recommended the heartfelt message. He wanted to hear her voice. Gaze into her eyes.

He'd heeded her advice. *She's probably wondering about Cinnamon. I can't wait to see her again.*

He considered Rachel's cinnamon-colored gift to him. She'd given him what she loved most. She'd also confessed her dream to him. The first two parts, anyway. He contemplated her question about wanting children. As he imagined a house full of kids, he wondered about her third wish. What was the rest of Rachel's dream?

Rachel cut up bell peppers and set them to the side as she considered how her relationship with Jarred had blossomed since she'd met him. She smiled a little. She always did things in steps, and freezing vegetables was no exception. A warm breeze floated into the kitchen through the window in front of her. The pleasant aroma of fresh produce and newly cut grass filled her nostrils, and she breathed in satisfaction.

As she sliced peppers into strips, she looked out the window. Her gaze automatically drifted to Old Sam's pasture before landing on the Kauffman barn. Outside, Paula looked over the fence. As Rachel studied the filly, she thought of Jarred and pictured his pickup leaving their drive. She could envision him waving good-bye and hear the crunching of loose gravel under his tires.

The recollection prompted a smile, and she thought of when he'd join the church with her this fall. She loved conversing with him. They could talk about Cinnamon. About animals he healed.

While the large fan behind her purred lightly, Rachel continued cutting the red and green veggies into cubes on the large wooden board, then rinsed the white seeds off and laid the clean slices onto doubled paper towels.

I'm not sure when I'll see him again. I miss him terribly. I miss Cinnamon.

She rolled her shoulders to relax. She'd wanted to repay him with something wonderful for his special attention to Cinnamon. As she'd watched them together inside his barn, she'd known without a doubt that they belonged together. She'd given him what she loved.

She took a deep breath and let it out as she held her hands under the faucet. She ran the nearest dish towel over her palms to rid them of moisture. Then she continued her task at hand, still contemplating the kind animal doctor and that they loved each other.

As an Amish girl, she'd been taught to look at a person's heart and not to focus on a person's good looks. But her approval of Jarred's physical appearance came without thought or planning. She couldn't help it. In fact, she admired everything she knew about him.

His compassion. Patience. Kindness. Faith in God's power to heal.

She'd never been courted by anyone, but she looked forward to spending time with him. Jarred's kind, gentle manner was so comforting, their moments together passed quickly. When she watched him with Cinnamon, she saw a man who truly loved her horse with all his heart. Thank goodness, he'd come to her aid. But she'd never expected to fall in love with him.

She contemplated her encouragement to write his parents. While she stared out the window, she considered the dire situation between Jarred and his parents and frowned, wondering if her advice had been the right course of action. *I should have considered the consequences before I advised him. I'm hardly qualified to tell him what to do, especially in such a fragile situation, despite that the suggestion came from Old Sam. At the time, contacting them seemed the obvious thing to do.*

She raised an eyebrow. *Why did I advise him? How on earth would I even guess what he should do? I'm not in his shoes. I haven't suffered the past twenty years because my parents blamed me for the loss of a sibling.* She lowered her gaze to the floor. *And his heart has already been broken.*

When she looked up at the countertop, she took in the plate-sized piles of green and red. With great care, she slid the peppers into freezer bags, laid them into long rows, then sealed the bags. She imagined their contents in chili this winter, but to her dismay, even that delicious thought didn't chase Jarred and his agonizing situation from her thoughts.

She hadn't known him long. At the same time, it seemed like they'd known each other forever. *The length of our relationship doesn't matter. I care about Jarred. A lot.*

Because of that, she feared her advice to him might worsen his family situation. *Look at the glass as half-full.* She didn't know Jarred's folks, so she couldn't predict their reaction to his attempt at communication. It was possible that the message could harm their relationship.

Rachel prayed with all of her heart that his honest words would spark the love they surely had for their child, and that the three hearts could mend.

She pressed her lips together as she thought about her dream. She'd told him the first two parts, but the third would stay her secret, safe within her hope chest.

The following morning, Rachel sat opposite Old Sam in his barn and poured out her concerns about the advice she had offered Jarred.

Buddy's soft hair tickled her wrist as she stroked his head. Pulling her hand away, she giggled as he made himself comfortable on her shoes. His softness reminded her of a baby blanket Mamma had knit for a neighbor.

Every once in a while, a cricket chirped. Birds flew in through the opened doors and perched on the upper windowsills. The fresh aromas of oak and straw filled her nostrils. Rachel eyed the new bales lined up against the wall by Ginger's stall. She had glimpsed the filly in the pasture before coming inside.

"Sam, I wonder if I should have stayed out of this."

A long silence ensued until he looked up from his work. He furrowed his brow as their gazes locked. "Why? You did your best to help."

She interlaced her fingers and leaned forward. "*Jah*, his situation with his parents is dire. It's also sensitive. I mean, they sent him away. He and his folks haven't seen each other for two decades. I suggested to him that he write to them. Like you advised."

She gave a quick shrug and shook her head. "But I shouldn't have done it. What I'm afraid of is . . ."

Sam looked at her to continue.

"That their response will make him feel worse than he already does." She lifted her palms in the air helplessly.

After another long pause, Sam put down his tool and eyed the others, as if deciding which one to use next. A breeze floated in, moving some loose pieces of straw to the area around her feet.

Buddy stayed put. Rachel sat very still while her awareness of the severity of the dilemma of Jarred's relationship with his parents grew inside her until she had to shift to a more comfortable position. She sat back in her chair, stretched her legs, and sighed in relief that she'd unleashed what worried her. With a reproachful glance, Buddy adjusted his position, too.

As Sam stood at the end of the bench to sand a corner of wood, Buddy pawed at a fly buzzing around his nose. While slow steps took Sam away, Rachel mentally coached herself to be positive. She tried to be patient while Sam returned to his seat. The bottom of his chair made a brief, irritating noise as he pushed closer to his bench. With a slow, deliberate motion, he pulled a small knife from his carving tool box and cut into the wood. As he spoke, his voice was reflective.

"God presents us with challenges, Rachel. But this situation you've shared with me . . ." He shook his head and his voice softened to a tone that was a combination of regret and reality. "It's something that can never have a happy ending, you see."

She frowned while he pressed his legs together in a straight line. "You've got to know that."

Rachel's heart sank. As she considered the disappointing words, she lowered her gaze to the now-sleeping canine. After a long pause, she offered a nod of agreement.

"You're right, Sam. It can never be good."

Creases deepened around his eyes. "The brother's gone. No matter what the parents say in response to the letter, there's no way to bring him back. And his death happened at Jarred's party. That can't be changed, either."

He paused before leaning into his work. The knife cutting into the oak made a light whistle that was barely audible. His thick brows knit together as he etched. Finally, he laid down his tool and glanced up.

"I'm sorry, Rachel. I know you expected something more positive. But the way I see it, there's no one to blame for what happened. Not really the parents, because sometimes things happen that we don't prepare for. Accidents."

"And certainly not the four-year-old or the seven-year-old. You're sure the adults weren't responsible, Sam? They're our protectors."

Sam shook his head before giving a slight shrug. "Responsible, yes. After all, they were in charge. But I don't believe they're to blame. There's a difference."

He brushed some chippings off the board. "It's odd that they sent the other son away after the death. With the one already gone, one might think they'd want to keep the living child close. It's not an easy thing to comprehend."

"But, Sam, the parents blamed Jarred."

He tapped his tool lightly against the bench. "Are you sure about that?"

Rachel leaned back and rolled her tense shoulders while contemplating his question. "If they didn't, why would they send him away?"

She leaned forward and rested her elbows on her thighs as she waited for him to explain. Buddy whined and turned over onto his back. Dutifully, Rachel ran an affectionate hand over his belly.

"You're high maintenance, you know that?"

Sam rested his hands on his lap. His gaze locked with Rachel's while she sat very still and listened.

"There could be a number of reasons to send their offspring away. Of course, I wouldn't understand any of them, but, young one, I'm not a mind reader. And neither are you. Only they can answer that."

At four the next morning, Jarred emptied Cinnamon's trough and stepped back while dirty water flowed down the small incline next to the barn. He proceeded inside and grabbed a rake from a metal hook. Letting out a deep sigh that was regret mixed with happiness, he made his way into Cinnamon's stall.

He glanced at the attentive horse and smiled a little. "I'll give you the best life I can, boy." He chuckled. "But Rachel set the bar high."

Without thinking, he raked dirty straw into a pile. Cinnamon pushed his nose against Jarred's arm. In response, Jarred laughed.

Flies buzzed around manure. A mouse scurried to the corner. In the distance, the tomcat looked on. From Jarred's perspective, the scene in his barn looked perfect because the story of the sick horse had a happy denouement. Cinnamon's recovery was nothing less than a miracle, and he gave God all of the thanks and praise. Now it was time to move on to his mother and father.

As he worked, he considered his horse. The straw dust pooled around Jarred, forcing a sneeze. He sniffed and considered the thousands of horses he'd help in the future and hoped his career would be filled with blessings like this one, because there was nothing as satisfying as watching a struggling animal pull through.

He was fully aware that it wasn't really his talent that saved them. It was all about his Lord and Savior taking over. With human hands, Jarred's abilities couldn't compete with God's touch.

He closed his eyes a long moment in satisfaction as he breathed in the familiar barn scents. He considered the earthy smells a natural remedy for stress.

They eased his mind. The aroma of oats calmed the tense speed of his pulse.

His thoughts migrated to the letter he'd mailed. As he focused on Rachel's advice, he could almost hear her soft, encouraging voice.

I miss her. I miss my parents and Matt. My attention to animals can't compensate for what happened at my birthday party, but at least helping them is therapeutic.

The realization prompted a dull ache in his chest. *Be positive.*

He lifted his chin with new determination and paused for a moment. His fingers lingered on the oversized rake while he focused on contentment.

Rachel's a large part of Cinnamon's happy story. He leaned forward to rest both hands on the handle, recalling the day he'd fallen in love with the cinnamon-colored gelding.

"You're unique and special in every way, boy."

Cinnamon threw back his head.

But intense emotions accompanied that love because Jarred had never been able to separate his heart from his mission to save the sick. Each time, he invested every part of himself into healing. And in that very process, he'd met a girl whom he'd come to lean on.

Rachel drifted into his thoughts while he continued to rake the pile of straw near the entrance. He'd been up most of the night thinking. Opening up to Rachel about Matt's death and writing his parents had stirred up a mixture of emotions. Last night, he had slid back into a place where terrible guilt overcame him.

He squeezed his eyes closed and whispered,

"Dear Lord, Please help me. My burden's too heavy
for me to bear alone."

When he opened his eyes, he mentally relived
happy moments from yesterday. As he eyed a bag of
oats, he focused on the only person he'd confessed
his past to.

He stopped a moment to envision the rosy glow in
Rachel's cheeks. The honesty and sincerity in her
blue-green eyes. The loose strands of hair that escaped
from her kapp and caressed the sides of her face
while she'd worked. What piqued his interest most
was her sincere intent to support him. And above all,
her optimism.

In his lifetime, he'd experienced very few close
relationships. Even with Tom, Jarred hadn't been
comfortable enough to disclose the details about
Matt's passing. Of course, his conversations with
Tom had pertained to animals. No one had really
brought up Jarred's past until Rachel.

As he thought back on what he'd told her, it
wasn't his confession that surprised him nearly as
much as her unexpected interest and reaction. He'd
never forget her expression, a strong combination
of shock and devastation. When she'd finally
thought of something to say, her voice had quivered.
Obviously, she'd taken to heart what he'd told her.

The light morning breeze came in through the
open doors of the barn to caress the back of his
neck. He grabbed the bottom of his oversized T-shirt
to wipe sweat from his forehead. While the breeze
lifted the ends of his hair, he closed his eyes to enjoy
the welcome relief. He soon forgot about the unusually high summer temps and envisioned Rachel.

I've never met anyone like her. She's so thoughtful. Insightful, especially for her age. Caring. When I glimpsed her reaction, it was as if she'd taken my confession personally. As if she was in my place. I trust her. But what I told her; it was emotionally heavy. I was selfish for dumping so much on her.

He dug his hands deep into his pockets. *I shouldn't have. But she's so easy to talk to. The story just came out. I've kept it inside for so many years.*

Should I be concerned about her? My story's powerful, especially to an innocent Amish girl. I'm sure she's never listened to anything so horrifying. Should I have kept my problem to myself?

His dependence on Rachel was a good thing. At the same time, it wasn't, because being close to her didn't necessarily guarantee a happy ending.

He already struggled with one major loss.

Life doesn't come with a warranty. I would buy one, if I could, to ensure I don't lose Rachel. Before I think of marrying her and raising children, I need to resolve my situation with my parents. Otherwise, I won't be whole. And I must be a complete person to make Rachel's life everything she deserves.

Chapter Twelve

Early the following morning, Rachel swatted away a mosquito before proceeding to pick pumpkin blossoms. The sun made a shy appearance in the sky, causing the beads of dewy moisture on the plants to glisten. The wetness gave the blossoms a deep gold appearance. She yanked the bottom of her navy dress to stop it from brushing the plants, but keeping them off of her large apron and sleeves was impossible.

As she cut the blossoms from the vine, she carefully placed them in the basket at her feet. She loved how Mamma prepared pumpkin blossoms in the frying pan, dipped in egg and followed by a toss of crushed saltines. The trick was to pick them before they closed up. Of course, she was accustomed to being up early.

While she breathed in the vine's pleasant scent, her thoughts turned to her dream. Jarred had automatically become part of it. She grinned and tried to focus on the vegetables, but it was difficult when her heart pumped to the "Jarred beat."

As she laid delicate orange blossoms onto the paper towel, she imagined a crew of little ones following her from the home she would share with her husband and children to her parents'. She envisioned loading up her family in two buggies to head to church.

And in the center of her vision was Jarred. She closed her eyes a moment, recalling his words of affection to her. For some reason, today, her dream seemed more real than ever. An Amish husband who loved her. A bunch of children. And even what she considered the icing on the cake.

The late-August sun lingered in the western sky as Jarred pulled into his drive, got out, and closed his truck door. Quick strides took him to his box, where he reached inside to retrieve the day's mail.

He closed the cover and proceeded to the house. The hot afternoon temperature was fast dropping. Thunder crackled. The damp air smelled like rain.

Without thinking, he flipped through the stack of envelopes. The moment he glimpsed his handprinted address, his heart skipped a beat. He stopped and stared in a daze at the self-addressed stamped envelope he'd enclosed with his letter to his parents.

While lightning bolts flickered, he stood very still. The pulse on his wrist sprinted at a pace that could win a race, he was sure. Finally, he continued to the patio door to the kitchen, where his thoughts were an odd chaotic mixture of optimism and pessimism as he stared at his name in the center of the white envelope.

He opened the blinds to glance at his barn for reassurance. Before the storm set in, he'd pay Cinnamon a visit. He gave a helpless roll of his eyes when he realized that he was merely postponing what needed to be done.

Open it. Frustrated, he gave the piece in question a thoughtful wave and squared his jaw.

They must want to get in touch with me. Otherwise, they wouldn't have responded. Envelope in hand, he paced to the living room and back. *But a reply doesn't necessarily mean good news. What if they still blame me for Matt's death?*

Look at the glass as half-full. A few sprinkles dotted the window and glass door, making an uneven tapping noise that sounded like Ping-Pong balls meeting a table. As he remembered Rachel's constant advice, he wished she were with him to read his parents' response. She was so reassuring and logical.

Faith. He struggled to stay calm while he pulled the nearest chair from his kitchen table and sat down, nervously tapping his boot against the tile.

He stayed very still while the enticing smell of curry from last night's dinner lingered in the air. He breathed in the spicy scent and swallowed. When the pace of rain hitting the roof accelerated, Jarred leaned forward and carefully picked up the envelope with both hands. While contemplating its contents, he squeezed his eyes closed to keep calm.

When he opened them, the tomcat appeared. Aware that the stray would be outside in the coming storm, Jarred went to the door and cracked it open. To his surprise, the cat stepped inside.

Jarred quickly made him a soft, warm spot in

the corner of the room. "You're safe in here. Don't you worry."

As his new friend got comfortable on the oversized pillow, Jarred's heart warmed, and he relaxed a little. He knew that God protected His flock. Jarred was a member. So was the stray. So what was there to be concerned about? He vividly recalled a scripture to not fear, for God was with him.

He'd heard in a church sermon that God never turned anyone away from His door. That awareness slowed his pulse to a calmer, less urgent pace. Jarred carefully opened the envelope and pulled out the neatly folded paper. He read the written message and caught an emotional breath. Tears flowed down his cheeks.

The following morning, as soon as Rachel's gaze met Jarred's, she sensed good news. Holding her breath, she made her way to his Ford while he stepped quickly to meet her between the house and the Kauffman barn.

When they met face-to-face, his expression was an exuberant combination of relief and immense joy. His eyes sparkled with newfound excitement, and the uncertain, stormy depths were gone.

Rachel brushed her hands over her apron to rid it of straw. She motioned to the barn. "You heard from them?"

As the sun played hide-and-seek from behind a cloud, he blinked before offering a firm nod and a wide grin. "Rachel, they want me to come and see them Saturday."

She led him to the bench beside the barn, and

they sat at the same time before turning toward each other.

A laugh of relief escaped his throat. "I can't believe it."

"So you'll drive to Ohio?"

"Yeah."

She jumped up and down. "Jarred, I'm so . . ." She laughed because she couldn't think of a word strong enough to describe what she was. "Happy!"

He smiled widely.

A long, satisfied silence ensued while Rachel took in the great news.

Finally, Jarred cleared his throat. "This would never have happened without you."

She slightly raised an eyebrow. "You mean Old Sam. Writing them was his idea, you know."

Jarred stood and dipped his head. "And I intend to personally thank him. But first things first."

She looked at him to continue.

"I'm going to ask your father if he'll allow you to celebrate with me."

Before she could say anything, he lifted a hand and continued. "I know I'm not a member of the church yet, but I will be soon." He winked.

"I'm sure Dad will let us celebrate, Jarred! What do you have in mind?"

He paused, then slapped his hands decisively on his thighs. "I'd like to bring Cinnamon over for a nice, leisurely buggy ride."

Rachel closed her eyes and drew her hand to her chest. "I would love that. So would Cinnamon." With determination, she hugged a hand to her hip.

"But first, we've got to talk about what you'll say to your folks."

When he didn't respond, she added, "It's been a long time since you've seen or talked to them, Jarred. And Saturday's only two days away."

A familiar, enthusiastic voice interrupted their conversation. "Good to see you, Dr. Zimmerman! Won't you two come in and enjoy fresh-squeezed lemonade?"

Rachel looked from Mamma to Jarred and lifted a hopeful brow.

"To be continued," he said and turned in the direction of the new voice. "I'd love to, Mrs. Kauffman."

Inside, Rachel helped with three beverages before she and Mamma joined Jarred at the table. Rachel sat opposite Jarred, with Mamma on her left.

"To what do we owe this pleasure?"

Rachel and Jarred smiled at each other. Finally, Jarred adjusted in his chair, returned his glass to the napkin, and squared his shoulders.

He explained his situation to Rachel's mother. While he talked, the battery-powered clock on the wall ticked to an even beat.

The fresh scent of wood soap lingered in the air. All sorts of fresh produce covered the kitchen countertop, which was within view.

After Jarred poured out what had happened, Mamma's jaw dropped. "My, you've been through a lot!"

Rachel took a drink and returned her glass to the table. She glanced at her mom before focusing her full attention on Jarred. "This is definitely a reason to be happy."

Jarred pressed his lips together and looked down at the table. For several moments, his lips stuck in a frown.

Rachel rested her elbows on the oak. "What's wrong?"

She glanced at her mother, who also watched the kind doctor.

He tapped a hand against the table nervously, and Rachel quickly noted the pink flush in his cheeks.

"I'm excited. I'm also a little bit unsure of myself."

Mamma broke the long silence that followed. "Of course you are. I understand why you would be. You haven't seen them for years."

Rachel cut in. "Jarred, to have a relationship with them might take some effort on your part. I mean, you're not close to them, and they don't really know you."

Even so, she added with enthusiasm, "What's happening is wonderful!"

Mamma leaned forward and jumped in. "That's right. What's important is that you're all still alive and able to get to know each other again." Her tone was thoughtful. "Just think of the time you spent apart as a long pause."

Jarred nodded and chuckled. "That's certainly one way to look at it. A break that spanned most of my childhood."

He fidgeted with his hands. "But yeah, I'm grateful to see them again."

Rachel beamed and stood. She reached for Jarred's empty glass. "Refill?"

"Sure." As Rachel stepped into the kitchen, she

could hear Jarred and her mother. While Rachel listened, to her surprise, the conversation reminded her of a mom-to-son conversation. Rachel's heart warmed.

"I don't know what to say to them. What to wear. How to act."

Reassurance edged Mamma's voice. "They're your folks. Your own flesh and blood. And even though you might feel like strangers, that will change the moment you're face-to-face, I'm sure. Want to know something?"

Rachel glimpsed Jarred's expression of hopeful curiosity.

"I'll bet they're as nervous as you are."

When Rachel returned, Mamma and Jarred faced each other. Rachel knew all too well that her mother loved offering advice, and it pleased Rachel that Jarred had opened up to her.

"You really think so?"

She offered a firm nod. "I'm sure. Let me tell you, I don't know your mom or dad, but I'm a parent. I'm sure that they must feel awful about what happened."

Jarred's voice lowered with emotion. "I don't know." He shrugged. "They've had plenty of time to reach out to me."

A combination of seriousness and concern infused Mamma's voice as she and Jarred locked gazes. "Jarred, I can't even begin to imagine how you must feel about everything that happened. And I'm sure your parents dealt with it as best they could. Of course, I don't know what's going on in their minds, but I can assure you of this."

Jarred and Rachel both looked at her to continue.

"They love you and always have."

Rachel studied Jarred's reaction. His look was difficult to read. She wasn't sure that Mamma's statement had convinced him.

Rachel thought of Old Sam and what he might say to ease Jarred's uncertainty. As she tried for the right words, the bright sunshine coming in through the windows lightened the shade of Mamma's and Jarred's faces.

And suddenly, Rachel knew what to offer. "Jarred, pray for God to guide you and help you with your visit. You've made huge progress just by contacting them and getting a reply."

He nodded. "I know."

"So go and be yourself."

Mamma piped in with enthusiasm. "They'll be so proud of you." She gestured with her hands. "Even though your situation's difficult, I can assure you that God will be with you. He is your Shepherd. With the Lord as your guide, how can things not work out?"

Saturday came quickly, and Jarred parked in his parents' drive. His sweaty palms lingered on the steering wheel. He was home.

He said a silent prayer as he approached the front door, placed his pointer finger on the doorbell, and pushed it. When he dropped his arm to his side, his hand shook. He suddenly wondered again if reconnecting had been a mistake.

The warm August breeze caressed the back of his neck. The pleasant aroma of grilled steaks filled the neighborhood. As he stood, he could hear children laughing and screaming. He turned to take in the street where Matt's accident had occurred.

He closed his eyes, recalling his birthday party. The moment he opened them, the door opened, and he faced his mom and dad. Their expressions were difficult to read as they stood very still. But as soon as his dad waved him to come in, his mother threw her arms around him.

Love filled Jarred's heart until he was sure it would burst as he relished his mother's touch.

"Son. Welcome home." His dad joined in the long, emotional embrace.

His father was the first to break the silence when they dropped arms. His gaze traveled from Jarred's toes to his head. He nodded approval. "You've become a handsome man, Jarred. Your hair's darker than when we last saw you, but that smile . . . and those eyes." His dad shook his head as if undecided about what to do. A short, tense silence ensued.

Jarred's mom eyed her husband before lifting a decisive brow.

His dad cleared his throat. "Before we catch up, there's something we need to say." He motioned to the living room.

Jarred followed them in and took the seat on the end of the couch.

When his father spoke, his voice cracked with nervousness. His words seemed to stumble out. "We regret what we did to you, Jarred. We're so deeply sorry."

While Jarred took in the huge significance of that statement, he held his flesh and blood's gaze. He watched his father look down at his shoes and study them. When he finally met Jarred's gaze, his eyes watered. The creases in the corners deepened.

"I'm afraid this apology's long overdue." He paused before lowering his voice to a level that was barely audible. "We can't change what we did. We're so sorry . . ." He stopped to catch a breath. "For sending you away."

For long thoughtful moments, his parents regarded each other. Their faces were an odd combination of agony and relief. During a long pause, his dad laid a hand on his wife's wrist and squeezed it. All the while, Jarred sat completely still, not sure how to act or what to say for fear that his father would take back those very strong words.

Mrs. Kauffman's advice echoed in his mind. "God is your Shepherd. With the Lord as your guide, how can things not work out?"

Those words from Rachel's mother seemed to land on Jarred's tense neck like a soft cotton blanket. His shoulders relaxed and his pulse slowed to a much more comfortable pace.

The room was so quiet, he could have heard a pin drop. His heartstrings pulled so hard, his chest ached. To his surprise, he knew with full clarity what needed to be said.

Sitting up straighter, he regarded his mother before his gaze landed on his father's face. "I'm the one who needs to apologize. It's all my fault."

He threw his hands in the air before looking down at the cream-colored carpet. When he lifted his head, he struggled to maintain his composure. "I'm the reason Matt's gone. How can I ever forgive myself?"

For long moments, Jarred stared at his parents,

who gazed back at him. While the heavy silence
ensued, Jarred noted the obvious differences in how
they had changed. His dad's jet black hair had
grayed. His mother had aged at least three decades.

The biggest difference in both of them was their
sad expressions. He'd never forget his mother's smile
and laugh. His dad had been commonly known as
the joke teller, but noting the lines of devastation
etched around his mouth, Jarred guessed that laughter had been rare since Matt had died.

At that moment, Jarred immediately knew without a doubt that they had suffered as much as he
had.

His mother's voice hinted at huge remorse as she
laid a fragile-looking hand on Jarred's arm. "Honey,
we were to blame. Not you." A slow shake of her
head followed while she gazed regretfully at Jarred.

Jarred suddenly remembered their apology. "I
thought you hated me. The first night away from
you, I turned to God. I was so scared. I missed you
terribly. I had nightmares for years about Matt and
the driver who'd hit him."

His dad's fingers shook as he leaned forward.
"Son, we sent you away because we couldn't face
what we'd done. You were such a haunting reminder
of the fatal mistake that was ours. The accident
could have been avoided."

Jarred watched in agony as his parents turned
toward each other and clasped their hands together
in what appeared to be a means to gain strength.
Their faces went void of color. His dad choked
before straightening his shoulders in what looked like
forced bravery.

"We should have put up a fence. We'd talked

about it. It was no secret that you and Matt played ball in the yard. And you were both so young. We were terribly naïve as parents."

He paused to blow his nose. A tear slid down his cheek as he went on. "We're certainly not trying to make excuses for our negligence, but one day you'll know, son, that there's no perfect science to being a parent. Grief overcame us, and we did what we believed was right. At the time, we weren't thinking straight. What we did was wrong, Jarred. So wrong. I hope God can forgive us. We'd known for years that the road in front of our house was busy. We let you down, I believe, more than we did Matt."

Jarred tried to make sense of that last statement and finally offered a helpless shrug. "I don't understand."

"Matt's accident was just that. On the other hand, what we did to you was deliberate."

"Matt's death . . ." His mother choked. For long moments, the grief-stricken couple held each other with their eyes closed. When his mom finally released him, his father spoke.

"Afterward . . . we felt we didn't deserve to be parents. We love you, Jarred, but we're not worthy of your love. I hope you can find it in your heart to forgive us."

Jarred couldn't move. His parents obviously awaited a reply. While Jarred processed their words, his heart filled with an emotion that was a mixture of disbelief and relief.

Before today, he hadn't been sure what to expect. He'd believed the worst for so many years, it was hard to react. Jarred knew his brother was with the Lord. Jarred couldn't bring him back. Neither could the distraught couple in front of him. No matter how many prayers Jarred sent to God, Matt would never return.

But after all of Jarred's lonely, sad years, his mom and dad loved him. Hearing that was so unexpected. When reality sank in, Jarred's pulse pumped to a joyous beat edged with relief. He bowed his head and fought emotional tears. When he looked up, the words came. "I love both of you. I forgive you."

Immediately, his parents joined him on the couch and embraced him. He relished their love. When his tears finally stopped, he caught his breath and tried to regain his composure.

"I miss him so much." He lifted his chin with forced confidence. "But now I've got you and dad back." A grin tugged at the corners of his lips. "And to be honest, that's a blessing I never expected."

His mom's expression turned to relief. His dad's voice hinted of newfound confidence while he gave Jarred a hard, affectionate pat on his shoulder. "There was never any reason for you to feel guilt. We accept full blame for your brother's death. We can't take back the lost years, but we'll have the future. And we intend to make wonderful new memories with our son."

Jarred parted his lips with hope.

"We'll do whatever we can for you, Jarred. We'll be the parents you deserve." After a slight hesitation, he added, "If you'll let us."

Jarred contemplated the offer and stood. "Of course." He paused. "There is something I'd like to do."

"What?"

"See Matt's room."

With one hand, his dad motioned to the circular stairwell. As slow steps took Jarred and his parents upstairs, time seemed to stand still while Jarred drifted back to the happy days when he and Matt had chased each other up and down.

At Matt's door, they stopped. Jarred squeezed his eyes closed and braced himself. His heart hammered like a runner's at the finish line. *Dear God, You are my Shepherd. Please comfort me and give me strength. Amen.*

His mom gave a gentle turn of the brass knob, and they went inside. Automatically, Jarred flipped on the light. His gaze traveled to walls filled with horse pictures, Little League trophies, Matt's second grade picture. Finally, Jarred's attention landed with great affection on the twin bunk beds.

As he went to the upper mattress to rest a hand on the blue comforter, his heart pounded with an odd combination of relief and anxiety.

"We didn't touch anything," his mother whispered. Jarred half heard the words while memories of Matt flooded his heart and soul until he could almost feel Matt's existence.

As Jarred squeezed the soft covering, it seemed like Matt joined him in spirit. Jarred knew from a church sermon that souls that had passed on couldn't come back; still, his brother's presence seemed to sweep through Jarred until he closed his eyes to savor the special, much-needed sensation. Long moments passed before he opened his lids and regarded Matt's personal things.

He moved close to the horse drawings and nodded. "Someday, I'll start an animal shelter in his name."

"Jarred, that's a wonderful idea." His mother glanced appreciatively at her spouse. "Let us help."

Jarred barely heard his own words or those of his parents as he envisioned himself with Matt on the soft tan carpet in the middle of the room. On this very spot, they'd read animal books together. They'd both been most interested in stories about lost animals. Early on, the two had yearned to rescue and protect the abandoned.

His mother's voice broke his reverie. "We have something for you, Jarred."

Not wanting to break away from precious memories, he turned.

"Matt made you something special for your birthday."

A hard knot formed in Jarred's throat.

His mom nodded. "He wanted to give it to you after the party."

Jarred stood very still while his mom opened the drawer on the nightstand. She looked up, teary eyed. "He wrapped it himself."

She retrieved a box and handed it with great care to Jarred. The drawer remained open.

As his parents looked on, Jarred stared in amazement at the present wrapped with plain white tissue. There wasn't a card. With a combination of great care and anticipation, Jarred untaped the sides and pulled out the cardboard box. Before removing the lid, he glanced at his mom and dad. Their expressions were difficult to read.

When he pulled off the cover, his heart skipped a beat. He claimed the empty chair next to the nightstand and studied the picture of a beautiful white horse with tan markings.

"An Arabian. His favorite. And he drew it just for me."

Jarred's gaze drifted to the bottom right-hand corner of the picture. The printed words stirred every emotion inside Jarred until he felt his heart break: TO MY LITTLE BROTHER. LOVE, MATT.

With a combination of happiness and regret, Jarred waved good-bye to his parents before proceeding to I-90. As they disappeared in his rearview mirror, he lowered his window and tried for a more comfortable position on his bucket seat.

He eyed the box on the passenger's seat holding Matt's drawing. Jarred rested his fingers on the cardboard with love and took in the significance of the gift.

This is the most precious thing I own.

He contemplated Matt's special talent, which was displayed in each stroke of colored pencil. Matt had given him the best gift he could think of: a picture of an Arabian horse.

Jarred's grip tightened on the steering wheel as he realized that his fierce determination to start a shelter in his brother's name was now a must.

He would fulfill Matt's dream.

Jarred stepped on the brake pedal to slow for I-71 South, smiling a little at how this much-anticipated day had changed his life. His conversation with his father and mother, and their complete honesty, filled his chest with a great sense of relief and happiness.

He loved them so much. Despite what he'd gone through, he understood their actions and forgave them. At the same time, it relieved him to know that they had never blamed him for Matt's death.

"Dear God, thank you. Amen."

Prior to this visit, Jarred had feared that being inside the home would be eerie and uncomfortable. To his astonishment, the opposite had occurred. What he'd experienced was an unexpected closeness to his brother. The sensation had calmed Jarred to the point where he hadn't wanted to leave.

He tapped his hand to a few country music beats and wondered what his folks would say about his plan to become Amish. Before coming, he'd been fully aware that twenty years couldn't be covered in one visit. Today's focus had been on Matt, on the long-awaited opportunity to take in everything that Matt had loved. To be in the room where they'd played and read stories.

Suddenly, he yearned to talk to Rachel. He grabbed his cell phone and dropped it back onto the seat, grinning in amusement. Of course she didn't own such a modern convenience. There was a phone in their barn, but he was fully aware that Mr. Kauffman checked messages only twice daily.

He yearned to talk to her like never before. He rested the back of his head against the seat. Today was a turning point in his life because he knew his parents loved and cared about him, and also because his belief that they blamed him for Matt's death was in error.

He couldn't wait to watch the expression on

Rachel's face when he related the details of his visit. He would share everything with her. How the house looked. What it was like being back in the very bedroom where he and Matt had slept on bunk beds. What his parents had said. Their remorse. And how Jarred's heart had melted the moment he'd opened the special gift that Matt had wrapped for him so many years ago.

He glimpsed his cell phone and smiled a little as he acknowledged certain conveniences that he'd voluntarily surrender once he joined the Amish church.

He glanced down at his means of transportation and rolled his eyes. His cell phone would be history. Electricity, too. He'd certainly miss the Discovery Channel on his small living room television.

He'd be able to keep his truck. The Amish in their particular area needing transportation were allowed to have cars titled in their names—a must for fear of their vehicles being stolen—however, he would be required to have a driver. Not driving would take getting used to. In fact, relinquishing his place behind the wheel might be his biggest challenge in joining the Plain Faith.

He looked around the small cabin of his truck and thought of Cinnamon and the buggy he would have for non-working occasions. A chuckle escaped him. He enjoyed traveling that way. However, that particular mode was a far stretch from his Ford, with its automatic transmission. *I won't be listening to country music.* He silently chastised himself. He moved into the other lane. He braked to slow for construction.

As he leaned forward in his seat, he returned to

his mental challenge. *I won't watch television at night. On the upside, I'll invest that time studying to become a better veterinarian.*

To his satisfaction, he never questioned his choice to join the church. He would compromise, that was for sure, but in the end, he had no doubt that he would be a more satisfied, complete man. And he would focus only on serving his Lord and Savior.

His sacrifices would lead to a more fulfilling life. He imagined that to most, relinquishing material things might be unimaginable. But to him, becoming a member of the hardworking Amish would be worth every sacrifice. His decision wasn't just because of Rachel. Over the years, he'd considered joining the group he so admired.

Rachel's kind face swept into his mind like an unexpected ray of warm sunshine. He smiled a little. It would be best to discuss his visit with her face-to-face. He tried to put things into perspective, focusing on Rachel's dream: To marry a good Amish man. To raise a large family. And the last part, whatever it was.

He hadn't known the girl with the heart-stopping smile long, but he was sure that he wanted to make her dream come true. He sighed with relief. *Settled. That will never change.*

What had taken an unexpected turn was his relationship with his folks. Jarred flipped on his headlights and kept in the right lane on I-71. As he turned the volume higher to hear Randy Travis, he drummed his fingers against the wheel in time with the music.

Jarred reached inside the compartment between the seats for a hard candy. Popping the treat into his mouth, he squeezed the wrapping and tossed it on the floor of the passenger side.

As he enjoyed the red candy, he tried to relax, but his heart still pumped excitedly. *My mom and dad don't blame me for Matt's death. My parents love me. And I love Rachel. But what is the last part of her dream?*

Chapter Thirteen

The following Saturday, Rachel smiled at Jarred as Cinnamon pulled them in her family's buggy. Jarred's visit with his parents had changed him. Reconnecting with his folks had lifted his joy to a whole new level. She noted the new sparkle in his eyes. The confident lift of his chin.

The beloved horse traveled along the narrow blacktop road at a slow, comfortable speed. There wasn't much traffic in the country. As Cinnamon trotted with his head held high, his tail moved gracefully back and forth. So did the hair on his mane.

Rachel said a silent prayer of thanks for his good health and for Jarred's rescue, too. She pressed her palms against the soft velvety seat covering, taking in the tall corn and beans on both sides.

The clomp clomping of Cinnamon's hooves and an occasional whinny were the only sounds. Large white puffy marshmallow-like clouds decorated the sky.

When the full sun appeared, she blinked to adjust

to the unexpected brightness. The warm breeze coming in through the open carriage caressed her neck and face. She breathed in, trying to savor the comforting moment.

Right now, she was completely satisfied. At ease. After long weeks of concern about Cinnamon followed by not knowing when she'd see Jarred again, this togetherness was a welcome relief. She certainly didn't take this blessing for granted.

As she considered the kind, gentle man beside her, she decided to voice her thoughts. "God has answered our prayers. He reconnected you with your parents. What more could we want?"

Before he could respond, she went on. "Jarred, I'm really happy to see you again." After the confession came out, she smiled a little, fully aware that her flat-sounding words hid the excitement she felt.

At the same time, she recognized that her parents most likely wouldn't approve of her boldness. Although she practiced openness and honesty, Old Sam had once told her that there was a difference between honesty and boldness. Somehow, she was certain she'd just crossed that line.

Assertiveness was a little out of character for her, but to her astonishment, she had no regrets. She'd thought about Jarred and written about him in her journal from the moment she'd met him. "I've missed you."

His response hinted at satisfaction. "I've missed you, too."

She nodded. "And I'm dying to hear about your visit with your parents. Don't you dare leave out a single detail."

She listened attentively as he began with his arrival at their home and told her about his time inside the house.

Sometime later, he darted her a wink. "This happened because of you, Rachel. Because of the letter." With a grin, he added, "And of course, huge thanks to your friend, Old Sam."

The corners of her lips pulled upward and she let out a grateful sigh. "I'm so happy for you, Jarred. After I gave you that piece of advice, I had second thoughts. In fact, I actually regretted telling you what to do."

His voice softened. "Why?"

She gestured with her hands before resting her palms on her thighs. "Because I don't have much experience to draw from to be offering such important stuff. Your situation with your parents was serious. Fortunately, your message led to a happy ending. But what if it hadn't?"

He shrugged. "No worries. Rachel, that's something you had no control over. Neither did I. Before I did it, I thought a lot about the repercussions. About their reaction, if they responded, and if so, the worst that could happen."

After a long, thoughtful silence, he offered her a thankful glance. "God answered our prayers. I can't begin to tell you what it's like being back in the home where Matt and I played, Rachel."

She watched a joyous expression sweep across his face and parted her lips in awe.

"It was like he was there. I felt so close to him."

"That's understandable. After all, it's where you

two spent the first years of your lives. Where you bonded."

"Now I'm convinced of something I sort of knew before."

She turned to lift a curious brow.

He guided Cinnamon to the side of the road to stay clear of an oncoming car. The buggy wheels bounced because of the unevenness. After the vehicle went by, they returned to the middle for a smoother ride.

"Now I'm more convinced than ever of God's plan for me." He paused. "It was for Cinnamon to bring us together so you could help me get my parents back. Rachel, I owe you so much."

Warmth invaded her cheeks. "I'm glad I could help." She lifted her chin a notch. "Just like you came to Cinnamon's rescue for me."

She glanced at him. The look in his eyes was reflective. Confident.

"You know what I think, Rachel Kauffman?"

She giggled at how he said her name. It came out with a respectful tone that she matched with her response. "What do you believe, Jarred Zimmerman?"

They shared a laugh.

"That the two of us complement each other." After a slight pause, he went on. "We make a great team."

Not sure how to respond, Rachel drew in a surprised breath not just because of what he'd said, but the way he'd said it. The words had been edged with admiration but also a strong hint of affection.

Afraid to speak, she bit her lip, fearful of breaking their special bonding moment.

As he leaned closer, the breeze stopped, and

suddenly, Rachel's long dress seemed uncomfortably warm. Dressed in blue jeans, Jarred wore a short-sleeved shirt buttoned down the front.

"Rachel . . ."

She sat very still, trying to stay calm. Her heart beat so quickly, she was afraid he would hear it. "I really look forward to joining the church and to spending more time with you."

Rachel ordered her lungs to continue pumping air, but they were struggling. "Jarred, I can't wait to spend more time with you. You must know that." She hesitated, not sure she should verbalize what she was thinking.

His smile widened. "I love you."

"Oh, Jarred, I love you too! So much."

He breathed in before continuing. "This may come as a surprise, but I've contemplated being Amish for years."

"Really?"

He nodded. "Working with animals has provided me exposure to people of all types of faiths, and I've always felt a strong sense of belonging with your group. They all seem to be honest and hardworking. And . . ."

He paused to cup his chin with his hand. Several heartbeats later, he sighed satisfaction. "Since I was four, I've craved being part of a family. Wanted to be with people who love and care about me."

His confession pulled at her heartstrings until her chest ached and tears welled up in her eyes. "You've got your parents back, Jarred. Now you can enjoy that unconditional love again. It's what you deserve."

"And I'm grateful. But there's something I want you to know. Since I've gotten close to you and your family, I've experienced that wonderful sense of belonging that I went without for most of my life. You're fortunate. You've always had that emotional support, Rachel. It's a true blessing, one that all of the money in the world can't buy. When I'm at your home, something very strong and comforting comes over me. I can't explain it. But when I leave, I feel a huge void. I've wondered what it would be like to be in a family again, Rachel. And now I have my answer."

Her throat tightened with emotion. "Jarred, I don't know what to say. I can't begin to tell you how much it means to me that we Kauffmans have made a positive impact on you. And you joining the faith that's everything to me . . ."

She drew a hand over her chest and closed her eyes before opening them again and giggling. He joined in the laughter.

"Such a serious conversation!"

"It is, but I'm glad we had it. Rachel . . ." His cheeks turned a light shade of rose as the flecks on his eyes danced with a combination of honesty and hope. "You're my dream come true."

That evening, Rachel pulled her journal from her hope chest. When she was seated, she flipped to the first empty page. Pressing the sides of the journal to keep the paper flat, she neatly printed the date at the top right-hand corner.

As she recalled the day's blessings, she squeezed her eyes closed and said a quick prayer of thanks. When she opened her eyes, she wanted to shout with happiness. It was hard to sit when she would rather run outside and throw her hands in the air with immense joy.

She eyed the empty page and drew in a deep breath. Old Sam always stressed the importance of discipline. Now was the time to practice it because there was much to be thankful for. But where to start?

Letting out a happy sigh, she crossed one bare foot over the other and focused on her entry. *Today was the most wonderful day of my life!* She went on to write about her buggy ride with Jarred and their conversation that had spanned his visit with his parents to Jarred's confession that she was his dream.

> *God is blessing me with every piece I need to see my goal come true! This wonderful man has asked my parents' permission to date me. And he'll join the Amish church after we go through our classes, even though it seems like we have to wait forever to start them.*
>
> *As far as living next to my mother and father, we've never really talked about it, but it will make sense for him to stay here after he joins the church. And fortunately, my parents own enough land for my siblings and me to build on.*

She laid her pen next to her journal, sat back in her chair, and crossed her arms over her lap in pure contentment. For some time, she imagined a glorious future with Jarred, children, and a house by her parents'. Her heart pumped with excited energy when she returned her pen to the paper.

> *I'm so happy when I'm with Jarred. I liked him from the moment I met him. Now we're in love.*

But there have been obstacles. Big ones. First of all, he's not Amish. For a while, that alone gave me reason to believe a relationship with him was not possible. But amazingly, that will be resolved. Secondly, he didn't feel he deserved to be loved because of the situation with his brother.

She frowned. That his parents had deserted him made her choke up. She caught a lone tear that started down her cheek. *Look at the glass as half-full.*

Jarred has reconnected with his folks. They apologized. Thank goodness Jarred won't go through the rest of his life thinking his parents blame him for his brother's death.

She leaned forward as thoughts filled her head, and wrote faster to capture them on paper.

How fortunate I am to have been raised in a loving home. I've never been given reason to doubt my parents' unconditional love for me. I wonder if I would be bitter had I been in Jarred's shoes.

I would hope not. But I'm not sure I would have handled it with the grace with which he has. I know that when I have my own children, situations will arise that test my judgment. And I will pray for guidance so my kids will never doubt my love for them.

The thought of having a large family warmed her heart. She laid down her pen to draw her hand to her chest in joy. For long, happy moments, she imagined the little ones she would have. Would they be girls? Boys? How many?

She turned, stood, and stepped with excitement to the window where she looked out at the clusters of stars in the sky. In awe, she knew that, in many ways, she was like each of those very stars. God was in charge of where they were.

She closed her eyes and pressed her palms together. "Dear Lord, I trust Your plan for me. Thank You for letting Cinnamon live. And I give You all of the praise and thanks for reconnecting Jarred with his parents. I know their situation will never be perfect, but only You know what the end result will be. I say a special thank-you for bringing Jarred and me together. And thank You for helping my dream to come true. Amen."

Later that week, Jarred wondered what was going on. His mother had phoned earlier in the day, her tone extremely urgent. All day, he'd contemplated the purpose of the last-minute visit. So here he was, at his small kitchen table. *With my parents. They're at my house.*

Jarred pulled the meat loaf he'd prepared ahead of time from the oven and set it on the pad in the middle of the table. After saying the prayer, he passed his father the entrée.

Automatically, his gaze drifted to the empty corner. His new furry friend enjoyed his independence.

Jarred's mother broke his reverie. "It always was your favorite."

Jarred looked at her to explain.

"Meat loaf."

He nodded agreement.

"There's something you should know." After a brief pause, she continued, "This is the first time I've had it since we lost Matt and you."

She choked up, then quickly composed herself.

Jarred's throat constricted. He swallowed and closed his eyes to focus on the advice Old Sam had given Rachel. *Look at the glass as half-full. I was not responsible for Matt's death. My parents love me.*

His mother drew in a deep breath. "I'm sorry, Jarred."

His father cut in. "You're back in our lives. And we're grateful. We're finally going forward."

A long silence ensued. The only sound was the clinking of silverware meeting plates and an occasional ice cube moving in a glass. The air smelled of pepper and onion.

Jarred leaned forward and lowered his voice to his most convincing tone. "Mom and Dad, Matt is no longer with us. But we have each other. And, Mom . . ." His gaze traveled to his father. "Dad, we've wasted so much time. God doesn't let us stay here forever. I've missed too many holidays and birthdays with you."

He closed his eyes a moment to think of the right words. When they came, compassion edged his voice. He wanted to reach his parents because what he was trying to tell them was so important.

"I don't doubt God's plan is for us to be together in the end. But I don't know what will happen up to that point. We'll take it in stride. And during that time, I'll trust Him."

Jarred looked on as his parents regarded each other. He smiled because he'd said exactly what was on his mind. With Rachel's help, he was now able to focus on the right things.

His dad cleared his throat. "Now, son, what we came here to tell you . . ."

Days later, the warm sun caressed Rachel's face as she pulled the mail out of the Kauffman box at the end of the long drive in front of their home. As she flipped through the pile, she caught her name on one of the envelopes.

A closer look showed Jarred's name in the return address corner. She stopped and pressed her lips together.

Why the letter?

Quick steps took her back up the drive and into the kitchen, where she laid the mail in the center of the kitchen table. Except for hers.

With a combination of fear and uncertainty, she rushed up the stairs, envelope in hand. *Why is he writing me? Maybe he's too busy to stop by. Or perhaps something happened.*

Once inside her bedroom, she closed the door. With shaky fingers, she sat at her desk, tore open the envelope, and removed the sheet of paper. Nervous breaths escaped her lungs while she held the paper in front of her with both hands and read the neat black print.

Dear Rachel, I feel compelled to write you before getting your thoughts in person. I'd like for you to have time to take this in before we talk.

What?

So much is happening right now, and I'll share what's going on.

Her desktop glistened with extra sheen from an earlier coat of Murphy's wood soap. She breathed in the fresh, pleasant scent; still, her pulse zoomed with an uncomfortable sense of urgency.

My parents paid me a visit. There wasn't time to tell you. It was last minute. I was stunned at what they said.

Rachel's arms stiffened. Her senses told her that she didn't want to hear what was coming.

I told you how connected I felt to my brother when I was in the home where we grew up. I'd said the same to my parents. They've decided to offer me something I never expected. I'm not sure why they're doing this, but my guess is that it's to apologize for the years we spent apart. Rachel, they're gifting me their house.

After finishing her chores the following afternoon, Rachel bounded through the open doors and shouted, "Old Sam!"

He looked up from his workbench and smiled.

"Rachel! I was just wondering how you were. I haven't seen you for a while."

She plopped herself down into the chair opposite him and caught her breath, pushing some loose hairs back under her kapp.

"What's on your mind?"

She launched into an explanation of her dilemma. As she did so, Buddy whined for attention, making himself comfortable on her shoes. Automatically, she stroked the canine's head.

As she relayed the brief contents of Jarred's letter, her heart pumped faster to keep up with her desperate words, which started to run together. When she'd finished, she said, "Old Sam, you've got to help me. I don't know what to do."

She watched with intense anxiety while he carved into the oak board in front of him. She wondered how he could stay so calm and focused while her own thoughts were in absolute chaos.

At last, his thoughtful voice broke the silence. She straightened. As she did so, she moved her shoes closer to the chair, and Buddy let out a disgruntled whine.

"Young one, do you recall the advice I always give you?"

It didn't take Rachel long to reply. "Look at the glass as half-full."

He offered a slow nod while he worked. She noted the steadiness of his hands, his concentration, the serious lines around his eyes, and she wished she could be as in control of herself as he was of himself.

She crossed her legs. *Be patient. Old Sam will know what to do. He's the wisest person I know.*

"Rachel, let's talk this situation out."

In the background, Ginger snorted, but Rachel couldn't give the spoiled horse a treat until she and Old Sam resolved the issue at hand.

"Okay."

Buddy moaned his disapproval when she stretched her legs. "Sorry, boy." It didn't take long for the Irish setter to content himself again.

"First of all, does the doctor know you'd like to live near your parents?"

She shrugged. "We've never talked about it. I just assumed we would."

Old Sam stopped his work. For long moments, they looked at each other until he sighed and slid his chair back to cross his hands over his lap. For long moments, he lowered his gaze to the floor. When he finally lifted his chin, he raised an eyebrow. "Rachel, I'm not sure I understand the problem."

"Old Sam, Jarred's moving back to Ohio!"

"Did he say that?"

Rachel shook her head. "But I'm sure he will. He loves the thought of being close to memories of him and his brother. And after all he's been through, I'm sure his childhood home offers him a certain comfort that he's been without."

"Yes, yes. But I'm not sure I understand your dilemma."

"Old Sam . . ."

The creases around Sam's eyes deepened. "Let's say that he decides to move to Ohio." He waved a hand to silence her when she tried to speak. "And you must realize that this is the worst that could happen."

He hesitated. "Would you give him your blessing?"

It didn't take her long to respond. "Of course. I mean, I'm not selfish. He's finally getting his relationship with his parents back on track. I'm sure that for him to live in their home would please them. Not to mention, the close connection to his brother."

"I understand. How could he not be comfortable where he and his brother played? But I'm concerned about you. What about Rachel?"

She considered the question and drew her brows together with uncertainty. "Of course I'd like him to stay here. But this isn't about me. If living there brings him joy, that's what I want for him. How could I deny him something I've always taken for granted?"

Old Sam finally offered a firm nod of acceptance. As she waited for him to speak, a brown squirrel rushed into the barn and stood on his hind legs as if he, too, awaited a reply. When he quickly rushed back out, Sam cleared his throat and said in a more serious tone, "Then this is how I see it. You'd give your blessing for him to move. Then, if he decides to do that, of course, you'd have to let him go. However, if you're determined to be with him, your situation with the doctor becomes much more involved because that would require you to go, too."

He looked down at his tools. His voice was soft as he kept his gaze on the box. "I know that's not what you want to hear, but the way I see it, there's no other option. And love is about making sacrifices." He paused to look up. When he did so, his eyes glistened with moisture.

Rachel's heart sank because she was certain Old Sam was thinking about Esther. He missed her so much. Every time he mentioned her, he teared up. Rachel realized that she could at least be with Jarred, but Old Sam had no option that included being with Esther. No matter how much Sam compromised, it was impossible for him to be with the woman he loved dearly and had shared most of his life with.

His voice cracked with great affection. "Young one, if I could have Esther back, I'd move to the other end of the world to be with her."

They locked gazes.

Suddenly, a pang of guilt swept up Rachel's spine to the base of her neck. The uncomfortable sensation prompted a quick roll of her shoulders.

"Search your heart. And pray. Perhaps God presented this situation to test your love for Jarred."

She sat very still while she contemplated Sam's theory.

"Put all things aside, including what happened to his brother. All of that is irrelevant, really. There's one question you must ask yourself. Would you move with him? And when you have your answer, you'll know what to do if the worst scenario materializes." After a lengthy pause, Old Sam stood and started slowly toward the area where he kept extra tools.

Next to her, he stopped. When he spoke, his tone was matter-of-fact. "Perhaps your doctor will stay here. Then you've worried for nothing. But let's say that he decides to accept his parents' offer. Do you love him enough to live away from your family?"

Chapter Fourteen

When Rachel glimpsed Jarred's pickup coming down their long front drive on the first day of September, she steadied her wicker basket of late tomatoes and carefully made her way toward him.

As he parked his truck, she returned his wave. Normally, she would feel great excitement at seeing the Ford, but under the circumstances, a rush of uneasiness replaced it. Uncertainty that they'd join the church together.

"Hey, there." He met her and reached out his hand. "Let me carry that for you."

"Thank you."

After she handed him the basket, she eyed him with skepticism. "I've been thinking a lot about your letter."

As they walked to the side door of the house, he steadied the heavy produce in front of him with both hands.

"How wonderful that your parents want you to have the home you and Matt grew up in."

When he turned to her, a sense of great relief swept across his face. "You think so?"

She swatted away a black bug. "What is there to say, really? I want it for you, Jarred, if it's what you'd like. But I'd miss you terribly."

A long silence ensued. Rachel stepped around a chicken. Gravel crunched under their shoes as they crossed the drive that led to the sidewalk.

He stopped to face her. "If we were married, would you consider coming with me?"

Her jaw dropped in surprise.

She'd thought about that very question too many times to count. She just hadn't expected to hear the actual words.

She considered an answer. Long seconds passed before she knew what to say.

"Jarred, we'd have to rethink everything. It wouldn't make sense to join this church and then move to Ohio. Look. I want you to be happy. This offer from your folks . . . it's so much more than a gift. For you, it's a chance to live where memories of your brother come alive. I think that, if I were in your shoes, I'd want to be there. If it gives you comfort and peace, then how could I not encourage that?"

"But, Rachel, it's not that simple. I'm sure you've always wanted to live by your folks, but we could visit as much as you'd like. I want to make you the happiest girl in the world and make your dream come true."

She struggled to not let emotion take over. Getting worked up over what was inevitable wouldn't accomplish anything. "Jarred, ever since I read your letter, your move to Ohio is all I've thought about. You have my blessing to go." She blinked back a tear. "Of course, I'll miss you."

"You wouldn't consider coming? Ever?"

Her heart jumped with a combination of joy and sadness. She was so close to having her dream, yet so far away. "I would love to spend forever with you, Jarred. And I understand how being in your parents' home makes you complete. Every memory you've ever shared with Matt is there. At that house, you experience a part of your life that you lost long ago. I respect that more than you can ever imagine."

He looked at her to continue. For long moments, she wasn't sure what else to say, but as she considered what she'd just told him, for the first time, she could answer Old Sam's question.

For once, her beloved surroundings didn't comfort her. Chickens and goats traversing the yard. Daddy's beautiful garden. Cherry trees. Paula hovering near the fence in the pasture. The buggy parked next to the house.

"Old Sam asked me if I loved you enough to move with you."

"What did you tell him?"

"At the time, I didn't have an answer. Now I do. Yes, Jarred, I love you enough to move with you. But there's a stronger reason I can't."

The corners of his lips dipped.

"As I said, being with your roots makes you complete. But being here with my family makes me whole. I can't imagine life elsewhere. I love you, but all of my memories are here. It's where I want my future to be. Despite my strong love for you, this is where I belong."

* * *

The moment Rachel stepped inside the Mast home, the sweet, enticing aroma of sponge cakes filled the air. Her mouth watered. As Annie Miller closed the front door, Rachel grinned.

"This has to be the best-smelling house I've ever set foot in."

Annie motioned to the dining room table. "It's so good to see you, Rachel. What a pleasant surprise. Have a seat." She put her hands on her hips and straightened her shoulders. "How 'bout some sun-brewed tea?"

Rachel nodded. "*Jah*, sounds delicious."

After quick steps took her to the kitchen, Annie raised her voice. "I want to hear all about Hannah. How's she doing? When's her baby due?"

Rachel updated her while Annie returned with two glasses and with a swift, graceful motion, placed one in front of Rachel.

"Rachel, you got here at the perfect time! I've got a batch of sponge cakes in the oven for Old Sam." She turned to the battery-powered wall clock. "They've got another ten minutes or so."

"I'll wait as long as they take." Rachel giggled and Annie followed suit.

Rachel glanced down and motioned to the table. "It's beautiful."

"Thanks. Levi's father made it for our wedding. He knows we love cherrywood. My folks like it, too, so we're using it here until we move into our new home."

"Levi's dad's a builder, right?"

"That he is. And fortunately, Levi inherited that

talent." She pointed to the window. "Our home should be ready for move-in by fall. So, as you can imagine, it's standing room only here at my folks'!"

Rachel knew the Mast family well and she was sure it was a happy home, even if they could use an extra bedroom or two.

"It's nice being with my family—Levi and I've got no complaints—but on the other hand, it will certainly be great to finally have our own place."

She stopped to eye Rachel. "Enough about me!" She shoved aside a pile on the table to clear the space that separated them. "I'm so excited we have a chance to catch up. Old Sam keeps me up to date on Cinnamon." Annie gave a low whistle. "That was a close call."

Rachel nodded. "I'm so thankful." She cleared her throat. "That's what I came to talk to you about."

Annie took a drink. "Your horse?"

Rachel looked down before meeting her gaze. She flicked her fingers in uncertainty. "Sort of." She decided on complete directness and honesty—after all, she was here for an important opinion, and skirting the issue wouldn't help. "Actually, it's about Jarred, Cinnamon's veterinarian."

Annie's jaw dropped.

Rachel waved both hands. "Don't worry. Nothing terrible has happened. It's not like that. I'm just a little confused, and I thought you were the one to talk to."

Annie pointed to her chest. "Me?"

Rachel shrugged. "Yeah. I know bits and pieces about what you went through with Levi." She lowered her voice to a more confidential level. She wasn't sure why. No one else was there. "I figured that you must have loved him a lot."

Annie nodded confirmation.

Rachel lifted her shoulders in enthusiasm. "Just look at how happy you are!"

Annie blushed and lowered her eyelids a notch.

"So I'm sure I can use whatever advice you give me. I have to say . . ." She sighed. "I'm just a beginner when it comes to relationships."

Annie stood and put a hand on her hip. "I can already see that this conversation is going to require some edibles." She rocked on the toes of her sturdy black shoes before moving forward. "Sponge cakes comin' up!"

Rachel smiled a little. When her gaze dropped to her lap, she noticed that her fingers shook. And they were cold. She focused on the positive.

Don't be ridiculous. It will be okay. Look at the glass as half-full! This girl went through a lot to be with the man she loves. She's not going to breathe a word of this conversation to anyone. She will tell me what to do. I've known her forever, and I trust her.

The second hand made a few sweeps around the large black numbers of the wall clock before Annie returned with two cream-colored plates and set one in front of Rachel.

"Enjoy!"

As Rachel stuck her fork into the dessert, the soft morsel separated.

"It's still hot."

Rachel blew on the piece. "It looks and smells delicious. And if what Old Sam says is true, your desserts give Esther's a run for her money. And those are mighty strong words, my dear!"

Annie gave a bashful roll of her eyes. "I think that's a far stretch, but I'm glad he likes them. Of course, I always save one for Buddy." She giggled. "Have you ever seen such a spoiled dog?"

Rachel shook her head.

There was a slight pause before Annie cleared her throat. "But you didn't come here to talk food." She winked. "Tell me what's on your mind. We've got a good forty minutes or so till everyone comes home. They're in town doing errands."

Rachel laid her fork on the table and sat back in her chair to cross her hands over her lap. "Okay. Here it goes."

Making the details as succinct as she could, she spilled out her story about how she had bonded with the kind veterinarian.

When she had finished, Rachel leaned forward and rested her elbows on the table. "Annie, I think I'm truly in love with Jarred. Does that mean I should move to Ohio?"

To Rachel's surprise, Annie didn't respond, but sipped her tea with a pensive look on her face. Rachel wasn't really sure what she'd expected. *Patience.*

Annie was unusually outspoken for an Amish girl, which was why Rachel firmly believed she'd offer honest, from-the-heart advice.

While the silence ensued, Rachel sighed with relief. She had just shed a ton off her shoulders. The tight knot in the back of her neck went away, and to her surprise, she'd developed a sudden appetite. She tested the cake, closed her eyes in delight, and savored the sweet, delicious taste. After she swallowed, she complimented the cook before finishing the treat.

At last, Annie broke her silence by taking a drink. Ice cubes clinked when she returned the glass to the table. When her gaze locked with Rachel's, she lifted her palms in a helpless gesture.

"I don't know if I can give you an answer, Rachel."

Rachel stopped to consider the unexpected. "So how did you know when you were in love with Levi?"

"Realizing that I loved him wasn't the issue." She sighed. "In fact, it wasn't long after we reconnected at his cousin's wedding that I found myself wanting to be with him every minute I could. As you know, his time here was temporary. To put it mildly, it was frustrating to know that he would eventually go home. And let me tell you, that was on my mind twenty-four seven."

She shrugged. "What was at stake was spending the rest of my life with someone who was outside my faith. Not only that, but for years he had blamed the Amish for shunning his father."

Her mouth curved in amusement. "Until he learned that his dad knew all along that he was breaking the Ordnung. That shocking revelation changed everything."

Rachel propped her cheek on her hand, with her elbow on the table. "But I thought that his driver quit and he was looking for another one. Of course, in the meantime, he had to drive himself because his customers were depending on him."

Annie shrugged. "Sort of. As it turns out, my father-in-law actually relished his newfound independence, driving and not having to pay someone to do it for him. Certainly he would have needed to hire another driver, but he could have done that in a week or so. He never did. And in all honesty, Rachel, he didn't intend to."

"You mean that Levi never knew this?"

Annie shook her head. "Not until recently. For years, Levi had blamed our church for shunning his dad. Thank goodness Levi approached him about it. I'm so glad he did! Our future depended on the outcome of that conversation."

She snapped her fingers. "But back to when I knew I was in love with Levi. As you're probably aware, our relationship started with our friendship. When we were kids, we were inseparable. So when we met up at his cousin's wedding, we were strangers, really. At the same time . . ."

She lifted her palms. "That we hadn't seen each other for a decade really didn't matter because we had established such an unbreakable bond when we were young."

Although Annie was a couple of years older than her, Rachel vividly recalled the strong bond she had shared with Levi.

Annie laughed. "It's kinda funny, Rachel, but people in our community never understood our friendship because it wasn't typical for a boy to be best friends with a girl."

Rachel interrupted. "It still isn't."

Annie laughed. "I know. People always expect certain things because you're a girl or because you're a boy." She offered a helpless shrug. "Why can't we just be who we are?"

She went on, "Some don't realize that we're not all cookies made from the same cutter." Her eyes brightened. "It's just the way it is."

"I like that, Annie. It's so true. And you're right about the cookie cutter."

"I guess it would be safe to say that most of us are the same shape. But my interest in Levi wasn't the typical 'Amish boy marries Amish girl' thing. So obviously, my situation created a bigger challenge for us to be together."

Rachel paused to digest what Annie had said.

"So . . . if I want to marry Jarred, my situation will become a different-shaped cookie!"

Annie's eyes brightened with amusement. "*Jah.*" She stood and pushed her chair back from the table.

As Annie meandered into the kitchen with their empty plates, she talked. Rachel strained her ears to ensure she didn't miss a word, and when Annie returned, Rachel leaned forward to stretch her arms onto her thighs.

"Rachel, I've heard so much about Dr. Zimmerman. People speak quite highly of him. In fact, word has it he's the vet of choice." Before Rachel could respond, Annie went on. "That he's great with horses. That he can save animals other doctors write off. And he's well respected. I know he doesn't live in the community. Is he Amish?"

"No."

Confusion flickered across Annie's face. "Have you ever discussed which church you would go to?"

Rachel nodded. "Soon he'll join the Amish church with me."

Annie grinned. "That's wonderful! Oh, Rachel. Don't despair. It sounds like you're taking the right steps. I mean, thinking things out. You're going at the relationship the smart way. Of course, you don't have every answer. That's really not possible, anyway.

But if you love somebody, there are ways to fix even the most difficult challenges. Compromises need to come from both sides."

She paused to press her finger to her chin. "I remember something Old Sam told me once. It was when we were trying to raise money for that little boy who had the heart defect."

"Amos."

"*Jah*. He needed surgery, which required lots of green stuff. And Old Sam said what he always does."

Rachel beamed. "To look at the glass as half-full."

Annie giggled. "Yeah. But he mentioned something else, too. 'That hard work will get you the prize.'"

Rachel considered the statement. "Does that mean Jarred's the prize?"

Annie shrugged. "I see it that way. Actually, it's good advice. Even Mamma always told me that nothing can compensate for hard work."

After a slight pause, Annie went on. "Let's face it—relationships aren't easy. And, my dear, the more obstacles there are, the more you have to persevere!"

Rachel relaxed in her chair and crossed her legs. Annie was touching on things Rachel hadn't really thought about. But she was right.

Annie lowered the pitch of her voice a notch. "Rachel, don't be like me and get discouraged."

Rachel waited for her to explain.

"For a while, I gave up on being with Levi." She shook her head. "To be honest, I just couldn't fathom it happening. But I prayed *so* hard for God to fix our situation so we could be together."

To Rachel's surprise, Annie paused as if deciding

whether or not to continue. Finally, she spoke in a much softer, hesitant voice.

"Rachel, I'm going to tell you something in confidence. Promise me this is just between you and me." She gestured back and forth between them. "Not even Old Sam knows."

Rachel's heart picked up to a more excited speed. "You've got my word."

Annie leaned forward a bit and tapped the toe of her sturdy black shoe against the floor. "After I realized a relationship with Levi was impossible, I was devastated. Mamma couldn't even get me to smile. Or eat! And I didn't visit Old Sam for what seemed the longest time."

"Really?"

Annie nodded. "I keep a journal, Rachel, and I store my secrets inside the hope chest from Old Sam. Anyway, if I wasn't going to have Levi as my husband, I decided to let him know exactly how I felt about him so he could keep a part of me inside his heart."

Annie stopped a moment before grabbing her drink. Her fingers lingered on the cold glass.

"If there's one thing I've learned, it's to not hide your feelings for someone you love. If they truly love you, they won't shame you for doing so. On the contrary, they will respect your words of openness."

She returned her hands to her lap. "Rachel, if you can't be honest with the man you want to be with forever, it's not true love. I decided that I wanted to tell Levi exactly how I felt. And in the end . . ."

She closed her eyes and pulled in a deep breath. When she opened her eyes, her voice was barely more than a whisper. "I even offered to give up what

was most important to me so we could be together."
A long silence ensued before she said, "Joining our
church."

The statement took Rachel's breath away. She
couldn't find her voice while she tried to accept that
Annie would even think of forfeiting joining the
church to be with Levi.

"Rachel, please don't judge me."

Rachel was still processing the potent words.
She straightened and raised a hand defensively.
"Oh, no. I would never do that. Annie, what you
did . . . it was so bold."

Annie smiled mischievously. "I'm sure that doesn't
surprise you. You must remember that I was constantly chastised for speaking my mind. I must have
driven Mamma crazy. But she never gave up on me."

"Would you really have done that for Levi?"

A slow nod followed. "I'm not saying it would have
been easy, and it would have brought huge disappointment to my family, but I had given me and
Levi a lot of thought. To be honest, since his dad's
shunning, I had blamed our church."

Rachel glanced at her to explain.

"Losing Levi at such a young age was terribly hard
on me. In fact, I never really got over it. And then,
like I said, I had the story backward. It wasn't the
fault of our church. On the contrary, John Miller
was to blame. I wasn't aware that the bishop had
warned him to follow the Ordnung."

Rachel laughed. "Sounds like Levi's dad really
enjoyed driving his own truck." The statement
drew a frown, because the man she loved would
be required to sacrifice the very same thing. She
wondered if Jarred had considered how not driving

would change his life and if that sacrifice would be difficult to adjust to.

Rachel suddenly remembered her purpose. She regarded Annie.

"Rachel, I'm fortunate that the truth about Daniel and the bishop surfaced. If it hadn't, my life would have been much different. It wasn't until Levi straight out asked his dad to tell him what had happened that he got the story in its entirety."

Rachel chimed in. "At that point, he realized that the Amish church wasn't to blame."

Annie nodded. "To be honest, Levi really longed to get back to his roots." She drew her arms over her heart and smiled. "He truly loves his little cousin, Jake. Do you know they hadn't even met until Levi came back for his cousin's wedding?"

"Really?"

"It's true. And of course, there was extra bonding time after Levi rescued little Jake from the barn fire." Annie continued, "Looking back, when Levi saved Jake's life, that must have been God's way of bringing Levi back to us."

Rachel digested this and lifted her brows in surprise. "You've been through a lot, Annie. I had no idea that your relationship with Levi faced so many obstacles."

"Rachel, I prayed more than ever. Old Sam has always instilled in me how important faith is."

Rachel grinned. "Look at the glass as half-full."

Annie returned the big smile. "Exactly. I'm sure we've heard that a thousand times. But I tell you, Rachel, he's right. I truly believe that God answered my prayer to be with Levi because I prayed and had faith."

She lifted her hands in gratefulness. "Just look what happened, Rachel. I've got everything I've ever wanted. But it didn't come without a struggle." Her expression turned serious. "Does anything worthwhile?"

Rachel shook her head. "I guess not."

"Mamma always told me that God rewards the faithful."

"You're such an inspiration, Annie. I don't even know why I'm here now. I feel a bit ashamed. I haven't come close to what you went through." Rachel shrugged. "At the same time, I wish I knew exactly what to do."

Annie arched an eyebrow. "I don't believe it's really as difficult as you're making it out to be, Rachel. But in time, you *will* know. And when you do, you'll be happier than you've ever been in your life. It's funny, being in love is complicated, but at the same time, it's simple."

"I'm not sure I understand. How exactly did you know when you were in love with Levi?"

Annie looked away. A few moments later, when she locked gazes with Rachel, she smiled bashfully. "I think I always knew it, really. But it hit me on the head when we spent the day together at Six Flags."

"Yeah?"

"Uh-huh. We'd talked about going when we were kids. And Levi wanted to take me before he returned home." She drew in a happy sigh.

"What happened?"

"It became clear to me that the only person I

could see as the daddy of my future children was
Levi."

Rachel let out a surprised breath. "Oh!"

Annie leaned forward. "Rachel, think about when
you have babies. When you get down to it, you try
your whole life as a mother to raise them to believe
in God and to follow His word. Sometimes, I can't
even fathom what a huge responsibility it is to raise
children to know God and to follow Him, because
there's nothing more important than eternal life in
heaven. And eternity's an awful long time!"

A few heartbeats later, she went on in a softer
voice. "Try to imagine going to church with Jarred
and your little ones, Rachel. Imagine loving a man
so much that you would rather be alone the rest of
your life with no husband and no children than to
settle for raising a family with someone else. And if
you decide that being alone is the only other option,
you'll know Jarred's the one."

"Whew. Those are strong images. You've given me
a lot to think about, Annie."

When Rachel stood, she was still absorbing their
interesting conversation and realized that Annie had
offered her some heavy stuff to think about.

At the door, Rachel thanked her. They said good-
bye, and slow, thoughtful steps took her home. While
she walked, she dared to imagine herself with a
bunch of little ones at her feet.

She imagined Jarred as the father. And she had
her answer.

Chapter Fifteen

Side by side, Jarred and Cinnamon rounded the pasture behind their barn. As they walked, a sigh that was a combination of relief and anxiety escaped Jarred's throat while he loosened his hold on Cinnamon's lead. Relief because the emotionally rough week was finally over. Anxiety because if he moved into his parents' home, he'd be there without Rachel. He frowned.

His folks' generous offer should have brought him joy. Happiness. Instead, it had challenged his relationship with the woman he loved, throwing their plans into chaos and creating an unknown ending for them as a couple.

He loved Rachel. That he was sure of. She added a bright spark of happiness to his life that he'd never known. At the same time, he loved his brother and his parents, and being inside his childhood home seemed to gift Jarred with a comfort and renewed sense of belonging he hadn't known in two decades. He recalled vividly the unconditional love he'd experienced as a child. He'd had no worries because the warmth and tenderness of his family had given him such a sense of security.

Jarred patted Cinnamon on the head. "What Rachel said is right on, boy. A person's roots make his or her life complete." He scratched his chin and muttered, "I bet she got that from Old Sam."

When the horse started picking up speed, Jarred tightened the lead. "Whoa! This is just a leisurely walk, boy." He dug his right hand into his jeans pocket. "Cinnamon, I've got a big dilemma. About Rachel."

The leaves on the tall oaks moved gracefully with the gentle breeze that soothed the back of Jarred's neck while he contemplated his past and his future. As Jarred breathed in the light, refreshing scent of clover, he said a special prayer of thanks for being healthy and for the knowledge and the opportunity to serve God through healing. Then he said to the horse, "Even with my struggles, God has blessed me with the ability to help others. There's plenty of food on my table. I live where it's safe. D'ya know there are people in the world who don't get enough to eat? Some go to bed at night just hoping to wake up safe the following morning."

Jarred swallowed with emotion as he realized how fortunate he was. Still, his situation wasn't easy because Rachel's words about memories were true—and because of that and his love for her, he was unsure which path to take. Whichever road he chose would determine the rest of his life. With all of his uncertainties, he was convinced that his childhood home helped to fulfill him as a person.

A family and memories make a person whole. Rachel's

open-minded; even so, she couldn't truly understand my situation and how strongly I need the love and security I experience when I'm in the house where Matt and I grew up.

He rolled his shoulders to rid the uncomfortable knot in the back of his neck. *Of course, I can't expect her to. How could she fully grasp my dilemma? She's been blessed with love and security her entire life.*

I don't hold that against her. In fact, that's a large part of what makes her who she is. How she feels within boosts my sense of well-being. She's taught me to view the optimistic parts of every situation. I know all too well what it's like to be without family and how it feels to finally have it back, and I prefer the latter.

Now that I have that much-needed reassurance again, I don't want to let it go. He rubbed a spasm in his shoulder before taking a deep breath. *At the same time, Rachel provides me with love and security. And she's good for my mental well-being.*

Cinnamon whinnied, startling Jarred from his thoughts. A laugh escaped him as he ran a gentle hand down the side of the horse's nose.

Cinnamon picked up speed again, holding his head high. Jarred tightened the lead. "Whoa, boy. Not now. You're not pulling the buggy. You miss that, don't you?" Not expecting an answer, of course, Jarred went on. "And you miss Rachel, too?"

He chuckled at the horse's energy that was nothing less than a miracle since a short time ago, he'd been close to death. For long, blissful moments, Jarred allowed his mind to drift to chasing his brother around their yard. To family cookouts and holidays. Going to Sunday school, where his brother always walked him to his class and stayed until Jarred was comfortable.

Jarred wondered if Matt would have been a veterinarian, too. They could have partnered. Moisture clouded Jarred's vision, and he ran the back of his hand over his eyes. He quickly ordered himself to stop the emotion. *Look at the glass as half-full. It's the only way to be happy.*

He and Cinnamon made a full circle of the pasture before finally approaching the area behind the barn. As the house came into view, his thoughts drifted back to Rachel and her theory on family and how a person's roots completed his life.

As he took in his home, he acknowledged that his place provided him with quiet and privacy. There was plenty of room in the barn to grow his animal family, and the pasture was pure beauty. He wanted everything to be calm and serene for Cinnamon and for himself.

It was as if God had designed the most tranquil landscape to compensate for what Jarred had gone through. But there were other properties, and the home he'd soon move to offered him something this one couldn't. Blessed memories.

He drummed his fingers nervously against his thigh and turned to lead the horse into the barn. Would they be enough? They came with a heavy price. Rachel.

It was a perfect Labor Day weekend for the annual Cheese Festival in Arthur. Many of the streets around the Welcome Center were blocked off for the popular celebration. As laughter floated through the air, Rachel lifted a small child to pet Cinnamon's head. Every year, Cinnamon seemed to enjoy the kids who visited the petting zoo. Jarred had brought him to her home this morning so they could ride to and from the festival together in the buggy.

There were horses, llamas, a cow, and rabbits. All tame. As a boy petted a llama, a mélange of voices filled the air. English wasn't all that was spoken here. She detected other languages, too, but didn't know their origins.

The enticing aroma of corn dogs and crepes filled the air. Rachel smiled while enjoying the sweet-smelling food. Corn dogs, hot pretzels, lemonade.

As Jarred talked to children about farm animals and pets, Rachel considered what he was saying. In her opinion, four-legged creatures were the most important part of the festivities.

To her, each species was put here by God to fulfill a specific role. She couldn't change the world, but she yearned for everyone to love and respect animals like she did. How would the Amish get around without horses? Even the tame rabbits were beautiful, special miracles. If God had taken time to design them, they must be important to Him.

And if they're worthwhile to the Creator of the universe, shouldn't they be to people? Rachel gave a slight nod.

One by one, Jarred held small children up to the face level of the horses to pet them. Rachel looked on as he placed sugar cubes in each child's palm to feed the gentle, hardworking Standardbreds.

For a moment, she disregarded the chatter and smells and dared to imagine Jarred as a father. Immediately, her heart warmed. She couldn't think of anyone who would make a better dad.

Jarred appeared to have all of the attributes of her own daddy, who she loved dearly. Even if he didn't always see the glass as half-full. Love for God, kindness, patience, and faith were must haves for whoever she married.

Without a doubt, Jarred possessed all of these qualities. Plus, he loved and respected horses, an extra-special bonus. As she watched him with animals and kids, her heart fluttered. She forced herself to stop daydreaming and to focus on what was going on.

In her peripheral vision, she glimpsed Old Sam and Ginger in the queue for buggy rides. It amused her that something she'd always taken for granted would be the most sought after attraction of the festival.

"Good day, Rachel!"

Rachel turned. "Martha!"

"It's a good turnout!"

"*Jah.*"

As Martha continued down the street, Rachel curved her lips in amusement, wondering if the kind, good-intentioned widow would ever add sugar to her pies.

As Rachel refilled the water bowls, she contemplated when she'd say a final good-bye to Jarred. As much as she looked at her glass as half-full, she was sure his move to Ohio was inevitable. That meant they wouldn't join the church together. Or get married. A wave of sadness filled her heart and soul. She wished there was a way to keep him here.

But he belonged with his memories every bit as much as she belonged with hers. She was fairly sure that without her large, strong support team, she wouldn't be the Rachel Kauffman Jarred knew.

In the distance, she glimpsed William and Rebecca Conrad in one of the cheese-tasting tents. She offered a big wave, but the tent was across the street, and the two appeared to be engaged in conversation with a local.

She recalled their struggle when William had considered becoming English. Wasn't that a stronger conflict than her situation with Jarred? She wasn't sure.

The day passed quickly. Before she knew it, she and Jarred were loading the pets into their carriers for the ride home. When that task was finally finished, Rachel hitched Cinnamon to the buggy.

As she did so, she planted a big kiss on Cinnamon's nose and ran an affectionate hand down his side. "Boy, I miss you." She closed her eyes. When she opened them, she whispered, "The good news is that you're well. Do you have any idea how many times I prayed for you?" She frowned and added in a softer tone, "The bad news is that I'll miss you terribly."

Old Sam's question replayed over and over in her mind until she closed her eyes and breathed in. *Do you love him enough to live away from your family?*

She whispered, "He saved your life, you know. In fact, he cares for you like I do. When God handed out love and attention, he gave you extra portions. Do you realize how fortunate you are?"

As the festival area began to clear out, Rachel wondered if Cinnamon would go to Ohio with Jarred. She ducked her head while she struggled to ascertain how she could live without both of them.

Jarred's voice interrupted her reverie. With a smile, he lent her a hand to step up into the family buggy while Cinnamon impatiently clomped his hooves and snorted. Workers cleaned up. Swept the streets. Picked up litter. The rest of her family had already left.

When she and Jarred finally began the ride to her home, Rachel said, "It was a wonderful day!"

Jarred nodded and continued guiding Cinnamon down the road that led to the Kauffmans'.

As they made their way out of town, Rachel took in the countryside and let an appreciative sigh escape. The tall corn made it difficult to see at the cross-road. The crops were only weeks away from harvest.

Rachel pointed to the kaleidoscope of colors in the western sky. "Have you ever seen such a beautiful sunset?"

After a slight hesitation, Jarred answered, "It's a miracle. If only people paid more attention to sunrises and sunsets."

"Nothing can trump either of them."

Jarred nodded agreement. "Humans can't create them, yet there are people all over the world who don't believe in God. It's hard to figure."

"I know. His presence is undeniable, but I think that some things happen so subtly, they go unnoticed."

"Think of it, Rachel. I mean, a sunset is something most take for granted. When you really think about what's happening, it's more powerful than almost anything in our day-to-day lives, yet it happens without drama."

She smiled at his reasoning.

"I'm aware that your family doesn't own a television. Every night awful things are reported on the news. Yet

something so huge as a sunset isn't even mentioned."
He chuckled in amazement. "Go figure."

She considered the depth of his observation. To
her astonishment, it was something she'd never
really contemplated.

She turned to him. "I like the way you see things."

He darted her an appreciative wink. "I'm glad."

"By the way, this was the most fun I've ever had at
the Cheese Festival." Her voice took on a bashful
tone. "It's because you were there, Jarred. I couldn't
believe the huge interest in the petting zoo."

"It was a nice turnout. Farm animals might seem
like a small thing—like sunsets, I suppose—but it's
important that people understand and respect animals because that will lead to better care for them."

Her heart warmed. For several moments, an
emotional knot blocked her throat. Finally, she
swallowed and said, "I love your caring nature for
animals. I want you to know that."

His brow curved in amusement. "It pleases me
that my Amish friend commends my special bond
with four-legged creatures."

She grinned at the tone he used. It was kind of . . .
goofy.

"What else do you like about me, Rachel?"

The unexpected question caught her off guard.
She drew in a breath while she contemplated an
answer. She was open with Jarred and had been
from the moment she'd met him, but there were
reasons for that. He had helped her beloved Cinnamon. He made her feel at ease. From their first meeting, she'd sensed that she could speak her mind,
and no matter what was on it, he would respect her
opinion and not pass judgment.

She suddenly realized that he awaited an answer and lifted her shoulders with newfound confidence. "What else do I like about you?"

Without responding, he held her gaze before returning his focus to the road.

She held out her fingers, cleared her throat, and lifted her chin a notch. "Where do I start? Who knows? There might be too many to name!"

They laughed.

She ticked off a short list. "You're down-to-earth. Caring. Kind to animals." She lowered her voice. "And to children. When I watched you with kids today, I was thinking what a great daddy you'll make."

His jaw dropped. A long, thoughtful silence passed. The only sound was the clomp clomping of hooves against the black top and the light creaking of the large buggy wheels.

Finally, he broke the silence. He turned to look at her. "Were you really?"

She crossed her arms over her lap and offered a firm nod. "Uh-huh." She softened her voice. "But that must not come as a surprise. You're a natural with kids. They relate to you. And vice versa."

He guided Cinnamon closer to the ditch to allow a car to go by them. The driver of the vehicle waved, and Jarred and Rachel returned the friendly gesture. After the Buick passed, they returned to the middle of the road.

Rachel closed her eyes to better appreciate the steady rhythm of Cinnamon's trot. The scent of horse that was on her clothes. The soft caress of the seat's velvety material at the nape of her neck.

When Jarred glanced at her, emotion touched his

voice. "Kids bring out the dreamer in me, Rachel. Today, while I told them about animals and how to care for them, the animal shelter I'm planning became a stronger image in my mind. I always wanted it to happen, but seeing kids and their obvious love for pets makes me want my dream more than ever."

He drew in a slow, steady breath before releasing it. "It's what Matt would have wanted me to do."

"Your hope will come true, Jarred. I know it will. Pray every night. And I'll do the same."

"I was thinking . . ."

As the front wheel hit a pothole, they bounced in their seats. Automatically, they laughed.

"Things like today play an important role in shelters everywhere. Really, if people understand animals, they'll be comfortable with them. Give them love. Treat them well. And when you think about it, Rachel, in the grand scheme of things, being educated greatly affects the number of shelters."

Pressing her lips in a straight line, she considered his philosophy. Several heartbeats later, she offered a firm nod. "*Jah.* I get it. What you're saying is that the more people know about pets, the fewer the pets that will end up without homes."

"Exactly. People will offer them better care if they know how to. Unfortunately, though, that takes money." He gave a quick shake of his head. "Folks have trouble covering their own medical bills, so it's even more of a strain on their pocketbooks to provide their pets with medical necessities because that green stuff comes from their own wallets. Of course, there are different types of insurance . . ."

He chuckled and eyed her. "But you wouldn't know about that."

"Oh, yeah. I know all about insurance, even though we Amish don't purchase it."

He veered Cinnamon to the right again as they encountered another horse and buggy. Rachel and Jarred waved to the Mast family before returning to the center of the blacktop.

While the Kauffman home loomed in the distance, Rachel lowered her voice and looked at Jarred from beneath her eyelashes. "When you go to Ohio, you and Cinnamon will leave a huge void."

As she awaited a response, a wave of emotional agony flooded her until she thought it would overcome her. A fierce pounding in her temples prompted her to press the area above her eyes to ease the sudden pain.

Surely Jarred would say something to make her feel better. Things would surely be okay. *Look at the glass as half-full.*

His lack of response made her longing to be with him even stronger. Why had God put her with him knowing they couldn't stay together?

Rachel's dream was falling apart. As she hollered for Old Sam, she seriously considered her situation with Jarred. "Old Sam!"

"I'm here, Rachel. Come see what I've finished."

Quick steps took her to his workbench, where he proudly displayed a new hope chest lid. As she took in the carving in oak, her jaw dropped with a combination of surprise and great admiration.

"Sam, it's your most beautiful work yet!"

"Ah, young one. Just wait till you hear the story behind it."

Suddenly forgetting her dilemma, she claimed her seat opposite him and continued to take in the precise detail that was etched so beautifully into wood.

"A couple in Indiana ordered a hope chest for their firstborn child. Apparently, they'd been told they couldn't have children."

"Oh!"

"So when Callie, the wife, learned she was pregnant, she and her husband considered their baby boy a miracle."

"What did they name the baby?"

"Chance."

Rachel imagined being told that she couldn't have children and drew her brows together into a frown. "Old Sam, it would be horrible to not have kids. I'd be devastated."

"Oh, but this couple had faith, Rachel. Despite the bad news, they continued to pray for offspring."

"Just like I prayed for Cinnamon to get well."

Sam nodded. "Rachel, there isn't a situation in the world that God can't handle." He paused. "Unfortunately, when we get right down to it, we can't control most of what happens in our lives."

She gave thought to his statement before finally offering a nod of agreement. "I guess you're right, Sam."

"When you think about it, faith is all that can save us when we have so little say in what happens. What we do have control over, though, is how we react."

"Sam, I'm not sure what I'd do if I couldn't have babies."

He gave a shake of his head before following it with a dismissive shrug. "You would pray for strength and believe in God's purpose for you. And you would trust in Him to guide your life."

After considering Sam's take on her destiny, she acknowledged that he was right. When it came down to it, producing children was all a part of God's plan.

He chose the size, the eye color, the gender, even the time of the little one's arrival into the world, provided that the delivery was natural. The mother didn't have a say about any of these things. All a mamma could do was pray for a healthy child and do her best to eat right.

That statement prompted Rachel to straighten. "I'm so glad I talked with you, Sam. I'm ashamed to say that I lost faith for a while."

He looked at her to continue.

She went on to talk about Jarred's parents' offer and Jarred asking Rachel to move out of state with him. They'd discussed it before, but now the situation was even closer to materializing.

Then she crossed her arms and shook her head. "Sam, I'm ashamed that I didn't trust God enough to take care of this for me."

His brows drew together with uncertainty. "Did you forget what the doctor did for Cinnamon?"

"No, of course not. But I think I got so overwhelmed at trying to fix how to be with Jarred, I forgot to have faith in God."

Sam chuckled.

"Rachel, I suggest you hand your entire situation over to God. He helped me get through the deaths of Esther and my sons. He'll surely help you to be with the man you love."

"I'll keep praying, because God creates miracles."

Jarred waved to the real estate agent who was backing out of his drive. Before the patio door clicked shut, his stray cat came from nowhere and slipped into the house, quickly making his way to the corner of the kitchen as if that particular spot on the cushion had been his forever.

To Jarred's happiness, the cat had put on weight. Soon, when he became tamer, Jarred would vaccinate him and give him a shampoo.

Jarred chuckled at the cat's adaptability to the home. He spoke in a low, gentle tone so as not to frighten the animal. "We've been roommates nearly all summer, and you still don't have a name." As Jarred's gaze locked with the set of beautiful, piercing green eyes, he pressed his pointer finger to his chin and considered what to call the golden creature.

"I'll name you for your eye color. How 'bout Jade?" A quick shake of his head followed. "Or is that a girl's name?"

Jarred looked more closely at the color and decided. "Jade can be either male or female. And looking at the shade of your eyes, there's no other option. Settled."

As Jade got comfortable on his pillow, Jarred offered a nod of satisfaction. He cut up pieces of cold chicken and placed them in the metal bowl next to the cushion.

"Don't worry, I'm taking you to Ohio. You'll never

go hungry again. Cinnamon's coming, too." He hesitated. "Now all I've got to do is to convince Rachel to join us."

As soon as Jarred stepped away, the golden animal swished his tail and gobbled down the meat. Jarred considered the day's appointments as he removed salmon from the refrigerator and pulled the plastic off before sliding the fillet into a skillet and adding olive oil.

The day had been filled with routine checkups, vaccinations, and general questions. To his surprise, there hadn't been an emergency. Still, some of his patients struggled. Jarred kept a prayer list of those needing God's miraculous hand. He recalled his own horse's blessing of survival.

He contemplated the loving, generous gift from Rachel while he sprinkled lemon pepper onto the fish and reduced the heat to medium. She'd given him what was most precious to her. And in return, he was leaving the area with her beloved horse. How could he do that to her?

He frowned, covered the skillet with a glass lid, and took a seat at his table to review the real estate agent's paperwork. He stared at the black print in front of him, but all he could see was Rachel's face.

His heart warmed while he envisioned her kind, flawless smile. The warmth that emanated from her eyes. The optimism in her soft, gentle voice. Her decision to stay in Illinois had taken him by surprise. He'd talked himself into believing that she would go with him.

At the same time she'd declined his offer, she'd confessed her love for him. But didn't true love mean making sacrifices?

He could ask the same of himself. It was just that he'd been without family for so many years. Now he finally had them back, except for Matt—but memories of Jarred's brother came alive in their childhood home.

The slogan in bold print at the top of the page caught his attention: WE HELP MAKE NEW MEMORIES.

He leaned back and stretched his legs. Holding the paper in front of him, he focused on those five words: WE HELP MAKE NEW MEMORIES.

As the oil popped in the skillet, Jarred laid the paper down on the table and stepped to the stove to lift the pan's lid and turn the fish. After adding more lemon pepper, he covered the pan and sat back down.

Memories. He'd never really given a lot of thought to the word, but right now, they seemed to dictate his life. *Isn't this why I'm moving? To be with memories of Matt and me?*

He pressed his lips together and continued to study the slogan that practically shouted at him. *Rachel must have so many memories with her sisters and parents.* He lifted the corners of his lips. The girl had been blessed.

Jarred plated his dinner and sat down to eat. He said a quick prayer, but the simple statement about memories stuck in his mind. Jarred barely tasted the seasoned fillet as he continued to think about Rachel. Wasn't her decision to remain in Illinois a true test of her love for him? On the other hand, didn't it challenge his love for her?

The real estate agency's slogan was supposed to promote excitement and hope for the future. For some reason, it didn't. Why not?

Chapter Sixteen

Rachel yawned as she ran a duster over the stairway. She'd nearly finished her day's chores and looked forward to writing in her journal.

As she made her way down the uncarpeted steps, brushing them with her feather wand, she contemplated what to write and how to accept being so far away from the man she loved.

She was sure there was no magic solution. At the same time, there must be a way to cope with the situation.

As she looked up, her gaze fixed on the large paper commemorating her parents' wedding. The framed gift had come from one of Rachel's aunts.

Rachel regarded her father's and mother's neatly printed names, the six witnesses who'd attended, and the date and address of the Christian ceremony. She took in the bouquets of roses sketched in pencil around the borders. In the lower right corner was a small clock that ticked softly, barely audible.

For long, thoughtful moments, she sat on the step opposite the large oak frame and wrapped her arms around her knees. While she watched the second hand make its way around the numbers, she moved her fingers to her chin and allowed her imagination to travel to the day when she'd glimpse her own wedding paper.

Leaning forward, she brought her knees closer to her chest, her attention still on the beautiful gift. *Will I be married like Mamma? Will hundreds of people be at my wedding? I'd love to spend the rest of my life with Jarred and raise a family with him. But if he moves to Ohio, how can that happen? I can't give up.* She focused on the three parts of her dream.

She stood, let out a sigh, and sprayed Murphy's wood soap on the banister. She closed her eyes a moment to relish the fresh, clean smell. A smile tugged the corners of her lips when she took in the pleasant scent. The cleaning polish competed with the enticing, mouthwatering aroma of Mamma's yeast bread rising in the oversized porcelain mixing bowl on the kitchen countertop.

Rachel's thoughts were divided between the dust, the hot rolls, and her last conversation with Old Sam. What he'd said about most occurrences being out of her control made her press her mouth closed in doubt. If that were truly the case, she really didn't have much control of her life.

But you can control your reactions. And God rewards the faithful.

The door opened, and Mamma stepped inside with her lint brush in hand. "The buggy seats needed a good cleanin'. With the produce and canning, I've gotten behind."

As soon as the door clicked shut, her mother's cheerful voice continued. "Honey, there's more peppers ready for pickin'. And tomatoes. Good thing your father planted some late plants."

Her voice began to fade, and Rachel heard the faucet in the hall. She knew her mother was washing her hands.

When the water turned off, Rachel raised her voice so Mamma could hear. "Okay, Mamma. I'll get to them next."

She didn't encourage further conversation. How little control she had of things disturbed her to the point that she had to turn to Old Sam's familiar advice: *Look at the glass as half-full.*

Have faith. God is in charge of your life. As she stood and ran her duster up the banister, she turned to find herself face-to-face with Mamma. To Rachel's astonishment, her mother's brows drew together in skepticism, making a serious wrinkle above her nose.

"Rachel, you feelin' okay? You look a little washed out." She stepped closer and pressed her palm against Rachel's forehead. "You're not comin' down with a fever, are you?"

She grabbed Rachel's duster and laid it on the stair. "This can wait. Let's sit down. I'll make a cup of hot tea." Mamma put one hand on Rachel's back. With her free arm, she motioned to the sofa.

"I'm okay, Mamma. Really."

Her mother was too perceptive. Obediently, Rachel plopped down on the couch and stretched her legs. She rested her head against the soft, over-sized cushion and got comfortable.

While Rachel looked straight ahead at the fire-place and the battery-run clock above it, her mother slipped away. Barely noting the even ticking, Rachel contemplated her situation and let out an uncertain sigh.

Moments later, the spicy aroma of hot tea joined the other pleasant smells. Her mother handed Rachel the cup. "Sip it slowly, honey. It's hot."

Rachel didn't argue. She sat up straighter, squared her shoulders, and forced a hopeful smile. The last thing she wanted was to worry Mamma. Her mother had enough on her plate already.

Three of her young grandchildren were teething. While Hannah seemed to be doing fine, Rachel's father had a sore throat. And Mamma was trying to keep up with new aprons for the little ones on her old Singer sewing machine.

Rachel turned to meet her mom's inquisitive gaze. Rachel was certain that the comforting hand she placed on Rachel's wrist was intended to calm her, but she could feel her mother's fingers shaking.

An ache filled the pit of Rachel's stomach. She loved her parents so much and wished with all of her heart that everything could be 100 percent perfect. But she knew it wasn't possible, not even close.

Sam's theory about most things being out of our control floated through Rachel's mind, prompting her to draw her brows together in skepticism.

She looked down at the steam that rose from the cup and then quickly dissipated. If only the spiced beverage could cure every concern. Mamma believed it did.

As far as dealing with obstacles, Rachel considered herself a rational human being. Even though Sam had coached her to always view the positive, she tried to keep things in perspective and to not expect too much.

But she had a dream. She closed her eyes and focused on her longing. She believed that Jarred had been planted in her life to rescue Cinnamon. She was also sure that God had put him here to play a prominent role in her dream. She opened her eyes. Unfortunately, barricades blocked the way.

Right now, she and the man she loved faced a major obstacle. It involved his parents gifting him their home. What should have been a reason for celebration was instead preventing her wish from materializing.

She'd tried all she could to resolve their dilemma. Unfortunately, there was nothing, really, that anyone could do to make a happy denouement.

Not that she'd thought of, anyway. To her surprise, even Old Sam hadn't come up with a solution, and he was the wisest person she knew.

Rachel drew in a much-appreciated breath of relief as she sipped the hot tea. Holding the cup in front of her face, she tried to enjoy the spicy-smelling steam. Already, Mamma's solution for every problem was helping her to relax.

Mamma patted the top of Rachel's hand before crossing her arms over her lap, and encouragement edged her voice. "I tossed some honey in it. It has all sorts of nutrients, ya know. You'll feel better soon."

She cleared her throat. In a soft voice, she added, "But, Rachel, I can read you like a book, honey. And this is about you and Dr. Zimmerman, *jah?*"

Rachel couldn't stop the corners of her lips from dropping. She shrugged, hoping to deflect her mother's interest. "Mom, it's nothing, really. I'll work it out. But it's gonna take time."

A wistful expression crossed Mamma's face as she

looked off into the distance. "Rachel, I remember what it's like to be young."

Rachel eyed her with skepticism. She couldn't imagine her mother in her position. In fact, it was hard to envision Mamma facing any obstacle she couldn't overcome.

As if reading her thoughts, her mother drew in a sigh and smiled sympathetically. Tiny creases formed around her eyes. "I'm afraid I might not be able to help you, but would you give me a chance?"

Rachel nodded. Mamma straightened and she ran her hands over a slight fold in her white apron. "Tell me what's going through that head of yours." With a swift but subtle motion, she used her pointer finger to move a loose hair back under Rachel's covering.

After a slight hesitation, Rachel took a deep breath and lifted her head to take in the concerned expression on her mom's face. With slow, thoughtful sentences, she poured out her situation.

Settling back into the sofa, she crossed her arms over her lap and stretched her legs while she spoke, attempting only the most important details. When she was finished, she said in a tone that was a combination of challenge and inquisitiveness, "Mamma, can I ask you something?"

"Sure."

"Let's say that you and Daddy were my age and you wanted to live here, but Daddy asked you to go with him to Ohio. I know it's probably tough to even think of being in this predicament, but please try."

Rachel watched as her mother squared her shoulders.

"Would you have moved with him?"

Long moments passed while Rachel's role model gazed down intently at her black shoes. The only sound besides the wall clock ticking was the clucking of chickens that floated in from the outside. A bright ray of sunshine slipped in through the living room windows, and Rachel blinked to adjust to the light.

Several heartbeats later, Mamma smiled a little. "Honey, first of all, what did you tell Jarred?"

Rachel shifted for a more comfortable position. "That I love him, but that living here with my family completes my life." She lifted her palms in the air. "Taking me out of this environment would be like moving Cinnamon to the city."

She and her mother laughed before Rachel got serious again. "To be completely honest, I can't imagine not having the support and love I've always counted on. I belong with my roots, just like he does."

Rachel lifted her shoulders in a small shrug. "You would never have moved away, would you?"

Rachel's mother tapped the toe of her shoe against the floor before meeting Rachel's gaze. "I don't know. That's a tough question."

"But—"

Mamma lifted a hand to stop Rachel from interrupting. "You've got to realize that Jarred's situation is anything but normal. It's really his past that's making your situation complicated. The past, the present, the future . . . When you think about it, they're all connected. In fact, you can't really have one without the others."

Rachel contemplated this before nodding her agreement.

"But keep your faith, honey. God works miracles. He healed Cinnamon, and if you and Jarred want to be together, I'm sure our Heavenly Father will work out a way that's good for both of you."

Rachel pretended to study the floor as she considered her mother's words. Finally, she shrugged in disappointment. "Mamma, the only way I can see that happening is to move to Ohio. And to be honest, I just can't leave everyone I love."

A long silence ensued before Rachel's mom said in an emotional, yet firm tone, "Marriage is about give and take."

Rachel straightened her shoulders. Mamma was going to offer something about Rachel's relationship with Jarred. She listened with interest.

"I'm certainly not an expert in relationships. Fortunately, I love your daddy, he loved me, and there weren't any complications in our way. But in my opinion, I see some advantages to this offer."

"You do?"

Mamma nodded. "In fact, I'm glad his parents offered Jarred their house before the two of you joined the church together and got married."

Rachel stared down at her hands on her thighs as she contemplated Mamma's take on what had happened. Then she offered a nod of agreement. "You're right, Mamma. Because if we'd already married—"

Mamma interrupted and wagged a calming hand in front of her. "Everything would have been fine because you would have talked this over and made the right choice."

Rachel wasn't sure she agreed.

"Honey, I've told you before that when you become one, sometimes you sacrifice what you love most for your spouse. And when that happens, you become even closer as a couple. Marriage . . ." Mamma smiled gently as she raised her palms for emphasis.

"It's not just one single thing in a relationship. It's a continuation of life together, from start to finish, that grows your love and respect for each other. It's taking care of each other when you're sick. It's celebrating the birth of babies. It involves helping your friends when they need you. And the list goes on and on."

Rachel still couldn't imagine leaving her family and Old Sam. Right now, they were her security blanket. She couldn't consider ever giving them up.

"You know that if you moved, Rachel, you'd still have our love and support."

Rachel's jaw dropped in surprise. Was Mamma encouraging her to go to Ohio?

"Mamma? You and Daddy never planned on me leaving, I'm sure. Wouldn't you be disappointed?"

The corners of her mom's lips lifted into a sympathetic grin. "Of course we'd miss you, but we have plenty of memories that will never disappear. When you marry, you'll start a brand-new life and new memories with your husband."

She hesitated, crossing her legs at the ankles and holding Rachel's gaze. "I've no doubt of your love for Jarred."

"No?"

Mamma shook her head. "When I watch you together, I catch a strong bond that's a combination of respect and friendship. With those two things, the two of you can work out any problem. Just keep praying, Rachel, for God to guide you."

A long pause ensued before Rachel replied. "Old Sam told me something the other day that has been bothering me. He's making a hope chest for a couple that just had a baby."

"I don't understand. What's troubling about that?"

"Nothing with the baby. But they'd been told they couldn't have children." She sighed. "Mamma, if a doctor said that to me, I would be devastated." She gave a gentle lift of her shoulders.

"And according to Old Sam, most of what happens to us is out of our grasp. And the only thing that we have control of is how we react."

Mamma offered a slow nod. "Old Sam is wise. We're fortunate to have his expertise." She went on. "Rachel, your father and I have done our best to raise you to love and trust our Heavenly Father. That's our most important duty as parents. As far as other things?"

Mamma gave a slight move of her head. "It's up to you to pray for guidance to do your best. We truly are grateful to your doctor friend for everything he's done. Not only did he come to Cinnamon's rescue, but he's helped Paula get up to date on her vaccines. And d'you know he told your father to forget the bill?"

Rachel was sure her eyes had doubled in size. Because she was fully aware of the countless hours Jarred had invested in their horses.

"We'd love to have him for dinner to personally show our appreciation. Friday, the whole family's coming. We've invited Old Sam, too. Why don't you ask Jarred to join us?"

* * *

Talking and laughter filled the Kauffman home. As Jarred stepped into the kitchen, his reception was overwhelming. The home was practically shoulder to shoulder yet, oddly, there seemed to be enough room.

Enticing smells of homemade dishes filled Jarred's nostrils. He smiled a little. It was no secret that Mrs. Kauffman was a great cook.

Jarred met Rachel's sisters and their husbands and children. In her cooking apron, Mrs. Kauffman prepared the buffet while Rachel and Jarred chatted. A white cloth covered the big table. Card tables placed throughout the kitchen and the dining and living rooms were set with place mats and silverware rolled in napkins.

As two of Rachel's sisters laughed at something their children did, Jarred supposed that this many people for dinner wasn't unusual for this family. He mentally compared the noise and the loving camaraderie to his lonely upbringing. An ache pinched his chest as he wondered what it would be like to be part of such a large, loving clan.

Now he truly had a taste of Rachel's life, but to his surprise, this full house didn't leave him feeling out of place. On the contrary, a certain homespun goodness floated through the air, warming Jarred's heart and helping him to experience a strange, wonderful closeness.

A mixture of emotions filled him. He wasn't sure what they were; all he knew was that they were happy ones.

While three of Rachel's sisters talked with him

about the Cheese Festival and the petting zoo, Jarred absorbed the comforting, satisfying sensation that filled him.

It had been over two decades since he'd experienced such security, and it didn't take long for him to decide that being one of the Kauffmans would be a great blessing. Whoever married into this Christian family would be welcomed with open arms.

From the get-go, he'd been most intrigued by Old Sam. Jarred had taken the widower's hand in a warm greeting. Sam's grip was firm, yet reassuring. Jarred took note of his long, artistic-looking fingers.

Immediately, he had no doubt why Rachel liked him. The tall man with gray-white hair and a matching beard talked to Jarred about his horse, Ginger. As he spoke, a light halo lingered around his deep brown eyes.

"And your hope chest stories fascinate me." Jarred went on, "Rachel shares them with me."

When Old Sam grinned, his eyes sparkled. "I must be the luckiest man in the world with my three to take care of me. Rachel, Annie, and Rebecca."

As he said their names, his eyes glistened with moisture. "God never ceases to bless me. After my wife passed on, the trio stepped right in to make sure I was okay. By the same token, I feel a responsibility to make sure they're all right, too."

When Jarred met his gaze, he noted an especially protective expression in Old Sam's eyes.

A combination of seriousness and great affection edged his voice. "Rachel has an exceptionally large heart, Dr. Zimmerman. I love her like a granddaughter. And right now, she's afraid of losing you.

You're a bright young man, and I know that house in Ohio stirs great memories of you and your brother, but your whole life's ahead of you."

He hesitated, running his fingers over his beard. "Memories stay in your heart. But if I've learned anything throughout my life, it's that the future's all about making new ones. Give those words some thought, son."

Sam offered a slight nod and patted Jarred on the back with affection. As soon as he did so, two of Rachel's nieces ran into Jarred while they chased each other, nearly knocking him over. The moment that happened, an uncle stepped in to reprimand them, and Jarred found himself talking crops with Rachel's brothers-in-law.

Mr. Kauffman interrupted to say the prayer. As everyone gathered close, Jarred took in two long tables of food covered with large metal containers with candles burning beneath them, obviously to keep the food warm.

After the blessing, there was a unanimous "amen."

In the buffet line, Jarred's heart raced, but he couldn't pinpoint what was wrong as he kept up with the different conversations around him.

As he plucked a piece of fried chicken with plastic tongs and put it on his cream-colored plate, one of the mothers reminded her children to only take what they could eat.

While Jarred eyed the sweet potato casserole, mashed potatoes, gravy, dressing, chicken and homemade noodles, yeast bread, and meat loaf, he grinned at the realization that cleaning his plate wouldn't be difficult. The challenge would be fitting everything he wanted onto the regular-sized dinnerware.

He and Rachel sat with her parents, Old Sam, and two sisters and their husbands at the main table. Mostly, the conversation hinged around how Jarred had become interested in healing animals.

As Jarred explained his brother's love of horses from an early age, he found himself talking about Matt, about how he was committed to start an animal shelter in his name.

As they chitchatted about Cinnamon and Jarred's success stories, Jarred couldn't take his eyes off the young boys with suspenders over their narrow shoulders.

As the conversation continued, he found himself wondering what it would be like to have his own sons. With Rachel.

Chapter Seventeen

That evening, Jade closed his eyes as Jarred touched his golden head. "You trust me," Jarred said with a surprised breath. He squatted and stayed very still while he gently caressed the sensitive area behind Jade's ears.

As he studied God's special creature, he considered the huge progress they'd made in their relationship since the start of the summer.

When he was even with the kitchen table, he glanced down at the real estate paperwork and stopped. WE HELP MAKE NEW MEMORIES. Old Sam's low voice floated through Jarred's head: "The future is all about making new ones."

Not sure why the subject kept stealing his attention, Jarred quickly shrugged it off and turned his attention to the box at the side of the couch and the books from veterinary school neatly stacked inside.

He stepped to Matt's picture, took the frame between his hands, and held it in front of him while he got comfortable on the couch.

He laid the photo on his thighs and reached for

the remote. After flipping to the local news, he put the clicker to the side and once again took his brother's picture in his hands.

While he stared into Matt's eyes, the newscaster's voice competed with the evening's conversations that replayed inside Jarred's head.

"Memories stay in your heart. But the future's all about making new ones." As Jarred could almost hear Sam Beachy speaking those potent words, he muted the television. With great affection, he traced his pointer finger over the smooth glass and considered the old widower's take on memories.

Jarred smiled a little. He fully understood why Rachel liked Sam. The man was wise, and there was something about the sparkle in his eyes that convinced you he was taking in with interest every word you said.

But his opinion about memories struck a familiar chord. Still holding the photograph, Jarred stared straight ahead. He didn't pay any attention to the newscaster on the television. He suddenly realized why the statement was so recognizable: because he had heard it before.

Or seen it, anyway. It resembled the slogan at the top of the real estate agent's letter on his table.

Enjoying the pleasant scent of cut grass that drifted in on the evening breeze, Jarred relaxed against the soft sofa cushions, but Sam's words reverberated over and over in his mind until he frowned.

Why am I stuck on preserving old memories? Memories have made me who I am. They have everything to do with why I think like I do and how I form my opinions. But Sam does have a point: New experiences will make my future. Don't I need both?

Heaving a sigh of frustration, he laid Matt's picture to his right and leaned forward, crossing his arms over his legs while he pondered the value of memories and what role they played in his life.

Jade meandered into the living room and claimed the area on the carpet next to his feet. Jarred spoke in a low tone. "I'll bet you've got memories you'd rather not remember, boy."

But Jarred didn't want to forget his. Even the bad ones. For some reason, he yearned to hold on to everything that had contributed to who he was.

But did he really need to move to Ohio to savor the time he'd spent with his brother? As good as those days had been, could they sustain him throughout his life? Or was Sam right?

Rachel tried to pay attention at church in the Yoder home, but Jarred's inevitable move to Ohio filled her thoughts. Conflicting emotions hit her until she drew her eyebrows together with skepticism. It was common knowledge that there were plenty of Amish folk in Ohio.

As Rachel admitted the depth of her feelings for him, she couldn't bear the thought of losing him. *When you truly love someone, you give up what you love most for them.* She'd already given him Cinnamon. Should she also forfeit her roots to be with him?

Mamma had told Rachel that she would always have her family's love and support, wherever she lived. Moving away would be the biggest sacrifice Rachel had ever made, but it was the only way her dream could come true.

* * *

The following day, Cinnamon trotted with his head held high as Rachel sat next to Jarred in her family's buggy. As she contemplated his unexpected visit and asking permission to take Rachel for a ride with him and Cinnamon in the country, she ran her fingers over the soft blue seats that smelled of fresh fabric. The black metal interior shone like it had just been polished. The October sun hovered next to a large, fluffy cloud as if deciding whether or not to disappear.

"Today's one of the happiest days of my life."

A combination of true satisfaction and happiness edged Jarred's voice. As the breeze in the open carriage caused loose tendrils of hair to escape Rachel's kapp, she turned a bit to better view his face. "I can tell."

With a smile, he returned his attention back to the road and Cinnamon.

She wished she could be as contented as Jarred obviously was, but she couldn't. Everything about him shouted happiness. His ear-to-ear grin. The enthusiastic lilt in his voice. The way he walked with a confident stride. How could he be so joyful when she was conflicted?

Later, Jarred parked the buggy near the Kauffman barn and led Cinnamon to the nearest water trough. While Cinnamon drew up water, Jarred tied him to a post. In the pasture, Paula looked over the wire fence.

He motioned Rachel to the bench at the side of the barn, where they sat down. As the October sun lingered above them, he took in the sad expression on her face.

"There's a couple interested in buying my house."

He noted the worry lines that crept over her forehead and decided to change the subject. "I want to tell you how grateful I am to you and your family, Rachel."

She pressed her lips in a straight line and eyed him with a combination of appreciation and uncertainty.

"Spending time with your family and Old Sam, and especially being here with you, has made me see my life differently than I've ever looked at it. Remember our talk about moving to Ohio?"

She nodded.

"You said that a person's roots make him or her complete."

"It's true."

"It is. But something Old Sam mentioned the other night made me start paying deeper attention to memories and the future."

After crossing her legs at the ankles, she lifted an inquisitive eyebrow. "What did he say?"

"That memories stay in our hearts, but the future is all about making new ones."

Her lips curved in amusement. "He's always right."

"Rachel, there's something I want you to know." Before she could say anything, he went on. "I've given the transition a lot of thought, and I've finally realized that you're my future. And I want it to be filled with memories of the two of us together."

A combination of surprise and excitement flickered across her face. "But . . ."

He lowered his tone while they locked gazes. "I'm staying here."

She breathed in before pushing out a deep breath of relief. Her eyes reflected great joy. She parted her lips in wonder and drew her arms over her chest in surprise. "Oh, Jarred! Are you serious?"

"I've never been more truthful in my life."

"But your brother . . . All of your memories are in your childhood home."

He shook his head. "That's what I thought. Memories of Matt and me are right here." He pointed to his heart. "And that's where they belong. Wherever I am, I will always love my parents, but my place is here. With you. With your folks, and all of your nieces and nephews." He lowered his voice. "And Old Sam."

He chuckled. "How would we get advice from our wise mentor if we're in Ohio?"

She giggled.

"If it's okay, I'd like to stick with our original plan to join the church and get married. We'll build close to your folks."

"Oh, Jarred!" She placed her hands over her mouth as tears rolled down her cheeks. "I love you! You've made such a big sacrifice. For me."

"Just like you gave me Cinnamon."

She hesitated, as if digesting what he'd said.

"But I'm asking you a favor in return."

"I'll do anything for you, Jarred. Anything!"

"I want to know the rest of your dream."

She dropped her hands to her lap. "It's to cele-brate my seventieth wedding anniversary with you."

He paused before grinning, then let out a low whistle. "That's a lot of years! So . . . we'd better get married soon!"

They laughed.

"Rachel Kauffman, you're my future."

"Jarred Zimmerman, you've made me the happiest girl in the world."

"And there's nothing that I'd like more than to please you. In fact, from this day forward, let's start planning our wedding. The future is ours. I can't wait to build a house by your folks." He grinned in amusement. "One with lots of bedrooms."

After a long, thoughtful silence, he went on. "I've been thinking."

She looked at him to go on.

"Our lives will be filled with blessings from our Heavenly Father. And I will devote my life to making you happy." He hesitated before adding, "I've thought of the perfect two words to describe our future."

His voice expressed a combination of joy and excitement. "Our life will be a dream." He paused before grinning. "Rachel's Dream."

DON'T MISS

Rebecca's Bouquet

The last thing Rebecca Sommer dreamed her plan
to marry would bring is a heart-wrenching choice.
She thought she and her betrothed, William,
would spend the rest of their lives in Illinois's
heartland, raising a family in their close-knit Amish
hometown. But when he must travel out of state
to save his ailing father's business,
Rebecca braves her relatives' disapproval—
and her own fears—to work by his side.
And though she finds herself ever more in love
with the dedicated, resourceful man he proves to
be, William's growing interest in English ways
may be the one challenge even
her steadfast faith can't meet . . .

Annie's Recipe

Annie Mast and Levi Miller were best friends until
his father was shunned by the church.
Now, ten years later, Levi has returned to Arthur,
Illinois, for a brief visit, and he and Annie discover
their bond is as strong as ever. Spending as much
time together as possible, Annie finds herself
dreaming of a future with Levi. And Levi is soon
dreaming of building a home on a beautiful local
hillside—to live in with Annie. Yet their longings
are unlikely to become reality . . .

Available wherever books and eBooks are sold.

Turn the page for an excerpt from
Rebecca's Bouquet . . .

His announcement took her by surprise. Rebecca Sommer met William's serious gaze and swallowed. The shadow from his hat made his expression impossible to read.

"You're really leaving?"

He fingered the black felt on the brim. "I know what a shock this is. Believe me, I never expected to hear that Dad had a heart attack."

"Do they expect a full recovery?"

William nodded. "But the docs say it will be a while before he works again. Right now, they can't even guess at a time line. In the meantime, Beth's struggling to take care of him."

While Rebecca considered the news, the warm June breeze rustled the large, ear-shaped leaves on the catalpa tree. The sun peeked from behind a large marshmallow cloud, as if deciding whether or not to appear. In the distance, a sleek black gelding clomped its hooves against the earth.

Pools of dust stirred, swirling and quickly dis-appearing. Lambs frolicked across the parcel of

pasture separating the Sommer home from Old
Sam Beachy's bright red barn. From where they
stood, Rebecca could barely glimpse the orange
YIELD sign on the back of the empty buggy parked
next to the house.

"I'm the only person Dad trusts with his business."
William paused and lowered his voice. "Beth wants
me to come to Indiana and run his cabinet shop,
Rebecca."

The news caused a wave of anxiety to roll through
Rebecca's chest. She wrung her hands together in
a nervous gesture. A long silence ensued as she
thought of William leaving, and her shoulders grew
tense. Not even the light, sweet fragrance floating
from her mother's rose garden could take away
Rebecca's anxiety.

When she finally started to respond, William held
up a defensive hand. "It's just until he's back on his
feet. This may not be such a bad thing. The experience might actually benefit us."

Rebecca raised a curious brow. The breeze blew a
chestnut-brown hair out of place, and she quickly
tucked it back under her *kapp*. Her gaze drifted from
his face to his rolled-up sleeves.

Tiny freckles decorated his nose, giving him a
youthful appearance. But there was nothing boyish
about his square jaw or broad shoulders that tried to
push their way out of his shirt. Her heart skipped a
beat. She lifted her chin, and their eyes locked in
understanding.

William smiled a little. "One of these days, we'll
run our own company." He winked. "Don't worry."

She swallowed the lump in her throat. For one

blissful, hopeful moment, she trusted everything would be okay. It wasn't those simple two words that reassured her, but the tender, persuasive way William said them. The low, steady tone in which he spoke could convince Rebecca of almost anything.

The warm pink glow on his cheeks made Rebecca's pulse pick up speed. As he looked at her for a reaction, her lips lifted into a wide smile. At the same time, it was impossible to stop the nervous rising and falling of her chest.

She'd never dreamed of being without William. Even temporarily. At the young age of eighteen, she hadn't ever confronted such a difficult issue.

But her church teachers and parents had raised her to deal with obstacles. Fortunately, they had prepared her to be strong and to pray for guidance. As she stared at her beloved flower garden, her thoughts became more chaotic.

The clothes on the line rose and fell with the warm summer breeze. Their fresh, soapy scent floated through the air. She surely had greater control over her destiny than the wet garments, whose fate was dependent on the wind. She and William could get through this. They loved each other. God would take care of them, wouldn't He?

She glanced up at William. The way the sun hit him at an angle made him look even taller than his six feet and two inches. He'd always been bigger and stronger than other kids his age.

The gray flecks in his deep blue eyes danced to a mysterious tune as he darted her a grin. When she looked into those dark pools, she could drown in happiness. But today, even the warmth emanating from his smile couldn't stop the concern that edged her voice. "Don't worry? But I do, William. What about . . ."

"Us?"

She nodded.

He leveled his gaze so that she looked directly at him. "Nothing has changed. We'll still get married in November after the harvest."

Rebecca hesitated. She couldn't believe William would really leave Arthur, Illinois. But his reason was legitimate. His father needed him. She wasn't selfish, and asking him to stay would be.

Circumstances were beyond her control. What could she do? The question nagged at her until frustration set in. Within a matter of minutes, her world had changed, and she fought to adjust. She nervously tapped the toe of her black shoe against the ground.

As she crossed her arms over her chest, she wished they could protect her from the dilemma she faced. Her brows narrowed into a frown, and a long silence ensued. She looked at him, hoping for an answer. Seeking even a hint of a solution.

To her surprise, William teased, "Rebecca, stop studying me like I'm a map of the world."

His statement broke the tension, and she burst into laughter because a map of the world was such a far stretch from what she'd been thinking.

"Of course, you've got to help your folks, William. I know how much Daniel's business means to him. You certainly can't let him lose it. I can imagine the number of cabinets on order."

Surprised and relieved that her voice sounded

steady, Rebecca's shoulders trembled as the thought of William leaving sank in. They'd grown up together and hadn't spent a day without seeing one another.

She stopped a moment and considered Daniel and Beth Conrad. Nearly a decade ago, William's mamma had died, and Daniel had married Beth.

He was a skilled cabinetmaker. It was no surprise that people from all over the United States ordered his custom-made pieces. Rebecca had seen samples of his elegant, beautiful woodworking.

A thought popped into Rebecca's mind, and she frowned. "William, you seem to be forgetting something very important. Daniel and Beth . . . They're English."

He nodded. "Don't think I haven't given that consideration."

"I don't want to sound pessimistic, but how will you stay Amish in their world?"

He shrugged. "They're the same as us, really."

She rolled her eyes. "Of course they are. But the difference between our lifestyle and theirs is night and day. How can you expect to move in with them and be compatible?"

William hooked his fingers over his trouser pockets, looked down at the ground and furrowed a brow. Rebecca smiled. She knew him so well. Whenever something bothered him, he did this. Rebecca loved the intense look on his face when he worried. The small indentation in his chin intensified.

What fascinated her most, though, were the mysterious gray flecks that danced in his eyes. When he lifted his chin, those flecks took on a metallic appearance. Mesmerized, Rebecca couldn't stop looking at them.

Moments later, as if having made an important decision, he stood still, moved his hands to his hips, and met her gaze with a nod.

In a more confident tone, he spoke. "It will be okay, Rebecca. Don't forget that Dad was Amish before he married Beth. He was raised with the same principles as us. Just because he's English now doesn't mean he's forgotten everything he learned. No need to worry. He won't want me to change."

"No?"

William gave a firm shake of his head. "Of course not. In fact, I'm sure he'll insist that I stick to how I was brought up. Remember, he left me with Aenti Sarah and Uncle John when he remarried. Dad told me that raising me Amish was what my mother would have expected. The Ordnung was important to her. And keeping the faith must have also been at the top of Dad's list to have left me here. Nothing will change, Rebecca."

Rebecca realized that she was making too much out of William's going away. After all, it was only Indiana. Not the North Pole! Suddenly embarrassed at her lack of strength, she looked down at the hem of her dress before gazing straight into his eyes. He moved so close, his warm breath caressed her bottom lip, and it quivered. Time seemed to stand still while she savored the silent mutual understanding between them. That unique, unexplainable connection that she and William had.

"I've always read that things happen for a reason," William mentioned.

"Me too." Rebecca also knew the importance of the Ordnung. And she knew William's mamma, Miriam, would have wanted him to stay in the faith that had meant everything to her.

As if sensing her distress, he interlaced his fingers together in front of him. His hands were large. She'd watched those very hands lift heavy bales of hay.

"Who knows? Maybe this is God's way of testing me."

Rebecca gave an uncertain roll of her eyes. "Talk to your aenti and uncle. They'll know what's best. After all, they've raised you since your father remarried."

The frustration in William's voice lifted a notch. "I already did. It's hard to convince them that what I'm doing is right." He lowered his voice. "You know how they feel. When Dad left the faith, he deserted me. But even so, I can't turn my back on him."

"Of course not."

"Aenti Sarah's concerned that people will treat me differently when I come back. She wants to talk to the bishop and get his permission. If that makes her feel better, then I'm all for it."

"If he'll give his blessing."

William nodded in agreement.

"But we're old enough to think for ourselves, William. When we get married and raise our family, we can't let everyone make up our minds for us."

He raised a brow. "You're so independent, Miss Rebecca."

She smiled a little.

A mischievous twinkle lightened his eyes.

"Your decision shouldn't be based on what people think," Rebecca said. "If we made choices to please others, we'd never win. Deep down inside, we have to be happy with ourselves. So you've got to do what's in your heart. And no one can decide that but you."

The expression that crossed his face suddenly became unreadable. She tilted her head and studied him with immense curiosity. "What are you thinking?"

His gray flecks repeated that metallic appearance. "Rebecca, you're something else."

A surge of warmth rushed through her.

"I can't believe your insight." He blinked in amazement. "You're an angel." His voice was low and soft. She thought he was going to kiss her. But he didn't. William followed the church rules. But Rebecca wouldn't have minded breaking that one.

In a breathless voice, she responded, "Thank you for that."

As if suddenly remembering the crux of their conversation, William returned to the original topic. "I've assured Aenti Sarah and Uncle John that I won't leave the Amish community. That I'll come back, and we'll get married. They finally justified letting me leave by looking at this as an opportunity to explore Rumspringa."

Rebecca grinned. "I guess that's one way to look at it." Rumspringa was the transition time between adolescence and adulthood when an Amish youth could try things before deciding whether to join the faith for him—or herself. She even had a friend who had gone as far as to get a driver's license.

He paused. "Rebecca, I know we didn't plan on this." His voice grew more confident as he continued. "You've got to understand that I love you more than anything in the world. Please tell me you'll wait for me. I give you my word that this move is only temporary. As soon as Dad's on his feet again, I'll come home. Promise."

As William committed, Rebecca took in his dark brown hair. The sun's brightness lightened it to the color of sand. For a moment, his features were both rugged and endearing. Rebecca's heart melted.

Her voice softened. "How long do you think you'll stay?"

William pressed his lips together thoughtfully. "Good question. Hopefully, he'll be back to work in no time. His customers depend on him, and according to Beth, he has a long list of orders for cabinets to produce and deliver. He's a strong man, Rebecca. He'll be okay."

"I believe that. I'll never forget when he came into town last year to see you." She giggled. "Remember his fancy car?"

William chuckled. "He sure enjoys the luxuries of the English. I wish our community wouldn't be so harsh on him. He's really Amish at heart."

William hesitated. "I used to resent that he left me."

Long moments passed in silence. He stepped closer and lowered his voice to a whisper. "Rebecca, you've become unusually quiet. And you didn't answer my question."

She raised an inquisitive brow.

"Will you wait for me?"

Her thoughts were chaotic. For something to do, she looked down and flattened her hands against her long, brown dress. She realized how brave William was and recalled the scandal Daniel

Conrad had made when he married outside of the faith and had moved to the country outside of Evansville, Indiana. She raised her chin to look at William's face. Mamma had always told her that a person's eyes gave away his feelings.

The tongue could lie. But not the eyes. William's intriguing flecks had become a shade lighter, dancing with hope and sincerity. His cheeks were flushed.

"William, you've got to do this." She let out a small, thoughtful sigh. "I remember a particular church sermon from a long time ago. The message was that our success in life isn't determined by making easy choices. It's measured by how we deal with difficult issues. And leaving Arthur is definitely a tough decision."

He hugged his hands to his hips. "What are you getting at?"

She quietly sought an answer to his question. What did she mean? She'd sounded like she knew what she was talking about. Moments later, the answer came. She recognized it with complete clarity.

She squared her shoulders. "I promised you I'd stick by you forever, William. And right now, you need me."

He gazed down at her in confusion.

Clearing her throat, she looked up at him and drew a long breath. "I'm going with you."

Inside Old Sam Beachy's barn, Rebecca poured out her dilemma to her dear friend. Afterward, Buddy whimpered sympathetically at her feet. Rebecca reached down from her rocking chair opposite Old

Sam's workbench and obediently stroked the Irish setter behind his ears. The canine closed his eyes in contentment.

Old Sam was famous for his hope chests. He certainly wasn't the only person to put together the pieces, but he was a brilliant artist who etched beautiful, personalized designs into the lids.

Rebecca had looked at his beloved Esther as a second mother. Since she'd succumbed to pneumonia a couple of years ago, Rebecca had tried to return her kindness to the old widower. So did her friends, Rachel and Annie. The trio took care of him. Rachel listened to Sam's horse-and-buggy stories. Annie baked him delicious sponge cakes while Rebecca picked him fresh flowers.

Drawing a long breath, Rebecca wondered what advice he'd give. Whatever it was would be good. Because no one was wiser than Old Sam. She crossed her legs at the ankles. Sawdust floated in the air. Rebecca breathed in the woodsy smell of oak.

When he started to speak, she sat up a little straighter. "The real secret to happiness is not what we give or receive; it's what we share. I would consider your help to William and his parents a gift from the heart. At the same time, a clear conscience is a soft pillow. You want to have the blessing of our bishop and your parents. The last thing you want is a scandal about you and William living under the same roof."

Rebecca let out a deep, thoughtful sigh as she considered his wisdom. In the background, she could hear Ginger enter her stall from the pasture.

Old Sam's horse snorted. And that meant she wanted an apple.

Sam's voice prompted Rebecca to meet his gaze. "Rebecca, I can give you plenty of advice. But the most important thing I can tell you is to pray."

Rebecca nodded and crossed her arms over her chest.

"But remember: Do not ask the Lord to guide your footsteps if you're not willing to move your feet."

Rebecca was fully aware that William was ready to leave. In her front yard, she hugged her baby sister, Emily, shoving a rebellious strand of blond hair out of her face. Rebecca planted an affectionate kiss on brother Peter's cheek. "Be good."

Pete's attention was on Rebecca just long enough to say good-bye. As she turned to her father, the two kids started screaming and chasing each other in a game of tag. Emily nearly tripped over a chicken in the process. Rebecca was quick to notice the uncertain expression on Old Sam's face.

The sweet, creamy smell of homemade butter competed with the aroma of freshly baked bread. Both enticing scents floated out of the open kitchen windows. Tonight, Rebecca would miss Mamma's dinner. It would be the first time Rebecca hadn't eaten with her family.

Her heart pumped to an uncertain beat. But she'd never let her fear show. Ever since the death of her other little sister, Rebecca had learned to put on a brave façade. Her family depended on her for strength.

Rebecca's father grasped her hands and gave them a tight squeeze. She immediately noted that his arms shook. It stunned her to realize that his embrace was more of a nervous gesture than an offer of support. And the expression on his face was anything but encouraging. Rebecca understood his opposition to what she was about to do. Her father's approval was important to her, and it bothered her to seem disrespectful.

All of her life, she'd tried hard to please him. They'd never even argued. In fact, this was the first time she'd gone against his wishes. But William was her future. She wanted to be by his side whenever he needed her.

In a gruff, firm voice, her father spoke. "Be careful, Becca. You know how I feel. I'm disappointed that William hasn't convinced you to stay. You belong here. In Arthur."

He pushed out a frustrated breath. "But you're of age to make your own decision. We've made arrangements with Beth so that living under the same roof with William will be proper. We trust she'll be a responsible chaperone while you're with the Conrads. Just come home soon. We need your help with chores."

He pointed an authoritative finger. "And never let the English ways influence you. They will tempt you to be like them, Becca. Remember your faith."

Rebecca responded with a teary nod. When she finally faced Mamma, she forced a brave smile. But the tightness in her throat made it difficult to say good-bye.

Mamma's deep blue eyes clouded with moisture. With one swift motion, Rebecca hugged her. For long moments, she was all too aware of how much she would miss that security. The protection only a parent could offer.

Much too soon, Mamma released her and held her at arm's length. When Rebecca finally turned to Old Sam, he stepped forward and handed her a cardboard container with handles.

She met his gaze and lifted a curious brow. "This is for me?"

He nodded. "I hope you like it." He pointed. "Go ahead. Take it out."

Everyone was quiet while she removed the gift. As she lifted the hope chest, she caught her breath. There was a unanimous sound of awe from the group. "Old Sam . . ." She focused on the design etched into the lid. "It's absolutely beautiful! I will treasure it the rest of my life."

"You always bring me fresh flowers, so I thought you'd like the bouquet."

She glanced at William before turning her attention back to Sam. "I'm taking the miniature hope chest with me."

Sam's voice was low and edged with emotion. "I will pray for your safety. And remember that freedom is not to do as you please, but the liberty to do as you ought. And the person who sows seeds of kindness will have a perpetual harvest. That's you, Rebecca."

Rebecca blinked as salty tears filled her eyes. With

great care, she returned the hope chest to its box on the bright green blades of grass.

Old Sam's voice cracked. "You come back soon. And if you want good advice, consult an old man." A grin tugged at Rebecca's lips. Sam knew every proverb in the Book. She'd miss hearing him recount them.

"Thank you again. I can't wait to start putting away special trinkets for the children I will have some day."

When she looked up at him, he merely nodded approval.

William's voice startled her from her thoughts. "Rebecca, it's time to head out. It's gonna be a long drive."

Her gaze remained locked with Mamma's. Mary Sommer's soft voice shook with emotion. "This is the first time you've left us. But you're strong."

Rebecca squeezed her eyes closed for several heartbeats.

As if to reassure herself, her mother went on. "We hope Daniel recovers quickly. William needs you. In the meantime, God will keep both of you in His hands. Don't forget that. Always pray. And remember what we've taught you. Everything you've learned in church."

"Jah."

"It's never been a secret that God gave you a special gift for accepting challenges. I'll never forget the time you jumped into that creek to save your brother. You pulled him to shore."

Rebecca grinned. "I remember."

"Rumspringa might be the most important time in

your life. But be very careful. There will be temptations in the English world. In fact, the bishop is concerned that you will decide against joining the Amish church."

"I know who I am."

A tear rolled down Mamma's cheek while she slipped something small and soft between Rebecca's palms. Rebecca glanced down at the crocheted cover.

"I put together this scripture book to help you while you're away, Rebecca. When you have doubts or fears, read it. The good words will comfort and give you strength. You can even share them with Beth. She's going through a difficult time. Your *daed* and I will pray for you every day." She paused. "Lend Daniel your support. The bishop wants you to set three additional goals and accomplish them while you're gone. Give them careful consideration. They must be unselfish and important. Doing this will make your mission even more significant."

After a lengthy silence, William addressed the Sommers in a reassuring voice. "I'll take good care of her. You can be sure of that."

Rebecca's dad raised his chin and directed his attention to William. "We expect nothing less."

Long, tense moments passed while her father and William locked gazes. Several heartbeats later, Eli Sommer stepped forward. "I don't approve of my Becca going so far away. I'm holding you responsible for her, William. If anything happens . . ."

William darted an unsure glance at Rebecca before responding. "I understand your concern. That's why I didn't encourage her to come."

Rebecca raised her chin and regarded both of

them. "I've given this a lot of thought. I'll go. And I'll come back, safe and sound."

Rebecca listened with dread as her father continued making his case. She knew William wouldn't talk back. And she wasn't about to change her mind about going.

"Daed, it's my decision. Please don't worry."

Before he could argue, she threw her arms around him and gave him a tight, reassuring hug. After she stepped away, William motioned toward the black Cadillac. As Rebecca drew a deep breath, her knees trembled, and her heart pounded like a jackhammer. Finally, she forced her jellylike legs to move. She didn't turn around as William opened her door.

Before stepping inside, Rebecca put Mamma's scripture book inside the hope chest. William took the box from her and placed it in the middle of the backseat. Rebecca had brought very little with her. Just one small suitcase that her father placed in the trunk.

With great hesitation, she waved good-bye. She forced a confident smile, but her entire body shook. She sat very still as Daniel's second cousin, Ethan, backed the car out of the drive. Gravel crunched under the tires. This wasn't Rebecca's first ride in an automobile. Car rides were not uncommon in the Amish community.

Trying to convince herself she was doing the right thing, she gently pushed the down arrow by her door handle, and the window opened. Rebecca turned in her seat and waved until the sad faces of her family, their plain-looking wooden-framed house built by her great-grandfather, and Old Sam, disappeared.

William turned to her. A worry crease crept across his forehead. The cleft in his chin became more pronounced. "Rebecca, your dad's right. I should have made you stay. The last thing I want to do is create tension between you two."

"It wasn't your choice. As far as my father's concerned . . ." She gave a frustrated shake of her head. "I don't like displeasing him either. On the other hand, it's not right for me to stay here and send you off to save Daniel's shop all by yourself." She shrugged.

In silence, she thought about what she'd just said. She nervously ran her hand over the smooth black leather seat.

"You can adjust the air vents," Ethan announced, turning briefly to make eye contact with her.

She was thankful she didn't have to travel to the Indiana countryside by horse and buggy. She rather enjoyed the soft, barely audible purring of the engine.

Next to her, she eyed the cardboard and pulled out the mini hope chest, setting the box on the floor. She smiled a little.

"Old Sam is something else." William's voice was barely more than a whisper.

"*Jah.* I can't wait to tell him about our trip." Rebecca giggled. "I'll miss listening to him grumble while he works in the barn. I enjoy watching him make those elaborate chests that he sells to the stores in town."

William gave a small nod. "He loves you three girls."

"Thank goodness that Annie and Rachel will be around to keep him company."

The three friends had loved Esther. Now they took care of Old Sam. He was like an uncle to them. But Rebecca was leaving the world she knew. Would she fit in with the English?

Connect with Us

Visit us online at
KensingtonBooks.com
to read more from your favorite authors, see books
by series, view reading group guides, and more.

Join us on social media
for sneak peeks, chances to win books and prize packs,
and to share your thoughts with other readers.

facebook.com/kensingtonpublishing
twitter.com/kensingtonbooks

Tell us what you think!

To share your thoughts, submit a review,
or sign up for our eNewsletters, please visit:
KensingtonBooks.com/TellUs.

Books by Bestselling Author
Fern Michaels

___ **The Jury**	0-8217-7878-1	$6.99US/$9.99CAN
___ **Sweet Revenge**	0-8217-7879-X	$6.99US/$9.99CAN
___ **Lethal Justice**	0-8217-7880-3	$6.99US/$9.99CAN
___ **Free Fall**	0-8217-7881-1	$6.99US/$9.99CAN
___ **Fool Me Once**	0-8217-8071-9	$7.99US/$10.99CAN
___ **Vegas Rich**	0-8217-8112-X	$7.99US/$10.99CAN
___ **Hide and Seek**	1-4201-0184-6	$6.99US/$9.99CAN
___ **Hokus Pokus**	1-4201-0185-4	$6.99US/$9.99CAN
___ **Fast Track**	1-4201-0186-2	$6.99US/$9.99CAN
___ **Collateral Damage**	1-4201-0187-0	$6.99US/$9.99CAN
___ **Final Justice**	1-4201-0188-9	$6.99US/$9.99CAN
___ **Up Close and Personal**	0-8217-7956-7	$7.99US/$9.99CAN
___ **Under the Radar**	1-4201-0683-X	$6.99US/$9.99CAN
___ **Razor Sharp**	1-4201-0684-8	$7.99US/$10.99CAN
___ **Yesterday**	1-4201-1494-8	$5.99US/$6.99CAN
___ **Vanishing Act**	1-4201-0685-6	$7.99US/$10.99CAN
___ **Sara's Song**	1-4201-1493-X	$5.99US/$6.99CAN
___ **Deadly Deals**	1-4201-0686-4	$7.99US/$10.99CAN
___ **Game Over**	1-4201-0687-2	$7.99US/$10.99CAN
___ **Sins of Omission**	1-4201-1153-1	$7.99US/$10.99CAN
___ **Sins of the Flesh**	1-4201-1154-X	$7.99US/$10.99CAN
___ **Cross Roads**	1-4201-1192-2	$7.99US/$10.99CAN

Available Wherever Books Are Sold!
Check out our website at **www.kensingtonbooks.com**

More by Bestselling Author
Hannah Howell

Available Wherever Books Are Sold!

Check out our website at
http://www.kensingtonbooks.com